Seabreeze Inn

A Summer Beach Novel, Book One

by

Jan Moran

SUNNY PALMS

PRESS

Library of Congress Cataloging-in-Publication Data
Moran, Jan.
/ by Jan Moran

ISBN 978-1-942073-12-3 (softcover)

Cover design by Silver Starlight Designs
Cover images copyright Deposit Photos

Sunny Palms Press
9663 Santa Monica Blvd STE 1158
Beverly Hills, CA, USA
www.sunnypalmspress.com
www.JanMoran.com

Praise for
The Love California Series
"A captivating world of glamour, romance, and intrigue."
— Melissa Foster, *New York Times* & *USA Today* Bestselling
Author

"Jan Moran is the new queen of the epic romance."
— Rebecca Forster, *USA Today* Bestselling Author

"Jan rivals Danielle Steel at her romantic best." — Allegra Jordan,
author of *The End of Innocence*

The Winemakers (St. Martin's Griffin)
"Beautifully layered and utterly compelling." — Jane Porter, *New
York Times* & *USA Today* Bestselling Author

"Readers will devour this page-turner as the mystery and passions
spin out." – *The Library Journal*

"Moran weaves knowledge of wine and winemaking into this
intense family drama." – *Booklist*

Scent of Triumph (St. Martin's Griffin)
"A sweeping saga of one woman's journey through WWII. A
heartbreaking, evocative read!"
— Anita Hughes, Author of *Lake Como*

"Courageous heroine; star-crossed lovers; daunting saga; splendid
sense of time and place, capturing the turmoil of the 1940s; an
HEA...featuring a larger-than-life heroine."
– *Heroes and Heartbreakers*

For my all my beach-loving readers
and my friend Bennett Zimmerman

Chapter 1

"WHERE IS SHE?" Ivy muttered. Impatient to board the flight to the west coast, she stood by the boarding gate, waiting for her sister, Shelly, who had disappeared in the crowded Boston Logan airport.

A flight attendant in a crisp uniform approached her. "We need to close the gate, ma'am."

"My sister will be here. Just another minute, please?"

The attendant pressed her perfectly outlined lips together. "One minute. That's all. She can take a later flight, but we have a plane full of passengers and a schedule to meet."

"I understand." Ivy shot her sister a text, and then

leaned against a wall, willing her perennially late sister to make it. She didn't want to take this flight alone. Closing her eyes, Ivy imagined the beachside community of Summer Beach in southern California. She hadn't been there in several years—and frankly, she hadn't expected to be visiting now—but she could still conjure the pale gold sand squishing between her toes, the morning sunshine warming her shoulders, and the salty spray misting her face.

Even though she'd been living in Boston for more than two decades, the sound of the waves breaking on Summer Beach was an altogether different pitch to her ears than that of any shoreline along the New England coast. *And the sunsets!* What she coveted most of all was watching the sun set over the Pacific Ocean.

She recalled gathering on the beach with her friends to watch the sun slip beneath the horizon. Almost every evening was a spectacular show as the sun fanned golden rays into a cerulean sky. To her artist's eye, blazes of coral and rose and cadmium yellow spilled onto indigo waves like paint across a canvas. Her friends would argue about whether the green flash actually existed. Some swore they saw it when the sun set, while others called it a beach legend.

Ivy glanced at the sweeping minute hand on her wristwatch—a reassuring analog throwback in a digital age where you were only as connected as your phone's battery life.

Forty-five seconds. Breathe.

To Ivy, no two sunsets were ever alike. Watching majestic swirls forming in the darkening sky was like witnessing an artist's broad strokes on a masterpiece that all too soon vanished in the mild evening air. The thought of it sent shivers through her, and she remembered photographing sunsets and setting up her easel in the late afternoon.

However, this trip to Summer Beach and San Diego County would be nothing like that. She had her late husband to thank for that surprise. She pressed a finger against her throbbing temple.

Thirty seconds.

Where was she? Standing on tiptoe and craning her neck, Ivy spied Shelly—her sister was racing toward her, dodging travelers and airport trams with the nimbleness of a dancer.

Shelly thrust an arm of colorful bangles into the air. A pink shopping bag dangled from her fingers like a trophy, while her thick mane of chestnut hair looked intent on escaping from a messy bun.

"She's almost here," Ivy told the flight attendant, whose frown had deepened into one likely specially reserved for the tardiest of passengers.

Ivy caught a reflection of herself in the glass expanse overlooking Boston's Logan airport. Just when had her style become so outdated? Sometime between raising two children, planning college tours and family vacations, and caring for assorted dogs and cats and hamsters, she had disappeared into the safety of comfortable clothes—dark, stretchy bottoms with flowing, muffin-top coverage blouses, or trousers and untucked Oxford shirts, like today. She straightened, tightening her stomach muscles. If the forties were the new thirties, she had some work to do.

It didn't help that the mouth-watering, sweet cinnamon scent of her devilish downfall, Cinnabon, wafted through the airport terminal, tickling her nose.

Twenty seconds.

Ivy had been putting off this visit for months. Her real estate agent in Summer Beach had been insisting that she needed to inspect the house left to her after Jeremy's death—the only asset in his debt-ridden estate. Between private college tuition and board for their daughters and Jeremy's love of lavish travel, it was hardly a surprise. Still, she missed her husband so much—the way he'd tuck her loose hair behind her ear or wake her with coffee on the weekends. His faint French accent imbued even ordinary words with such a musical tone. When she'd complain about a birthday, he'd tell her fine wine only improved with age.

All those years, and now she wondered if she'd ever really known him.

But she couldn't think about Jeremy, not now. She had too much to organize on this trip, and now she had to add shopping to her I-Don't-Want-To-Do list. Ivy recalled the seashell embossed invitation her mother had sent them, along with a note, which had ultimately spurred this visit.

Just in case I don't make it to 70, I'm throwing myself a 68th birthday bash. I want you to come. There's something I need to share with you, but only in person, my darling. Do come. I won't take no for an answer this time.

Her mother, Carlotta Reina Bay—always the dramatic one—had invited the extended Bay family, as well as her coterie of friends, to a party at their home, which was about half an hour south of Summer Beach. Ivy's parents were avid globe trotters who scoured the world to import the work of undiscovered artisans—sweaters from Peru and Greece, embroidered silk from India, silver jewelry from Mexico—and share profits in an equitable manner. Ivy's niece, Poppy, had created a website for them to sell directly to consumers.

*Just in case I don't make it to 70...*Was her mother ill? Carlotta wouldn't say, so Ivy had booked tickets immediately.

Ten seconds. The flight attendant unlatched the door, preparing to close it.

Ivy grinned as Shelly's long legs carried her closer. Her sister exuded a bohemian New York vibe and kept her figure yoga-sleek, which meant she would fit right in with the summer crowd. What a party that will be, Ivy thought.

Maybe Shelly could help her find a party outfit at one of the ritzy boutiques in La Jolla or Del Mar, sun-drenched villages that hugged the coastline of North San Diego

County. Eight years younger and still single, Shelly was always on trend or creating the next one. Most of her friends were young hipsters, and although Shelly had a degree in horticulture, in New York she worked in a florist shop creating exotic arrangements for extravagant weddings, bar mitzvahs, charity balls, and Christmas parties. She also wrote a blog and filmed a vlog—a video blog—that together had garnered thousands of fans. What had started as a blog for gardening and floral arrangements had morphed into an emerging lifestyle brand.

Ivy's phoned buzzed with a text from her real estate agent confirming their meeting today. *The sun's out—see you soon in Summer Beach.*

She blew wisps of hair from her face in exasperation. What's taking him so long to sell a beach house? Her real estate agent in Boston had two cash offers on her Back Bay brownstone condominium the same day it was listed. The probate attorney in Boston had referred Claire Sidwell, saying she was one of the best real estate agents in the area.

Just sell it, Ivy had texted her. She didn't want to hear the details. Claire had obliged, until a couple of months later when she'd retired due to health problems and turned her real estate office over to Bennett Dylan.

Of all people.

Ivy knew she should have changed real estate agents right then, but at the time, she could hardly bring herself to get out of bed, let alone interview real estate agents thousands of miles away.

On our way, she texted back to him. *Meet you there.*

The summer before Ivy had left southern California for college, she'd had a huge crush on Bennett. They hadn't attended the same school, but she'd seen him on the beach with friends. He wouldn't know her by her married name, but still, she wasn't pleased about having him represent Jeremy's—no, *her*—house.

And now, thanks to her social media-happy siblings and their children, she could no longer hide on the east coast. The ever-connected Bennett had heard about the pending party and called to set up an appointment. *Since you're going to be in town anyway...*

There was no way out. Ivy pursed her lips, determined to take care of business. She had to face the situation that she'd tried to ignore for months.

Breathless, Shelly arrived by her side and hugged her.

"Must you always make me late?" Ivy asked, a little perturbed.

"I'm right on time. The plane is still here," Shelly said, laughing.

The flight attendant was sweeping the door behind their heels and executing the most spectacular eye roll Ivy had ever seen.

"I knew I shouldn't have let you out of my sight. What was so urgent that you had to get?"

"Some cosmetics," Shelly said. "I left most of my stuff

in the city at Ezzra's apartment. And this." She patted the pink bag, which emitted sweet, calorie-laden aromas. "Break-up goodies. Once we're airborne."

Last week, Shelly had taken the train to Boston. She'd broken up with her on-again, off-again boyfriend—Ezzra, a hipster podcaster with a double Z name—and needed to talk.

The flight attendant herded them into the boarding bridge tunnel. "Ladies, your flight is ready to leave now."

"See? Perfect timing." Shelly rushed in. "And I got us upgraded to first class."

"Great. First class into the abyss." Ivy followed her onto the plane, shaking her head, but grateful that Shelly had made it—and for the extra comfort and legroom on the flight. Her sister had the kind of personality that people gravitated toward. When you were in her sphere, the world bloomed in vivid Technicolor, which was just what she needed right now.

As Ivy trailed Shelly to the last row of the first-class section, she smiled as heads turned toward her younger sister. Ivy had once been considered attractive, too. Not glossy magazine-cover gorgeous, but certainly pleasant enough.

"May we have champagne?" Shelly asked before she slid into her seat.

"Once we're airborne," a new flight attendant answered. Another one rushed to close the aircraft's fuselage door.

"And we're off," Shelly said, her glossy lips twisting into a cute grin. "Let's get this beach party started."

Ivy stowed her carry-on bag and sank into her seat, thinking about their parents. She couldn't wait to see them again, and she regretted having stayed away for so long. Between her husband and her daughters, life had been so full and busy.

Occasionally her parents had passed through Boston on their travels—or rather, they would take the train from New York if they had an international flight routed through the east coast. Her parents, Carlotta and Sterling Bay, were two of the hardiest souls she knew, yet she couldn't ignore her mother's request. Even her older sister, Honey, and her husband Gabe were flying in for the party from their home in Sydney, Australia. Ivy's twin brothers and their wives and tribe of nine children would also be there, along with other family friends.

Too many Bays on that shore, Gabe often joked, but it was true. Their family was multiplying. Her brothers Flint and Forrest had continued her parents' humorous affection for names. So had she, although her daughters were actually named Mistral and Soleil, on her husband's insistence. His surname, Marin, wasn't too far from Bay, and they'd even laughed about it on their first date. He was from Cannes, and a love of the ocean ran through them like blood in their veins.

The only people missing from the party would be Ivy's

two daughters, nicknamed Misty and Sunny. Misty had studied voice and acting, and she had a critical understudy role in a new theater production in Boston, while Sunny was backpacking across Europe after taking a year off from college after Jeremy's death. The last postcard had arrived with a Venice postmark, so she was probably in Rome by now.

Once they were airborne, a flight attendant delivered two sparkling flutes of champagne. Lifting the glass, Ivy scrunched her nose to the bubbles. Was it too early to imbibe? She hadn't done this since a vacation with Jeremy, long before the children were born.

"You're going to love these." Shelly's green eyes that mirrored her own danced as she opened the pink bag and withdrew an assortment of cake pops. One was covered with swirls of white and dark chocolate and studded with slivers of peppermint. Another one sported gold sprinkles and tiny lavender fondant roses, while yet another featured a pink high heel.

Instantly, Ivy's spirits lifted. "These are miniature works of art."

"I knew you'd love them. And I couldn't resist." Shelly slid out one that sparkled with rock sugar along a flat rim and was topped with a yellow fondant straw. "And this one is a pistachio margarita."

Shelly picked up her glass. "To our new lives," she said, clinking Ivy's glass. "Now, choose one."

"A new life?"

"If only it were that easy. No, one of these dangerous little goodies."

"Hmm. The pink high heels." Ivy admired it before she took a bite. "These are delicious," she said, savoring the sweet confection and sipping her champagne. "Completely decadent."

Shelly chose a lavender rose cake pop. "And totally deserved," she said between bites.

Ivy sighed. "I'll say."

While they indulged, Ivy's thoughts returned to the house. "I told the real estate agent I'd meet him at the house in Summer Beach before we go home. I want to get this over with first." With Shelly along for emotional support, she could face this situation now.

"Sure. We can call a ride-share service from the airport when we land," Shelly said.

Ivy squeezed her hand, grateful that her sister understood.

For weeks after Jeremy's death, Ivy had sequestered herself in their brownstone condo, trying to process her husband's sudden death and the trail he'd left, which raised so many questions. Why had he drained his retirement account to buy a dilapidated house in Summer Beach without discussing it with her? Was the house to have been a surprise? An investment? Jeremy had always been impulsive and given to grand gestures, but this was far beyond his usual behavior.

She wouldn't have known about the house at all except for their accountant, who'd asked her why funds had been removed from Jeremy's retirement account. The taxes due on that transaction had forced her to sell the condo.

She took another sip of champagne. Evidently, the beach house was such an old monstrosity that it had lingered on the market without any takers.

Ivy also wrestled with suspicions that plagued her restless nights. She'd spent days in bed, reeling back scenes in her mind like an old movie and wondering what had changed in their last year. If anything, he'd become even more attentive toward her.

She'd gone through his phone looking for clues to his actions, but the mundane emails were conspicuous because of what she didn't find—nothing about the house. Nothing. As though he had been extra careful not to leave a trail. Wouldn't he have emailed a real estate agent, a closing officer, an attorney, an inspector, a banker—anyone? As an experienced technology security consultant, Jeremy was well versed in such tactics. He was always cautious about what he sent online, but in this case, he'd been too careful.

She was not just imagining this. And who could she confide in, aside from her sister? All their friends and family were mourning Jeremy, too. Besides, one didn't speak ill of the dead—wasn't that the old cliché? She had to get these thoughts out of her mind—and that house out of her life.

Shelly loosened her seat belt and leaned over. "Any offers on the house?"

Ivy bit her lip and stared past her out the window. The fluffy clouds beneath them masked so many problems on the ground. "Not a solitary one."

Shelly inclined her head. "It's a shame you have to sell it. Have you thought of living in it?"

She met her sister's question with a firm gaze. "Absolutely not."

"You really don't know what Jeremy intended to do with it."

"I can't even afford the property taxes." Ivy had already made the toughest decision in selling the beloved home she'd lived in for most of her adult life. This decision was easy.

Shelly stroked her hand. "I'm sorry. I know you thought your condo was your forever home, and you loved the neighborhood. Maybe there's something else in store for you. Another life than the one you'd planned."

"But I loved my old life." Ivy knew that sounded whiny, but it was the truth. She blinked back tears that still sprang, unbidden, to her eyes, even after almost a year. How long would it be until she woke in the morning without thinking of Jeremy?

"I know," Shelly said with compassion.

Over the last year, Ivy had learned to be practical. Without Jeremy's income as a technology consultant, what

Ivy made from her work as a freelance art teacher barely covered her expenses, even after she'd sold their Back Bay condo—heavily mortgaged, another surprise—and rented a room in a professor's home. She'd sold what she could and put the rest in storage, consoling herself with the idea that she was downsizing for more freedom.

Instead, she felt rudderless and inconsequential. A middle-aged woman—although she didn't feel like it inside. Most of her adult life, she had been something to other people and always in demand. *Wife, mother, teacher.* Yet since her daughters had left for college, they didn't need her much anymore. So where did she fit in now?

At the moment, nowhere.

Rediscovering herself now was frightening at times. And as much as she loved Shelly, her sister couldn't truly understand how she felt. Shelly had been accustomed to being on her own.

Yet in her heart, Ivy knew this is not who she was. She had once been a fearless woman, unafraid of seizing the life she wanted. That was when she had moved from San Diego, gone to school in a new state with no friends, and met Jeremy.

Ivy turned to Shelly. "Eleanor Roosevelt once said, 'Do one thing every day that scares you.' From now on, that's what we have to do."

Shelly touched her glass. "Deal."

First, sell that house. Ivy had to be careful with what

little money she had left. At least she knew where Jeremy's retirement fund had gone. *The nerve of him.* When had he planned to tell her?

"We'll start over together," Shelly said. "Maybe I'll move to Boston."

"Ha. You would never do that. You love New York." Ivy sipped her champagne and eased her seat back.

Shelly reclined her seat, too. "I might be having an early midlife crisis."

"Some of my friends' husbands went through middle age crises," Ivy said. "They bought trendy clothes, Harley-Davidson motorcycles, or went sky-diving. That would've been okay. My husband just spent our entire retirement on a beach tear-down on the other side of the country." She pinched the bridge of her nose.

"Don't go there. It only leads to pity parties."

"And costly therapy." Despite her complaints, Ivy had loved Jeremy. Surely they could have worked out their problems; they always had. If she had only known they'd had a problem.

Ivy had once been so secure in her life, and it still astounded her how quickly a seemingly happy, stable life could have crashed around her shoulders like a crumbling relic. She recalled the night it happened. Jeremy always took her out on her birthday, but a disgruntled client in Florida had demanded an urgent trip.

"I'll be thinking of you, my love," Jeremy told her as he

was packing his suitcase on the bed. "I didn't want you to be alone, so I've asked Misty and Sunny to join you. I've arranged a personal shopper at Neiman Marcus, and I want you and the girls to go shopping. After that, you have a reservation at Chez Jacques—don't worry about the check. I want you to have the best night of your life, my angel."

"How could I, without you?" She lounged on the bed beside his suitcase, watching him bustle around the bedroom. Still, the day and evening he'd arranged for her sounded like fun. Misty had just graduated, and Sunny was still in college. Having them both home for the weekend was an unexpected treat.

"I'll be back next week." A frown creased his brow. "Unless the client wants me to stay over. You know how these jobs go." Pressing a hand to his forehead and temple, he asked, "Did you buy more pain meds?"

"I did, and I put them in your briefcase." He'd been complaining about pressure—a headache, she supposed—behind his eye. "Promise you'll get enough rest. And make time for exercise." His father had died of a heart attack, and she worried about him, especially with the increased stress he was under. Of course, she should heed her own advice. She untucked her legs and rose to see him off.

"Thanks. I will, my love. Have a happy birthday." He slid his hand around her waist and kissed her with the same passion he'd always had for her, and then he was gone.

The next day, after spoiling Misty and Sunny with new

outfits—Ivy also found a flattering cocktail dress for the evening—the three of them were dressed in their new attire and devouring apricot-glazed *foie gras* at the best table at Chez Jacques when her phone rang.

"That's Dad's ringtone," Misty said.

Sunny leaned forward. "I need to ask him something."

Ivy fumbled in her purse for her phone. She'd meant to turn the ringer off before they were seated. She hated hearing people chatter away on phones in elegant restaurants. Why did they always seem to talk louder than with dinner guests? "I'll be right back."

Rising on her new heels, she whispered, "Hello darling, we're at Chez Jacques, and—"

"Mrs. Marin?" An authoritative voice cut her off. "This is Officer McClaren from Los Angeles."

"Yes?" She listened for a moment and then pressed her hand to her mouth. "It can't be…he's in Florida…"

"There's no mistake," the disembodied voice over the phone said before the phone tumbled from her hand.

And there, in the middle of the plum velvet-draped dining room, Ivy's world imploded. She recalled stumbling to her knees and tearing her new hosiery, and Misty and Sunny jumping from their chairs to her aid, along with waiters.

Ivy blinked back to the present. The rest of that night was a blur that she could barely remember now.

She wanted to believe the pressure from the brain aneurysm had hampered Jeremy's judgment. Perhaps it had been the stress he was under. But no, there was no excuse for his behavior, for not involving her in a decision that could impact her future.

Ivy swallowed against the lump that had risen in her throat. After soothing her throat with champagne, she turned to Shelly.

"I have to sell that house."

Chapter 2

"THAT'S IT?" Ivy's heart sank. She shielded her eyes against the sun's rays, taking in the sprawling property perched on a knoll that swept to the beach. The house was dated, and the landscaping—what was left of it—was thorny and overgrown. No wonder there hadn't been any offers.

"You're lucky that Mrs. Erickson's estate kept up the structural and system repairs, including the roof and electrical, before your husband bought it," Bennett said.

Ivy caught her breath. The sound of his rich, slightly gravelly voice brought back a flood of memories. She recalled hearing him sing, strumming his guitar, on the beach beside a fire with her friends so many years ago. In an instant, she was seventeen again, with a heart so tender and so swiftly broken. This is why she'd never taken his calls, but only corresponded through email with him.

She slid on her sunglasses to study Bennett, surprised at his metamorphosis from long-haired surfer to successful citizen. He was dressed in resort wear as if he were planning a yacht excursion later today. His cropped hair had sun streaks, and his face bore light tan lines on his cheeks from his sunglasses. With deck shoes, light blue cotton pants, and an expensive-looking, casual windbreaker jacket over a white cotton shirt, he looked like he had just stepped out of an ad for sailing craft.

She wondered if he still sang.

Ivy turned away to focus on the house. She wasn't there to look at Bennett Dylan.

The scene before her was a drab wash of dingy white and pale, straw-like grass relieved only by pink and purple bougainvillea blossoms that tumbled across the barren lawn like haphazard flower fairies. Just beyond where a grassy lawn should have ended, waves bubbled on the beach, and shore birds skittered along the water's foamy white edge.

Yet as run down as the landscape was, Bennett gazed at the house with obvious pride. "The original owners, Amelia Erickson and her husband Gustav, christened the home Las Brisas del Mar, which means ocean breezes in Spanish."

"Lovely name," Ivy said. At least that was appealing.

"That was the original name of Summer Beach when this part of California was under Mexican rule," Bennett said. "It was important to Mrs. Erickson that the name preserve the heritage of the past for the community's sake. Most people around town call it Las Brisas, or the old Erickson estate."

While the history was interesting, Ivy didn't want to spend any more time with Bennett than necessary. She dropped her bag on the ground with a thud. She and Shelly had taken a ride-share here directly from the airport, though Bennett had offered to pick them up.

Shelly glanced at Bennett's SUV, a large hulking vehicle with dark-tinted windows. "Can we put our bags in your car for safekeeping?"

"Sure, though the neighborhood's fairly safe," Bennett said in a confident, real estate agent tone.

"I live in New York," Shelly said. "Can't leave a penny out in my neighborhood." Her laugh rang out against the continuous, low vibration of ocean waves.

Ivy watched two women in colorful sundresses stroll by wearing twinkling diamonds on their wrists and at their throats. They were brilliant pools of color against a vivid blue ocean backdrop and looked as if they belonged in a LeRoy Neiman painting. "Those two are unlikely to covet our well-traveled luggage. Still, I'd feel better if it were safe."

Accommodating them, Bennett opened the SUV's rear hatch. His eyes flicked toward Ivy and focused on her. "You seem awfully familiar. Did you grow up in Boston?"

Ivy shot Shelly a look to squelch the comment she feared. "No, we grew up half an hour south of here near the beach, but I left a long time ago." As she spoke to him, a rush of emotion seized her chest, surged up her neck, and exploded in her brain, sending a thousand sparks prickling through her nervous system. She didn't want to relive her last summer after high school—or her crush on Bennett. Of all people for Claire to stick her with.

"So how do you know Flint Bay?" he asked Ivy. "I noticed you're connected on social media."

While Shelly looked amused, Ivy dismissed his question with a wave of her hand, which was all she could muster for a moment. "He's a relative. I don't see him often."

That was true. Ivy hadn't spoken to her brother much in the past few years and had been surprised that he and his family had flown to Boston to attend Jeremy's funeral. It wasn't that they weren't close. They'd just drifted apart, each of them busy with their own families. Aside from tapping a benign like on social media posts, they'd lost touch.

Ivy watched Bennett swing their suitcases into the rear cargo area with ease. He had the kind of solid, muscular build that men half his age aspired to. No muffin-top on that physique. He'd bulked up since she'd seen him last, but then, that had been more than twenty-five years ago.

Yet, more than his build, it was his small movements that took her breath away. The way he angled his head to listen as if hearing the rhythm in a person's voice. Or the way he tapped a finger on his thigh to some silent tune. These revealed the soul of a fellow artist she'd once fallen in love with.

Not that she should care, of course. She drew a deep, cleansing breath.

She hadn't felt this way since Jeremy. *No.* If she were honest with herself, she'd never felt such intense physical attraction to Jeremy. Her husband had been more of a curiosity—an intriguing, mercurial puzzle to piece together. Yet over the years, she'd loved the life they'd built together and how he'd always cared for her. That was the true mark of love, wasn't it?

She had no idea what this feeling was, but right now, it definitely wasn't welcome.

Bennett shut the rear hatch. "I've been keeping up the grounds—what's left to keep up, that is. The landscaping and the house need work to properly show your property."

"I asked you not to spend any money on it," Ivy snapped. She wondered how large of a bill he'd racked up on that. "How much is the yard service?"

"No charge for my labor," he said. His flashy, white-toothed smile was a little too quick for her. "You mentioned that you were on a budget, so I did what I could to help the house show better. I didn't do much except clear the weeds and debris outside and dust a few cobwebs inside. I turned on the electricity and water, but I'm afraid it's like watering hay."

"Oh," Ivy said, now a little embarrassed. "Well, thank you." That was kind of him. With looming property taxes, she had to keep costs down. If the house didn't sell soon, she would lose it to a tax sale. This was her only remaining asset now. She scrutinized the exterior, trying to decide what could be done on a budget to make it more appealing.

Bedraggled palm trees thick with dried frond skirts lined the walkway to the house, standing like loyal, gray-bearded sentinels on guard. Sandy dust swirled in a little cyclone near Bennett's For Sale sign.

She sighed. Her house was the neighborhood eyesore.

Down the block, neatly trimmed palm trees swayed above tiered fountains and picturesque beach houses. Farther down were local businesses, including a coffee shop named Java Beach and a hardware store called Nailed It, as well as resort fashion boutiques and beach gear rentals. Summer Beach had retained its lazy, beach village vibe despite homes that had soared in price and summer tourists who poured in for the golden beaches and horse races.

Ivy frowned. The faster she sold this house, the sooner she could get on with her life. What was left over would cover Sunny's last year of college, a little nest egg, and a cozy little one-bedroom studio apartment somewhere in Boston. Not trendy Back Bay, of course. An outlying suburb would do, even if Ivy didn't know anyone. She had to live somewhere.

An ocean breeze cooled her face. She filled her lungs with fresh air laced with the aromas of sea salt and kelp, which reminded her of the summer holidays she'd taken with Jeremy and the girls on Nantucket. She sighed. Those had been among their happiest days.

"This house was once a real beauty," Bennett said, his tone reverent now. "I've seen old photos of grand parties held here. Hollywood celebrities, artists, and the horse racing crowd used to come here. She was stunning in her day. Could be again."

At his words, Ivy's thoughts shifted. She took in the wide stone steps leading up to the entry and a row of palladium windows facing the sea. In her mind's eye, she imagined cocktail parties set against brilliant pink sunsets, languorous dinner parties held on the veranda by candlelight, and guests waltzing under moonlight reflected on sparkling waves.

Bennett's voice brought her back to reality. "It's been months without any showings at all. The listing contract is up for renewal, but we have to do something."

Fighting the effect Bennett had on her, she turned to him. "Let's reduce the price again."

"We can, but that's not the problem," Bennett said, leading the way up the wide steps to the front door. "It has zero curb appeal."

"I could manage fresh paint and landscaping," Ivy said, calculating how much room she had on her credit cards.

Could she get a loan to do more? Probably not on her income. She rested her hand on a stone balustrade, which radiated the sun's warmth. The structure felt solid and enduring.

"Might be worth more as a tear-down," Shelly added. "It's a large lot that's just steps to the beach."

Bennett shook his head. "Even though Mrs. Erickson hadn't lived in Las Brisas for years after the war, she had it designated as a historic building. The first licensed female architect in California, Julia Morgan, designed it." Bennett cleared his throat. "Your husband was trying to demolish it in order to build on the lot."

Ivy cringed. *What gall.* But knowing Jeremy, it didn't surprise her. He'd traded in his car for a new model every year.

Bennett went on. "Jeremy was lobbying the city to revoke the historic designation, arguing that it's a blight on the village."

This news was startling to her. When had her husband had time to do that? Then Ivy recalled the trips to Los Angeles he'd been taking to advise a client.

Jeremy had been leading a double life, indeed.

Ivy ran her hand along the stone railing. Suddenly, a strange, protective instinct surged within her. This house had been left alone, just as she had been.

"I would never dream of demolishing Las Brisas," she said, surprising herself. *Where did that come from?*

Shelly shot her a puzzled look.

"Then let's go inside," Bennett said with a note of relief in his voice.

Ivy gazed up at the two-story house and its stunning architecture. A round turret anchored one side, and a veranda wrapped around the house. Its position high on a knoll gave it an even grander appearance. The location on a sandy point was ideal, with only one adjoining property. Even in its current state, the house still had a graceful beauty about it that tugged at her emotions. She could understand why Jeremy had fallen in love with it and bought it.

Even why he'd spent every penny they'd had on it.

She only wished she'd known about it.

Her younger daughter Sunny's criticism still haunted her. *How could you have let Dad spend your retirement?* Sunny was also angry that Ivy had withdrawn Jeremy's offer of a new car upon her college graduation, but what could she do? Ivy gave Sunny enough frequent flyer miles to take her to Europe, where she was backpacking and visiting friends who had family or summer rentals. That had placated Sunny some and given them both space to heal.

Ivy paused at the top of the steps behind Bennett, who was sorting through a ring of keys. His cologne wafted behind him on the breeze. Sandalwood, she detected.

Pausing beside her, Shelly bumped her shoulder. "Reminds me of a Vanderbilt mansion."

Bennett nodded. "It has features of Spanish Colonial

Revival and Mediterranean styles, especially inside. The owners were from Europe." Bennett slid a key into the old front door lock. "Julia Morgan designed William Hearst's castle in San Simeon, too. He was a newspaper magnate in his day."

"We went there as kids," Shelly said. "The pool is spectacular."

Ivy smiled at the memory. They were the two youngest daughters of a rambunctious family that had roamed the California shores from San Diego to San Francisco surfing, camping, and sailing.

"The Neptune pool at the Hearst Castle is used in a lot of photo shoots," Bennett said. "Lady Gaga filmed a music video there, too." His eyes brightened. "Wait until you see inside. It looks better than the photos I emailed you. Even with good equipment, the photos fail to capture the grandeur of the spaces."

"I didn't really look at the photos," Ivy said in apology. She had been so hurt and angry at her husband that she had never opened the photos or read the listing description. Or approved the costs of cleaning or staging. At that time, she'd also been grief-stricken, dragging herself out of bed only long enough to deal with the most pressing issues of his estate. Now she regretted her short-sighted decisions.

The door creaked open, and Ivy and Shelly followed Bennett inside.

As Bennett crossed the wooden floor, his rubber-soled

deck shoes formed muted echoes in the empty room. He pushed aside old blue draperies on tall palladium windows to reveal a stunning ocean view. The sunlight illuminated shafts of dust mites swirling in the soft air currents.

Instantly, Ivy felt as if they'd stepped back in time.

"The drawing room is to one side and on the other, the ballroom." Bennett walked through the room.

Waving her hand, Shelly sneezed.

Following Bennett, Ivy gaped at the cavernous rooms and the intricately carved coffered ceilings. Each panel was a work of art, mellowed with the patina of time.

"It's still dusty, though not as bad as before," Bennett said. "The drawing room was where the original owners received guests, and of course, the ballroom saw its share of dances. This was the summer house for the Ericksons, a wealthy couple from San Francisco. They were art collectors and appreciated quality."

Art collectors. That Ivy understood. "I could easily fill a house this size with artwork."

Ivy knelt to run her hand over the intricate, parquet pattern of the wooden floor. As she did, her fingers seemed to vibrate against the smooth grains, and she felt a peculiar sensation emanating from the wood as if her touch were returning life to it. Or maybe that was a vibration from the ocean waves. "The wooden floors are exquisite. They feel warm."

Bennett carried on with his commentary. "Julia Morgan was the first female graduate of the Ecole des Beaux-Arts Paris, so you'll see many old-world touches throughout. The Ericksons had owned homes on Mediterranean shores, so they asked Morgan to incorporate many features they loved. Built with love, Las Brisas is a truly unique home," he added, his deep, melodic voice resonating in the vacant space.

Feeling drawn to the home through his words, Ivy drank in the heady details of the house. Curved arches divided the rooms and art niches punctuated the walls. Overhead, chandeliers hung motionless, laced with spider webs. Risers on the curved staircase were fitted with vibrant hand-painted tiles. Despite years of abandonment and the shabby exterior, the home's fine interior fittings were well-preserved.

"The chandeliers are exquisite," Ivy said, craning her neck. The one she'd seen in the foyer was a grand statement piece, with hundreds of crystal pieces arranged in a stunning design.

"When was the house built?" Shelly asked. She whirled around, taking in her surroundings with awe.

"In the early 1920s," Bennett replied, returning his intense gaze to Ivy. "Not long after El Prado in Balboa Park for the Panama-California Exposition. The styles are similar."

Averting her eyes, Ivy filled her senses with an imaginary scene: A grand ball on a balmy summer evening, doors open to the long terrace outside. A lavish garden with white flowers that reflected the soft light of a full moon. The intoxicating scents of jasmine, gardenia, and plumeria perfuming the cool evening air.

"There's a lot more to see," Bennett said, interrupting her thoughts. He led them through a large kitchen that had two vintage O'Keefe & Merritt stoves, double sinks, and a large prep-island in the middle. Two hulking turquoise refrigerators stood like butlers on duty.

"Imagine cooking on these," Ivy said, running her hand over the dusty porcelain stovetops and keeping her distance from Bennett. The kitchen was well-equipped for parties. "I miss having everyone gather in the kitchen for holidays." She'd loved creating new dishes, planning meals, shopping for fresh food at farmer's markets, and seeing the delight on faces around her table.

Shelly touched her shoulder. "We'll do it again."

Bennett continued, leading them through an atrium sunroom, a formal library, an expansive dining room, and an intimate parlor.

In the library and dining room, Ivy noted that the wooden floors were darker around the edges of the rooms. "Looks like there were large rugs in here. That must have been stunning."

Ivy and Shelly climbed the stairs after Bennett. Upstairs was a long hallway of bedrooms, each one containing a private marble bathroom and claw-foot bathtub.

Bennett swung open each door. "It was rare back then, but each bedroom had its own *en suite* bath."

Ivy peered into the intimate bedrooms along the long corridor. Most of the rooms were empty, though one had old Art Deco furnishings and another had a wicker and beach theme. In a rocking chair sat a stuffed bear with a striped sailor shirt, posed as if it were waiting for a child to claim it before bedtime. Vintage children's books were stacked on a nearby shelf. She could almost hear the walls ringing with laughter.

"The owner's bedroom is at the end of the corridor." Bennett led the way and opened the door to a fully furnished Art Deco suite of curved furniture. Discolored splotches marked the walls where paintings must have hung.

Idly, Ivy wondered what they had looked like. The air was cooler in here, she noted, shivering a little.

"Cold?" Bennett shrugged out of his jacket and draped it across Ivy's shoulders.

"I don't need this," Ivy protested, yet the jacket was warm on her shoulders. The fibers held the fresh scent of his cologne, and she felt herself sinking into it like an embrace. What she would have given at one time for such a gesture from him. She shivered again. Though the sun was out, April could still be chilly.

"It can get cool here when the marine layer rolls in." Bennett crossed the room and lifted a window shade. "Here's a good view of the pool."

Looking out, Ivy sucked in a breath of awe. Below was a miniature-sized Neptune pool, complete with statues, though the pool was dry. "It's stunning," she said, aware of Bennett's gaze on her. "The entire place is a work of art."

"I'm glad you appreciate it. Las Brisas is a special, beloved landmark in this town."

After returning downstairs, they made their way to the servant's quarters behind the house. Adjacent to that, a stable-turned-garage still housed an old Chevrolet Deluxe convertible.

Ivy wiped dust from the curved fender. "Cherry red," she said, wondering when the car had last been driven. She could imagine careening down the coast with the wind in her hair. What a good life the owners must have enjoyed here.

"Goes with the house," Bennett said, holding her in his gaze a little too long. "Along with the furnishings. You could call an antique dealer for a quote."

"This is so swell," Shelly said, grinning. "Feels like we stepped back into the 1950s."

Ivy nodded, but what she felt was even more powerful than that. She felt a surreal draw to the house, but then, she'd always liked history. That's what had drawn her, in part, to Boston.

They walked back through the house, and Ivy and Shelly waited on the front steps while Bennett locked up.

Feeling sad to leave, Ivy faced the ocean drawing energy

from the breeze—energy she'd need to make critical decisions. She turned back, facing Bennett. "How long do you think it might take to sell?"

Bennett's eyes darted between them. "Most people are looking for modern houses, and rarely this large. It needs a lot of work. Since it's a historic home, new owners can't make many exterior changes. That's one reason interest has been low."

"So, what does that mean in terms of time?" Shelly asked.

"In this market, you should be prepared to wait for the right buyer," Bennett said. "A unique property like this could take a year or longer to sell. There haven't been any serious inquires."

That would never work, Ivy thought. "You said the historic designation is one reason why the price is lower. What are the other reasons?"

For the first time since they'd met, Bennett seemed flustered. "It's not important. Just local gossip."

Ivy and Shelly exchanged a look. Shelly pressed on. "What gossip?"

"About the previous owner, Mrs. Erickson," Bennett said.

A warning chill spiraled down Ivy's spine.

"Some say she had strange ways." Bennett sorted through his pocketful of keys. "Some people swear they've seen lights flicker inside, but that's just talk."

Shelly burst out laughing. "Are you trying to tell us it's haunted?"

Bennett chuckled. "Old houses often seem to have resident spirits. Nothing to it, though."

"Did the former owner die here?" Ivy asked.

"No, Mrs. Erickson closed Las Brisas when Pearl Harbor was bombed during the Second World War," Bennett explained. "The entire west coast was on high alert. She and her husband had fled Europe when the First World War erupted, and they feared another attack."

"That was 1941," Ivy said. "Has anyone actually lived here since then?"

"Mr. Erickson's husband died shortly after that," Bennett said, taking a step closer to her. "So Mrs. Erickson reopened it to house troops that were passing through the harbor. There was a shortage of lodging then. After the war, she returned to Europe for health reasons. The house was kept up, and older neighbors tell me she would visit from time to time, but less often as she grew older."

"Did she have children?" Ivy asked.

"None. However, after her death, the estate remained open. She had a young niece who had disappeared during the war, and she'd always prayed she would be found. Finally, the time expired, and the niece was presumed dead. That's when your husband bought it from her estate, which then donated the proceeds to charity. Claire brokered that deal."

Ivy shaded her eyes. Bennett was standing so close that the fine hairs on her arms prickled, and she stepped back, unnerved by her attraction to him.

Bennett pocketed the house keys and fished out his car keys. "Now, if you'll come back to my office, we can renew the listing and review the plan to sell it. Won't take more than fifteen minutes."

Ivy glanced back at the dowdy grand dame. She should let Bennett redouble his efforts to sell the house which had plagued her for months and was threatening her financial future.

Yet, after seeing the house, Ivy felt a peculiar kinship with it. Las Brisas seemed to beckon her into its past. And as large as it was, it felt like a real home. The teddy bear in the rocking chair, the solid stoves in the kitchen, the exquisite pool. The love that had once been lavished on this home was evident. She felt strangely conflicted.

Bennett seemed anxious to leave. "Would you like to wrap up the listing agreement today?"

"Not today," Ivy finally said, drawing a hand over her face. How many bedrooms were there in the house? She added the servants' quarters in the rear and did some quick mental math calculations, even as she could feel Shelly's concerned eyes on her.

"Thanks for showing us the house," Shelly said to Bennett.

He jingled his keys with impatience. "I can arrange

professional painting, cleaning, and landscaping for you. After the house is staged with new furnishings, it will have a better chance of attracting the right buyer."

As Ivy contemplated the house, a breeze whistled through the palm trees, drawing her in with a swish of their skirts and a promise to share their secrets. Just beyond, pelicans soared against a clear, cerulean sky while waves roared to the beach and rushed out again. Amidst it all, Las Brisas had stood guard for a hundred years. She wondered what had transpired within these walls. And why did she feel so attracted to the majestic old home?

When she didn't respond, Bennett said, "What would you like me to do?"

"Nothing." Despite her desire to distance herself from him in Summer Beach, on impulse, Ivy shot out her hand. "Actually, I'll take those keys now. I won't need your services any longer, Bennett. I'm moving into Las Brisas."

Chapter 3

"I THOUGHT YOU needed to sell the house," Bennett said, shifting his weight from one foot to another.

"What I need is income." Ivy felt dazed at the decision she'd just made to move into the house. Ideas were whizzing through her mind like comets, and she hadn't felt this alive in a long time. Maybe that's why her pulse kicked up a notch every time he spoke.

Ivy gave him a dismissive smile. "Thank you, Bennett, but we'll call a ride." She drew her phone from her purse. She had just enough battery power left. She tapped a rideshare app that she'd used from the airport. There was a car two minutes away. Perfect. Two minutes and she'd never have to see Bennett again.

He stood gaping at her. "If you can't afford the upkeep, why would you move in?"

"Why not? Looks like a good cleaning and a few plants are all it needs. We can do that." Ivy could hardly believe the words coming out of her mouth, but after she'd spoken, the idea sounded entirely plausible to her. Why was she paying rent to crowd herself into a professor's extra bedroom when she owned all this lovely space? "I'm taking Las Brisas off the market."

Shelly stared at her with rounded eyes. "I thought you needed to sell the house to pay the property taxes. And buy your condo."

"Bennett couldn't sell it, and he doesn't think it's going to sell anytime soon," Ivy said, anxious to get on with her plan. "As for the tax situation, I have other ideas."

Shaking his head, Bennett dropped the keys into Ivy's outstretched hand and shoved on his sunglasses. "Call me when you change your mind."

"I won't." Ivy spied their ride-share car easing to the curb. "But thank you for everything." Eager to leave, she rushed to the car and slid into the back seat. Shelly followed her.

Bennett swung into his SUV and left.

Sighing with relief, Ivy watched his taillights dim in the review mirror before leaning toward the driver, a young man with an awkward cowlick who was nervously checking his phone. "Hi, we're heading to—"

"No, you have to get out," the young man cried. "My wife—she just went into labor. I'm sorry, call another ride. I have to go. We're having a baby!"

Ivy and Shelly slid out.

"Hurry, but drive carefully," Ivy called back at the nervous young man.

"Are you feeling all right?" Shelly asked.

"Sure, why?"

"What's this about moving into...what's it called?"

"Las Brisas. Spanish for sea breezes."

"That's easier to remember," Shelly said. "Like the cocktail. But are you serious?"

"I am." Trying to regain her usual efficient balance, Ivy tapped her phone. "I'll get another car." Her phone blinked, then powered down. Pressing her fingers to her temple, she said, "Shelly, I need your phone. I forgot my portable charger."

"Mine's dead, too." Shelly angled her head toward Bennett's SUV, which was now a distant speck on the road. "And there goes our luggage. I could use one of those Sea Breezes now."

Ivy smacked her forehead. "How could I have forgotten?" She was the Great Organizer, the one who remembered every detail, who'd packed a family of four for a month's vacation on Nantucket and didn't forget even a band-aid. "I just wanted to get away from Bennett."

"I thought he was nice. What's up with you two?"

"If you have to know, I used to have a crush on him. He surfed with a friend of mine one summer."

"And?"

"And nothing." Ivy shrugged. "I don't think he ever knew I existed. Well, except for one time." And that heartbreak had been her first, though nothing in comparison to her husband's death. She shook her hair back. No, Bennett Dylan was nothing more than an irritant. And that's all.

Shelly stared at her with an incredulous look on her face. "Twenty-five, almost thirty years ago, right?"

"About that." Still, how could such old, forgotten emotions have lain dormant all these years?

Standing at the curb, Shelly spread her hands. "What's gotten into you? You're supposed to be the sane one."

"And look where that's gotten me." Ivy plopped onto the low stone wall in front of the house. Looking up at the forlorn old house, she began laughing.

Shaking her head, Shelly sat next to her. "I think the champagne has gone to your head. Did you win the lottery? Because otherwise, I have no idea how you're going to come up with the money for your property taxes."

"I'll figure it out." Ivy pushed aside her thoughts of Bennett. Except for getting their luggage back, she was finished with him. She poked her sister in the ribs. "Come on, you can stay as long as you like. Tell Ezzra you're helping me clean house."

At the mention of Ezzra's name, Shelly folded her arms. "That's exactly what I need to do—starting with Ezzra. I've let this one-sided commitment go on far too long."

Ivy slid her arm around her, thankful that Shelly was seeing the truth of her relationship with Ezzra now. "There's the fearless girl I've always loved."

Shelly tapped her forehead against Ivy's. "What have I been afraid of for so long?"

"Being left alone. Same as me. But better to be alone than to be with someone who doesn't respect you." Ivy looped her arms around Shelly. "What made you change your mind?"

Sniffing, Shelly leaned against her. "You did. Seeing how independent you've become after Jeremy's death—even when things didn't go your way. You inspire me." Her voice cracking, she added, "If you can overcome challenges on your own, so can I."

"I'm not perfect." Ivy dug a tissue packet from her purse and handed it to her sister.

"Perfect is overrated." Shelly took a tissue out. "I just wanted to have a baby before it's too late. Did you know that when women over thirty-five are pregnant, the medical community calls those geriatric pregnancies? I'm two years into my advanced maternal years. That's scary."

Shelly sniffled into the tissue. "Ezzra swore he wants a child, but every time we take a break from each other so he can be sure our future together is what he wants, he's off chasing other women. I don't think he'll ever change." Anger flashed in her eyes. "So in my advanced geriatric frame of mind, I've decided I'm over him."

This time, Ivy didn't offer any advice. Though she'd always seen Ezzra as self-absorbed, she'd thought he was what Shelly wanted. Now Ivy realized she should have spoken up more on Shelly's behalf. Told her the truth as she saw it.

Running her hand over Shelly's wavy hair, Ivy grew introspective. *That goes for me, too.* If she hadn't relinquished her decision-making authority over their financial life to Jeremy, she wouldn't be in this position now. He was a software engineer with an MBA; he was good with money—she'd had plenty of excuses, especially when the girls were young and she fell into bed exhausted every evening. Ivy blew out a breath. Spoiled as her daughter Sunny was, she'd had a point.

Shelly wiped her eyes. "You never liked Ezzra, did you?"

"I didn't think he was right for you. But I supported your decision to be with him."

"Next time, be honest with me."

"I promise." Ivy clasped Shelly's hand. "As much as we like to support each other's decisions, we also need to be honest with each other, especially when we see unfair or damaging behavior. Sometimes we miss obvious signs."

Maybe she had, too.

"It's hard to see the truth with my heart-shaped love blinders on." Shelly wiped her eyes.

How well Ivy understood that. There were only two men in her life that she'd ever fallen for—Bennett and Jeremy.

"It's okay," Ivy said. "The difference between us is that you just made an important decision to change your life. Mine was thrust on me."

"But look at you now." Shelly chuckled. "Making crazy decisions all by yourself. So, think you can spare a room here? I'm not quite as deft with a paintbrush as you are, but you should see me wield garden shears. I'm fierce against unruly nature."

"I'd like to see that." Ivy laughed and mussed Shelly's hair, which had almost escaped its messy bun. "You're on."

Shelly glanced back at the sprawling old home. "So what's your plan?"

"Besides teaching painting, I'd like to create serious work to sell. I've had a creative block—hardly a surprise—but I have some completed works I can ship out from storage. There are plenty of art fairs along the coast where I can show my work. Plus, I've fed and cleaned up after a family for years. How hard could it be to do that for strangers?"

When Shelly arched a questioning eyebrow at her, Ivy grinned. "We can rent out rooms. Run it as an inn. That's where the money for the taxes will come from." She pursed her lips. "I am not losing this house."

Ivy stood up and stretched, feeling fresh energy flowing through her. Being decisive felt good. She didn't need to ask anyone for permission. "Imagine the parties that were held here. It's a spectacular venue for events."

"Put me down for the flowers and decorations."

"I was counting on it. I might even put to use the skills I learned in all those Sur La Table cooking classes Jeremy used to sign me up for."

"Please, not the escargot again." Shelly waved her hand in front of her mouth. "I was breathing fire for a week."

"I've got reading glasses now. It won't happen again." She still didn't like them, but she wore them to read. "I calculated the number of rooms by what I think we can get per night. The summer season here is crazy busy. I'm sure we can make enough to cover the taxes and utilities—with some profit left over. "Are you in?"

"Why not?" Shelly brightened and stuffed the tissue into her pocket. "Surely we can handle a few vacationers. Really, how hard could it be?"

"That's the spirit. Let's do this." Ivy gripped Shelly's hands. Soon they were whirling around in the front yard like they used to do as kids, screaming and laughing until they fell onto the sandy lawn. Living in the moment and tossing off the baggage they'd each been carrying for so long felt exhilarating.

Shelly landed on her back and flung her arms out.

"You're crazy, you know that? Mom would be so proud."

"Mom! Oh, I forgot to call her." Ivy scrambled up. "We've got to get back."

"And get our luggage from Bennett."

Ivy made a face. "That's definitely your department." She held out a hand to Shelly and pulled her up. "Looks like we're walking."

Shelly slipped on a pair of dark sunglasses. "We passed a coffee shop on the way. Java Beach. They must have a phone."

As they ambled along the lane to the village, neighbors on porches waved to them, and people they passed said hello. After the harried bustle of Boston, Ivy welcomed the change of pace, though she knew that in less than six weeks, summer crowds would descend on Summer Beach.

She was betting on it.

"There's Java Beach," Shelly said as they neared the coffee shop they'd seen on the way in.

When they stepped into the coffee shop, heads swiveled toward them. Nautical nets were suspended from the ceiling, tiki torches anchored the counter, and vintage Polynesian travel posters of grass-skirted hula dancers covered the walls. Beach reggae played in the background, and the scent of roasted coffee and sweet pastries permeated the air.

An older woman in a gaudy rhinestone sun visor and dyed royal blue hair called out, "Mitch, you've got customers!"

A twenty-something man wearing flip-flops and a Hawaiian shirt pushed through a set of doors from the kitchen. "What'll it be, ladies?" Mitch's smile was warm and engaging, especially toward Shelly.

Ivy held up her phone. "I've got a dead battery. We're stranded. May I use your phone?"

"Sure." Mitch pulled his phone from his faded jeans. "What's the number?"

"Um, I don't remember," Ivy said. "Our parents got a new phone number a few years ago, but it's on my phone. Shelly?"

"Sorry, I never remember phone numbers anymore."

Sheepishly, Ivy asked, "Do you have a phone charger?"

"Here you are." Mitch brought one out from under the counter. "Charges are free. You two from around here?"

"We just flew in from Boston," Ivy said. "And we're moving into the old Erickson house."

"Las Brisas." Mitch let out a whistle. "You're going to be busy."

"Why do you say that?" Ivy asked.

"Place needs a lot of work. A real beauty, though." He grinned at Shelly. "If you need help, I'm pretty handy."

"We can't afford much," Ivy interjected. "We'd planned on doing most of the work ourselves."

The woman with the rhinestone visor behind them spoke up, and her voice had a sharp edge to it now. "The new owner was trying to tear it down and build some fancy resort. Is that you?"

"No." Ivy stiffened. "That was my husband."

"Ladies, meet Darla," Mitch said, amused at the interchange. "Your new neighbor."

The woman stood and stalked over to them. Spangled necklaces around her neck jangled with each step. "You tell him that if one bulldozer crosses that property, we'll stop it in its tracks, you hear me?" She jabbed a bejeweled finger at them. "We're organized here, and we don't stand for people thinking they can buy their way in and destroy our community. A high-rise resort, my eye," she snorted. "This is Summer Beach, not Miami or New York City."

"I didn't come here to do that," Ivy said evenly. "And my husband won't either. He died last year."

"Well, can't say I'm sorry," Darla huffed. "You better watch yourself in this town."

"Hey, Darla," Mitch cut in. "They're new here. Give them a break, will you?" He turned back to them. "I'm really sorry to hear that. Coffee while you wait?" He poured two cups for them. "Medium roast. Sugar and cream behind you."

"How much do I owe you?" Ivy asked, ignoring Darla.

Mitch shrugged off her question. "Welcome to Summer Beach. Most of us are pretty friendly." He dropped his voice. "Even Darla, once you get to know her." His eyes rested on Shelly again.

"I'll pass," Shelly said, turning her back to the woman.

"She's still your neighbor," Mitch said.

Shelly threw a look over her shoulder. "Clearly we're not going to be best friends."

"Just when I thought things were getting quiet around here." Chuckling, Mitch nodded toward the deck, where rustic wooden beach loungers were facing the ocean, and the water lapped the shoreline. Beachgoers were strolling or lounging under umbrellas, and children were playing in the surf. "Nice view outside while you wait for the charge."

Ivy dug out a couple of bills and dropped them into a tip jar that had a Jimmy Buffett Margaritaville sticker plastered to it. "Sounds like my husband made quite an impression here."

"You might say Jeremy Marin brought the community together," Mitch said.

Shelly cut in. "Against him, you mean."

Mitch started to reply, but with a glance at Ivy, he changed his tone. "Awfully big place for one person. Do you have a large family?"

Ivy and Shelly exchanged glances. "We're going to run it as an inn," Ivy said. Might as well announce it. They'd need to turn a profit quickly, and word-of-mouth advertising was about all she could afford.

Darla narrowed her eyes. "We'll see about that, won't we?"

A grin spread across Mitch's face, and Ivy saw Shelly watching him with interest. "No doubt you'll have some interesting guests. Tack a flyer on the community board over there. Everyone checks it out. Y'know, that's a cool idea. Few people have enough room for all their friends that want to visit in the summer. You should be busy."

"Thanks," Ivy said. Mitch seemed kind, and he was a welcome change from Bennett.

The two sisters made their way outside and sat under a beach umbrella in a pair of beach loungers on the sand.

"Jeremy sure made a lot of enemies here," Shelly said, sipping her coffee and surreptitiously watching Mitch inside.

"Another one of his messes to clean up." Stirring her coffee, Ivy said, "What do you think he meant about interesting guests? Seemed like an odd comment."

"Maybe this place attracts a lot of characters."

"Guess so, if Darla and Bennett are examples." Ivy gazed out over the ocean swells and watched the waves rushing the shoreline. "That house seems like a lightning rod for controversy in this town. Think I'm in over my head here?"

"I've watched you handle a lot worse," Shelly said. "I have faith in you—and your crazy decision." She chuckled. "I told you I'm in. Not changing your mind already, are you?"

"Course not." Yet she had an odd feeling that there was more to Las Brisas than she knew.

A few minutes later, Mitch sauntered out to them holding her phone. "You've got a small charge now." He handed it to her. "And here's my card. I put my cell number on it if you need anything."

Ivy noticed that Mitch gave his card to Shelly. She attracted men like stray puppy dogs. Mitch clearly liked Shelly, but he also looked a lot younger. Still, it was good to know someone other than Bennett here.

"Thanks," Ivy said. "First, our luggage." She tapped Bennett's name and passed the phone to Shelly. "You're on."

Shelly took the phone from her while Ivy looked on. "It's ringing...wait, what?" Shelly snapped the phone off. "He just sent it to voice mail."

"Let me see about that." Ivy pressed his number again. This time it went straight to voice mail. "What nerve."

"Text him."

Ivy punched in a message and sent it. She waited a minute, but there was no reply. "How unprofessional. What if I had changed my mind about re-listing the house?" Now, even if she decided to sell the house, Bennett Dylan would be the last person she'd call for assistance. What kind of real estate agent sends his clients to voice mail, declines their calls, and ignores their texts?

"The big question is, how will we get our luggage?"

Ivy flipped through his emails. "Here's one with an address. But it's just a post office box. Let's try again tomorrow. We need to see Mom and Dad." She opened her ride-share app to call a car. After a few taps, she said, "Ten minutes."

Succumbing to a strange new desire, Ivy slipped off her loafers while they waited and dug her toes into the warm sand, connecting with the earth just to make sure she was really here and not imagining things. The sun blazed against her shirt, which now seemed too restrictive. She tugged at the stiff, medium-starch collar.

Ivy tented her hand against the sun and gazed back at the tired white structure that loomed on a point just beyond the village, once again wondering why her husband had never told her about this beachfront house. But then, Jeremy had always had his secrets. She breathed in the cool salt-tinged air blowing in from the sparkling bay. Summer Beach was a welcome respite from the cloying summer humidity of Boston.

She had come full circle.

Ivy swung around, drinking in the beach scene that she'd left years before for college. After her last summer on the beach, she'd been anxious to leave—thanks to Bennett Dylan.

Ivy's parents were quintessential Californians, rooted in the soil they'd been born on, yet she'd grown up watching historical dramas and longing for what she perceived as romantic, old-world traditions. When she was ready for college, besides the local university, those in Boston were among her top choices in the United States.

And so, with her first broken heart, she'd left her

hometown beach life behind, drawn to the east coast and the intellectualism of Boston. The summer vacations on Nantucket were the only brief reminders of the life she'd left behind.

She had been enrolled in a fine arts degree program when she'd met Jeremy, who worked for the French division of a major U.S. technology consulting firm.

She still remembered meeting Jeremy in a coffee shop in Harvard Square. He'd been pounding on a computer keyboard, his floppy, chocolate brown hair obscuring his eyes. Another patron bumped her, and she accidentally splashed hot coffee onto his black turtleneck sweater. He leapt up, exclaiming in French until he met her eyes. Later, they would laugh that this was the only way she could've drawn his attention from his work. He had a single-minded focus, and when he latched onto an idea, there was no dissuading him.

Is this how he'd felt about the house? If so, why? She wondered what mystery was at the heart of his intentions, or if she would ever know.

Ivy glanced behind her at the woman who'd been so rude to them. Darla, their new neighbor. She sighed. Jeremy had not made any friends here, and it would be up to her to repair the damage.

Chapter 4

BENNETT DROVE HIS SUV through Summer Beach, relieved to be rid of his infuriating client. As far as he was concerned, Ivy Marin was the most unappreciative, shortsighted, cheap client he'd ever had.

"Inconsiderate woman," he muttered to himself. He rolled down his windows to vent the car and let the ocean breeze cool his anger.

Ivy had inherited a house on the beach from her husband of questionable merit, and now, with a looming property tax bill and without any discernable income, she'd decided to move into it. What on earth was she thinking? He couldn't imagine or understand what went through her head.

Of all the days for a client to disturb his equilibrium, today shouldn't have been that day. Bennett glanced at the digital clock on the dashboard. Ivy had wasted his precious time today. He was due at the Summer Beach marina soon, and he still had to stop at Blossoms for flowers.

As he drove, he rested a hand on top of the steering wheel, lifting it and nodding to folks he passed. He waved at George, who ran the hardware store, Nailed It, with his wife, and at Arthur from the antique shop, Antique Times. His wife Nan was the receptionist at City Hall.

Summer Beach was the kind of small town where locals and tourists alike still waved to each other. Of course, many people knew him, recognizing his face and name from the campaign and the televised city meetings. He had them to thank for his position, and he'd vowed to represent them to the best of his ability.

Even Ivy Marin, he begrudgingly acknowledged.

That woman hadn't even had the professional courtesy to open the photos he'd emailed to her. As her real estate representative, his job was to represent her, market her property, and find a qualified buyer. But with the derelict condition of the house—thanks to Jeremy Marin, not Mrs. Erickson's estate—he couldn't take photos until it was cleaned. Ivy had refused to pay for anything, so he had no choice but to clean the property himself if he expected to attract a buyer and close a sale.

At first, he'd felt a certain kinship with her when Ivy told him that her husband had passed away. He'd worked with other widows to help them maximize the value of their property, or even advise them not to sell if they had a low tax basis and prices were escalating, helping them realize the most value from their asset.

He prided himself on putting the interests of his clients before his own, which was why he'd spent two weekends hauling debris from Ivy's property and pulling weeds. Inside the house, he'd removed a thick layer of dust and cobwebs, and then cleaned the floors. Finally, he'd borrowed professional photography equipment and taken well-lit photos throughout the rambling house.

She hadn't even looked at the photos. And she'd even admitted as much, which was beyond rude in his book. Never mind that she hadn't thanked him.

Bennett banged the steering wheel. He should've known better than to take the listing. Referring it on to another agent would have been the prudent act, but he'd been soft on her situation and saw an opportunity to help. What a peculiar woman. Her husband had been strange, too.

Jeremy Marin, a millennial techie from Boston with a scruffy beard, black jeans, and expensive sunglasses had breezed into town one weekend, intent on finding a lot to build on. When he learned that the Erickson estate might be for sale, he made a cash offer, which was instantly accepted. Bennett's real estate partner Claire had clearly explained that the historic zoning precluded him from tearing down the house and building on the lot. He'd even signed an acknowledgment of the fact.

That should have been the end of it, but over the next year, Jeremy mounted a battle with the zoning commission to change the zoning. *How can you call this historic, or even historical?* Jeremy had huffed in his French accent. The man had ranted about the age of buildings in Paris, or as he'd said, *real historical buildings.*

If Bennett were given to violence, he'd have punched him.

To a person, Summer Beach residents were dead set against Jeremy's plan. Las Brisas del Mar was a cherished part of Summer Beach history. The local residents loved the old landmark, even though it had been shuttered for decades.

Occasionally Mrs. Erickson's estate and property managers opened the house for a fundraising event. The older woman had been partial to children's and medical charities and environmental causes. Supporters would flock to events because they seldom had a chance to see the property any other way.

Bennett had grown up hearing fabulous stories from neighbors who had attended parties at the estate. Mrs. Erickson had always been generous to the community. From donating money to establish a wildlife sanctuary to funding a children's hospital, she had long been a Summer Beach benefactor. He only wished he'd had the privilege of knowing the great woman.

Ivy Marin would never live up to the standards and generosity of Mrs. Erickson.

Even today, students of architecture still visited to sketch the exterior details Julia Morgan had incorporated into her design. All the old house needed was a thoughtful owner.

Not Ivy Marin. He pulled to a stop sign and waved at local teenagers who were carrying their surfboards across the street. As he waited, he tried to remember where he'd seen Ivy before. She was certainly attractive, although she downplayed her attributes. Maybe she reminded him of someone. Perhaps from his past. Sooner or later, he would remember. He seldom forgot a face.

After the teens passed by, he rolled the SUV forward. If he had the money, he'd buy Las Brisas. Summer Beach was a unique location that had been unspoiled by the growth of Los Angles to the north, where on the west side, charming bungalows on small lots had given way to monstrous McMansions that towered above their neighbors.

Bennett was convinced that Las Brisas should have another life, perhaps as a community center that all residents could enjoy. As he drove, he thought about that. It might still happen. Ivy Marin was in arrears on her tax bill—a dire situation. All the town needed to do was wait for a foreclosure sale and make a bid for the property.

He passed Rosa's fish taco stand, which looked busy today, and parked his SUV alongside the town's flower stand, Blossoms. The owner, Imani, had been an attorney who now made a good living with a far simpler life.

"Hey, Mr. Mayor," a woman in a tie-dyed T-shirt and a wide-brimmed straw hat over sisterlocks sang out.

"Hi, Imani. Could you wrap up your special bouquet of white roses and lilies?"

She looked at him with compassion. "For a special lady?"

Bennett drank in the sweet floral aromas, which reminded him of Jackie. "My wife. Today's our anniversary."

"Has it been a year again already?" Imani plucked the flowers, added one delicate pink rose in the center, and tied the bouquet with a length of pink ribbon. "Here, she'll love these."

"Always her favorites."

Imani's face lit with pride. "He had his choice, but he chose UCSD. And he has a full ride."

"Hard to pass up a university with an ocean view over ones with snow drifts in the midwest. Think we'll be calling him doctor someday?" He knew Imani must be pleased that her son was staying close and going to the university in San Diego.

"I'll let him decide where his passion takes him." She laughed. "Look at me. Three years of law school loans and now I run a flower stand. Although that career allowed me to do this now, so I can't bash it too much."

With an armful of flowers, Bennett made his way through the marina to his boat and boarded. Since he'd spent so much time with Ivy, he didn't have much time left before the sun set, which was the precise time he liked to scatter flowers on the water.

For at sunset, he'd made a vow to the woman he'd loved since college, and every year after that they'd toasted to their future on the boat exactly when the sun touched the horizon.

He smiled as he thought of Jaclyn, his Jackie. Just then, his phone rang, interrupting his bittersweet memories. Though he still thought of her often, this was a sacred time. Registering the name on the screen, *Ivy Marin,* he sent the call directly to voice mail. He'd soon be out of reach of phone service anyway. He turned off his phone.

When the sun kissed the horizon, he cut the engine. The world around him was quiet except for the waves gently lapping against the hull.

"Hey Jackie," he whispered into the breeze. "Didn't think I'd forget, did you?"

With each flower that he tossed onto the inky blue water, he thought about a cherished memory. Their wedding night, their honeymoon in Baja California, their walks on the beach. How she'd loved to sail, to feel the wind in her hair and the spray on her face. Each recollection warmed his heart, and he could almost feel her sitting beside him stroking the nape of his neck and his shoulders as he played guitar. More than anything, he missed her cute lopsided smile—the way one side of her mouth curved up higher until a dimple dotted her cheek.

When he came to the last flower in the bouquet—the blush pink rose—he paused to inhale the sweet scent before leaning over the starboard side and placing it gently on the water. "And for our little girl. I know you're watching over her."

After releasing the pink rose, he trailed his fingers in the water, sifting through the waves that swayed the boat. Finally, he bowed his head and placed his hand over his heart.

"To you, my love. Not to our future, but to our past. And always in my heart."

In her final hours, Jackie had asked him to find another woman to share his life with, but he had never found anyone he'd felt the same way about.

After ten years, he doubted he ever would.

Chapter 5

"WE'LL HAVE TO make do without our luggage tonight," Ivy said, shifting uncomfortably in the back seat as the ride-share driver neared their parents' home.

The adrenaline Ivy felt at the house had worn off. Now, she couldn't wait to ease into a warm bath to wash off the travel grime. "Bennett probably took off with it on purpose just to annoy me."

Shelly fanned her face. "I don't think so. It's not all about you."

"What do you mean by that?"

"You forgot about our bags, too."

Something she never would have done in the past. Seeing Bennett again had been disturbing. "Only because of his attitude."

"Seemed like he was being helpful," Shelly said. "Look, you're the most organized person I know, but you have to admit that in the last twenty-four hours, an impulsive, preoccupied woman who looks a lot like my sister has taken her place. It's okay to forget things. Relax, this gives us an excuse to raid Mom's closet. You know how much fun that is."

"I'll try Bennett again tomorrow." However, that was easily the last thing Ivy wanted to do. She leaned forward toward the driver. "You can let us off here, thanks."

The front steps to the home were a steep descent from the curb to the front door because the house was built on a sloping hillside, which was dotted with houses that opened out to a panoramic, edge-of-the-world view of the ocean.

Exhausted by the early flight from Boston and their afternoon in Summer Beach, Ivy started down the flagstone steps. The pathway was edged with delicate, green baby's tears and shaded by gnarled, silvery-leafed olive trees and pepper trees with pink peppercorns. Filtered sunlight shone through the arched canopy.

The coffee hadn't done much to revive Ivy, except make her jittery. Shelly dragged behind her.

Midway down the hillside, Ivy paused by a hand-carved stone bench her parents had brought back from one of their trips abroad.

As she waited for her sister, she glanced around at the familiar houses of her childhood. Noticing changes and up-grades—the Andersons had added a new Tuscan stone fa-çade, while the Levys and Chens had converted their lawns to stunning desert-scapes—she realized how long she had been away.

When Shelly caught up with her, Ivy asked, "Before we go inside, do you have any idea what Mom's big announcement is?"

"None at all," Shelly said, stopping beside her.

"Mom's nearly seventy," Ivy said, bracing herself for bad news. "You know what that means."

"Not sure I do."

"Her health is probably declining."

"She looked good at Jeremy's funeral," Shelly said. "Mom's pretty straight with us. If there's something wrong, she would've called us, not summoned us here like she did."

"I'm just saying we should prepare ourselves for the worst."

"You do *you*, sis," Shelly said, sounding tired. "I'm not going down that path until we have to."

"No, you never imagine the worst that could happen or plan for it," Ivy snapped. "That's why you've always ended up with men like Ezzra."

As soon as she uttered her words, Ivy regretted them. She was tired and frustrated that Shelly wasn't as concerned as she was.

"Didn't I just tell you that's over?" Shelly put a hand on her hip. "I might not be the uber-organizer you are, but at least I live in the present."

"And what does that mean?"

"Exactly what I said. Like the trips to Nantucket. That summer I joined you guys, you packed enough supplies for an army. You had every minute of every day so structured that you couldn't enjoy yourself without worrying about everyone else."

Ivy opened her mouth in astonishment. "That's what it takes to run a family. Not that you'd know anything about responsibility. You've been running from it all your life."

"And you took everything too seriously. No wonder Jeremy bought that house without telling you. You never would have agreed to it."

"If that's the way you feel, you don't have to move in." Ivy wished she could just shut up, but words kept tumbling from her mouth. "For all I care, you can go back to Ezzra."

Shelly glared at her. "If you were so sure that Ezzra wasn't right for me, you should've told me a long time ago. But then, I kept my mouth shut about Jeremy, too."

Fuming, Ivy crossed her arms. "Go ahead, say it."

Shelly turned away from her as if to end the conversation, but then she whirled around. "All right, I will. Maybe Jeremy wasn't the ideal husband you thought he was. Seems no matter what men do while they're alive, they suddenly achieve sainthood after they die."

"You were always jealous of what we had," Ivy charged, aware that their exchange was spiraling out of control, but too exhausted to stop the damage.

"Now you've got to be kidding."

A few steps beneath them, the front door opened.

Ivy shot Shelly a seething frown. "Not a word to Mom about this. We don't want to worry her." She blinked. How had they gotten into this sniping contest?

Their mother stepped outside. "My darling girls, welcome home," she exclaimed, holding her arms open wide, her gold and silver bangle bracelets tinkling just as Ivy had remembered. Carlotta looked more vital and alive than Ivy had recalled.

Ivy glanced at Shelly, who'd noticed that, too, and looked smugly triumphant.

"Mom, you look gorgeous," Shelly said. "New hairstyle?"

"And a week at the spa." Carlotta shook her fluffy dark hair. Glossy silver streaks framed her face, giving her an elegant appearance. "I feel fabulous."

Ivy was momentarily relieved. Carlotta Reina Bay was a woman who seemed to grow more striking with age. Ivy favored her mother with her petite frame and dark hair, while Shelly took after their father.

Their mother was descended from Spanish aristocrats who had once owned vast expanses of land in California before the state became part of the union. Carlotta carried herself with an air of authority. Even in a casual turquoise-and-white striped sundress and a chunky turquoise necklace, she looked as regal—and as fierce—as a queen.

As Carlotta observed the two of them, her smile waned. "What's wrong? You both look angry. Come here and give me a hug."

Ivy rushed to embrace her mother. "We're just worn out, Mom. It's been a long journey. Is everything okay? We came as fast as we could."

Carlotta looked amused at her daughter's worry. "Couldn't be better, my dear. Come, your father's waiting for you, too." Carlotta turned, her skirts swishing around her slim, muscular calves.

Ivy followed her, not daring to look back at Shelly. *This argument will blow over,* she told herself, though she couldn't help but wonder what Shelly had meant about Jeremy. An uneasy feeling pinched her neck. Did her sister know something she wasn't telling her?

Carlotta led them through the spacious Mediterranean home that her parents had built shortly after their marriage and expanded as their family grew.

Colorful, hand-embroidered pillows from Thailand punctuated long white sofas that rested on polished terra cotta tiles. Talavera Mexican pottery in deep blue hues, orchids in traditional Burmese pottery, and splashes of modern art blended to create a relaxed, comfortable atmosphere. The windows and doors stood open to the fresh ocean breezes.

Upbeat jazz piano music piped throughout the house. Ivy smiled in recognition. The recording was one of her father's own private sessions. He'd sent an audio file to her, and she had it in her music collection on her phone and computer.

"You haven't changed the house much," Ivy said, noticing everything.

"Except for the photos," their mother said, motioning toward a long hallway gallery where framed photographs and children's artwork told the story of the Bay family. "Lots of new photos from your nieces and nephews."

Ivy saw Shelly quickly glance away. Immediately, their silly argument diffused in her mind. What had they been thinking? She touched her sister's shoulder. *I'm sorry,* she *mouthed.*

Shelly nodded. *Me, too.*

Carlotta led them to the rear patio, where the Pacific Ocean sparkled in the distance, and they had all gathered to watch sunsets and roast marshmallows over the years.

Ivy folded back her sleeves, grateful for the sea breezes that cooled the hillside. The scent of honeysuckle from rambling vines mingled with those from orange blossoms, gardenia bushes, and Carlotta's roses, perfuming the air with a mesmerizing mélange.

Gazing around the lush yard perched on a promontory, Ivy breathed in. She'd almost forgotten the intoxicating scents. These were the aromas of her childhood, imprinted on her olfactory memory. This is where Shelly had spent hours helping her mother plant and propagate all manner of plants.

"Hi, Dad," Ivy called out.

Sterling Bay, a bear of a man with thick, steel-gray hair was at the barbecue pit assembling dishes for dinner.

Shelly raced toward their father, and he enveloped her in his arms.

"Two of my three favorite daughters," he said, chuckling. "Good to have you back on the west coast."

"Missed you a lot, Dad." Ivy eased into his generous embrace.

"My darling Ivy," he said, kissing her cheek. "Tell me, how're you doing?"

She knew what he meant. She hadn't seen her parents since Jeremy's funeral. "Every day is a little better. Sometimes I have setbacks, but I've been making the necessary changes."

"She made a huge decision today." Shelly scooped up a slice of fresh zucchini from a platter of raw vegetables and bit into it. "I'll let her tell you. I'm starving."

"Tell us what?" Carlotta asked.

"It's kind of a long story." Ivy wondered where to start so she wouldn't sound completely crazy.

Listening and waiting, Carlotta brushed a light veil of olive oil over the raw vegetables arranged in stainless barbeque mesh holders and finished them with a sprinkle of oregano from the herb garden. She handed the flat mesh holders to her husband, who positioned them over the flames with care.

When Ivy didn't go on, her mother said, "I also made a lime-cilantro aioli for the veggies."

Ivy peeked at the grill. Rosemary salmon and garlic shrimp were sizzling on the barbecue, sending out the most enticing aromas. With the three-hour time difference from the east coast, she realized they hadn't eaten in hours. No wonder she and Shelly were hangry.

"Are you painting again?" Carlotta asked, her voice laced with hope.

"I've been teaching." That's a valid reason for not painting, Ivy thought. Yet it was still an excuse. After Jeremy died, she'd thought she'd lose herself in her painting, but instead, her creativity had been at an all-time low. She'd been so lethargic that she had barely picked up a brush except to instruct a student.

Her mother saw through her thin defense. "Find time for your own work, *mija*," she said with a subtle nudge.

For years, Ivy's mother and father had marketed the crafts of indigenous people from around the world—Asia, North and South America, Europe, Africa, Australia, New Zealand. As they traveled, they discovered new and traditional artists and connected them to their network of retail stores. Carlotta understood the artist's journey.

Her father ignored her mother's comment. Shifting the vegetables on flame, he asked, "So what kind of momentous decision did you make today?"

"I finally visited the house that Jeremy bought in Summer Beach," she said in a light tone, minimizing the difficulty of the visit after she'd been avoiding it for so long.

Falling back into the familiarity of an old routine, Ivy picked up a stack of woven cloth napkins and silverware her mother had left on a table and began to set the places.

"Very glad you did," her father said, pride evident in his voice.

Shelly grinned at her in solidarity. Continuing to listen to the conversation, Shelly wandered around the yard, inspecting the roses and the garden.

"Any luck selling the house?" Carlotta asked, drawing her fine, dark eyebrows together.

Ivy folded a napkin and placed it at one end of the table. "Not even a showing."

"That's odd," Carlotta said. She was arranging a vase of her fresh-cut roses for the table. "Flint told me Bennett Dylan is quite successful in real estate."

"That's okay. I've decided to move into it." Ivy glanced at Shelly, who nodded. This decision solved both of their housing problems. "Shelly, too. We're going to fix it up and rent out rooms."

"Why, that's a wonderful idea," Carlotta said. "You'll be close to your brothers and their families."

"I'll ask your brothers to help," Sterling said. "I've heard the old Erickson estate needs a lot of work. Are you sure you can manage the finances?"

"Fairly sure. I've run some preliminary numbers. Without a mortgage, I only have to cover insurance, repairs, utilities, and taxes. There should be profit left over for both of us."

Ivy would have to create a spreadsheet and perform proper projections, which she had done in a business class that she'd taken as an elective. That had been a long time ago, but she'd managed the household expenses for years.

Ivy lit the candles on the table. "What do you know about the place, Dad?" Her father was a local history buff.

"Been vacant a long time." He removed the roasted vegetables from the fire and slid them onto a platter. "Lot of old stories about that place."

"Like what?" Ivy placed a salad and bread basket that her mother had brought out on the table.

Her parents exchanged glances. "The Erickson woman knew a lot of artists," Sterling said as he opened a bottle of wine and poured a glass for each of them.

Shelly carried platters of food to the table. "What? Is it haunted or something?"

"Not unless you believe in that sort of thing," Carlotta said.

Ivy looked from one to another. "What's that supposed to mean?"

"Only that Amelia Erickson was an avid collector," her father replied in a reassuring tone. "That place has a lot of history. Come, let's eat and celebrate your homecoming."

Ivy raised her glass of wine to theirs, though she couldn't help but wonder. Exactly what kind of history? And had she made a prudent decision?

Chapter 6

THE NEXT MORNING, Ivy stood in front of her mother's three-way mirror, which revealed more than she'd dared to view in years. Nearby, Shelly and Carlotta watched.

"What do you think?" Ivy had poured herself into one of her mother's sundresses. She'd left a voice mail for Bennett, but her mother, always the problem-solver, had hurried to her closets to choose outfits for them to wear until their luggage arrived.

Shelly was delighted, but Ivy was less enthusiastic.

"Wow, I haven't seen you in clothes like that in years," Shelly said.

"That's because I don't own anything like this." Ivy

wore a coral-colored sundress that her mother had brought out of her closet. The dress had a scooped neckline and a fit-and-flare silhouette that flattered her waistline. The hemline grazed her knees, showing off her legs, while the neckline displayed a little more cleavage than she was accustomed to sharing with the world. She felt awkward and bare, and it wasn't her style. She turned to the other side. Still, she had to admit that it was flattering, even a little sexy. The color brought out her green eyes and the highlights in her hair.

"And the *pièce de résistance.*" Her mother looped a handcrafted coral and turquoise necklace from an artisan she'd represented over Ivy's head. Carlotta turned her palms upward. "Stunning."

The jewelry added a certain flair to the dress, Ivy decided.

"You should have new clothes for your new life here," Carlotta said, her face lighting at the idea. "Let me splurge on you. Both of you. I know a fabulous little shop in La Jolla with plenty of dresses like these."

"I'm more of a jeans-and-T-shirt person," Ivy said. "Besides, I have plenty of clothes." When Ivy saw the pleasure on her mother's face dissipate, she paused. She hadn't meant her words to sound so defensive.

"It's just that I don't want you to spend your money on me," Ivy added with haste. "You've already done so much for the girls." And in the back of her mind, she couldn't help but wonder if her mother wanted to spend her money on her children while she was still alive. She softened her tone. "I'm just worried about you, Mom. Are you feeling okay?"

"I'm fine, and I assure you we can still afford our lifestyle," Carlotta said, sniffing at Ivy's comment. "I'd hoped to take all you girls, including Honey, shopping before the party."

Shelly was sorting through clothes in Carlotta's closet. She poked her head out. "When are Honey and Gabe flying in?"

"In a few days."

"I can't wait to see them," Ivy said. Honey was a few years older than Ivy, so Shelly was closer in age to Honey and Gabe's daughter, Elena, who lived in Beverly Hills and had made a name for herself as a jewelry designer to the stars. Since Honey lived on the beach in Sydney, Australia and owned a fashion boutique for resort wear, she had the casual beach look down.

"Actually I have something you might like." Shelly picked up the large leather purse she carried and pulled out a book. "A friend of mine sent this to me to review for my blog."

Shelly's gardening and floral arrangement site had morphed into a lifestyle vlog, with Shelly's 3-minute video makeovers for home, garden, and personal style being her most popular.

Ivy took the book and flipped through it. "*The T-Shirt & Jeans Handbook.* Are you kidding? I'm an expert at that."

Carlotta and Shelly traded exasperated looks.

"You can keep your basic style," Shelly said, tapping the cover. "But you really need to up your game."

Ivy closed the book, but not before she saw several photos of stylish outfits that caught her eye. "I'm through playing games," Ivy said. Especially with Bennett. Now that she thought about it again, where was their luggage and why wasn't he returning her calls?

Carlotta arched an eyebrow. "If you won't listen to me, listen to your sister."

"You have to live a new life now," Shelly added.

"And I am, as of right now," Ivy said, appraising herself in the mirror. Still, they had a point. "Mom, do you have some shoes to go with this?"

Carlotta bustled into her walk-in closet and emerged with a pair of handcrafted jeweled sandals with short kitten heels. "These look good with that."

While jeweled sandals were the last thing she'd buy, she tried not to cringe while she slipped them on. "Not bad," she said grudgingly. They were cute in a twenty-something way. Yet her mother got away with them.

"Wow, you rock those," Shelly said, clapping.

"You look fabulous," Carlotta added. "Very California chic."

Ivy slid another look into the mirror. Surprisingly, the color did lift her spirits.

Carlotta held up a yellow sundress for Shelly. "This is one of my lower hemlines. With your long legs, I'm afraid most of what I have would be too short on you."

Shelly slipped into the dress, which still hovered above her knees. "Perfect, Mom. Thanks." She gave her mother a peck on the cheek. "We have to be on our way. Will you stop by later to see the house?"

"If I have time after yoga," Carlotta said. "The keys to the old Jeep are on the rack by the garage."

"It's still running?" Ivy asked. "That car must have a few hundred thousand miles on it." The Jeep had been passed from one child to another when they were growing up. Ivy had good memories of that old vehicle. They'd carried all their friends to the beach in it.

"We replaced the engine, so it still runs fine." Carlotta smiled. "It's yours."

"Just until I can get a car." Ivy hadn't driven in months. She'd usually taken the subway in Boston, and she had sold Jeremy's BMW.

Carlotta shook her head. "As you wish."

Yesterday Ivy had been so certain of her decision about the house, but now trepidation crept over her. Could she really manage such a large undertaking? Her pulse quickened, and she sat on the bed, resting her chin in her hands. "What have I gotten myself into?"

"You'll find a way, *mija.*" Carlotta put her arm around Ivy. "Your father and the boys can help with cleaning and painting, and Shelly can manage the landscape."

"Already volunteered," Shelly said, turning to Ivy. "We'll figure it out together. That's what Mom always told us, so that's what we're doing."

Ivy reached out to hug her sister. "I needed that reminder."

"Speaking of that…" Shelly rummaged through her bag for a pen and a pad of paper that had a sparkly rainbow on the cover. "Here. You're the Great Organizer. Start with a list of what we'll need."

"You're on." Ivy grinned. With a pencil and paper in her hand, she felt grounded. How well her sister knew her.

Ivy and Shelly left their parents' home and drove along the coast to the smaller community of Summer Beach.

As Ivy drove, she thought about her decision. She was scared to death, but she had little choice except to forge on and give this project everything she had.

"What shall we call the place?" Shelly asked as Ivy drove.

"Las Brisas is the old name, but I'd like a new name to represent the new era. Summer Beach Inn is a bit plain."

"The Breeze Point Inn?"

"Maybe."

As she pulled into the long drive, Ivy had another idea. Once inside the house, she pocketed the key. "I've got it.

Welcome to the Seabreeze Inn," she said, trying to sound more confident than she felt. All she could think was how much money it would cost to open the doors to the public. The thought of it made her queasy.

"Hey, that's a sweet name," Shelly said, following her inside. "By the way, what was in those Sea Breeze cocktails?"

Ivy grinned at her. "Cranberry and grapefruit juice. Vodka optional. I used to drink the virgin version when I was pregnant with Misty."

Shelly chuckled. "I know you were being responsible, but you do see the irony in that, right?"

"I think the fully loaded version is how I got pregnant," Ivy whipped back at her.

"Seabreeze Inn it is. I like that. Sounds sunny and fresh." Grinning, Shelly flicked an old light switch, and the stunning chandelier in the entry blazed beneath layers of dust and cobwebs. "First on the list, glass and crystal cleaner."

Ivy shook her head. "To clean all the windows and light fixtures in this place would cost a fortune in product alone. I make a window cleaner with white vinegar and water. A lot cheaper and just as effective."

"Vinegar? You're kidding, right?"

"We had two children to put through college. I found a lot of ways to economize, especially on expensive branded cleaning supplies."

"While your husband was off spending your retirement

on colossal beach houses."

"Point." Ivy made a face. "But white vinegar still works well. Fewer chemicals, too."

"Point. Vinegar it is."

Ivy made her way into the ballroom and flicked another switch. The entire room blazed with light from the chandeliers. Her heart lit with them, and her mind raced with possibilities. She raised her hands to frame the room. "Reception desk here, sofa and chair grouping there."

"Wonder what all those chandeliers cost?" Shelly whirled around in a graceful pirouette, and her dress swirled around her like a bright sunburst.

Ivy eyed the grand chandelier in the foyer and jotted a note on her little pad.

They strolled through the downstairs rooms that comprised the public spaces: the dining room, the library, the drawing room.

"We'll create a library for the guests," Ivy said, smoothing her hand over handsome built-in bookcases in dark, carved wood. "We can contact local writing groups and host author's book signings here, or in the salon."

"I'll check in with libraries and local bookstores," Shelly added.

With their footsteps echoing in the nearly empty rooms, they continued to another room that still had a piano in it.

"Music room?" Shelly opened the wooden keyboard

cover on the grand piano and ran her fingers across the ivory keys. An off-key melody filled the room. "Must have
been beautiful in its day."

Ivy winced from the sound. "Still can be. Needs tuning." She scribbled a note on another page, imagining guests
mingling and listening to a pianist in the evening. "Maybe a
local music teacher would send students who want to practice. Until we can afford a regular pianist, that is."

"I should brush up on my old songs."

"You still play?"

"Not in years. Ezzra wasn't wild about my practicing.
The keyboard I wanted was fairly expensive, and New York
apartments are too small anyway." She lifted a shoulder and
let it fall.

"Playing the piano makes you happy." Ivy detected a
note of sadness in her sister's voice. What kind of man made
a woman give up her hobbies? Ezzra was worse than she'd
imagined. "You'll practice here whenever you want." If
Shelly could play again, Ivy could paint. With that, she
started for the kitchen. Shelly followed her, humming a
tune.

"This would house an army of cooks and caterers,"
Shelly said, glancing around the spacious kitchen.

"I'm sure it did." Ivy gazed around. Long tables, or
prep stations, ran down the center of the room. To one side,
an adjoining butler's pantry linked the kitchen to the large,
wainscoted formal dining room. She stepped into the pan-

try. "This is where the staff must have organized the dishes, stemware, and silverware."

Shelly opened a cabinet. "Look what's still here."

Ivy peered over her shoulder. Sure enough, vintage china and crystal filled the cupboard. She took out a plate and wiped off a layer of dust. A gold rim framed a delicate floral pattern. She turned it over to see the markings on the back. "Looks like these are from France."

"Fancy," Shelly said, surveying the collection of teacups, soup bowls, and serving dishes. She opened other cupboard doors and whistled. "There's more. Looks like Jeremy didn't touch a thing when he bought the place." She tugged on a cabinet door. "Locked. Wonder what's in here?"

"Maybe the silver?" Ivy stared at Shelly.

Ivy ran her hand over the inlaid wood. "We have to figure out how to open this. I wouldn't want to damage it."

"Bennett might have extra keys," Shelly suggested.

"Better to call a locksmith." The less she had to do with Bennett, the better. She jotted another note on her notepad.

"I'll call Bennett," Shelly said. "Locksmiths cost money."

"As long as I'm not around."

Shelly shook her head. "Whatever happened was a long time ago. He doesn't even remember you."

"Exactly." Ivy jabbed the pen in the air. "Let's check out the plumbing." She strode back into the kitchen and turned on the faucets over one of the large sinks. The pipes rumbled to life, and soon water spurted from the tap. Within seconds, the water ran clear.

Shelly did the same to another one. "This one looks good, too."

"The estate's property manager did a decent job of keeping up the plumbing." For that, Ivy was grateful. Plumbing and electrical would be her greatest expenses, she suspected. "Hope that goes for the toilets and tubs, too." She glanced around. Two vintage turquoise refrigerators flanked a tiled counter. "Think those still work?"

"They built appliances to last back then," Shelly said.

Ivy tried to shove one, but it barely budged. "Heavy, too. Help me with this one?"

Ivy and Shelly shoved a refrigerator from the wall. Ivy knelt to plug it in. As she stood up, brushing cobwebs from her hands, the refrigerator made a loud whirring noise. She stumbled back.

"Sounds like the fridge is getting ready for lift-off," Shelly said, inspecting the hulking appliance.

"As long as it works." Ivy opened the door, and a musty smell wafted out. "If it does, I need a truckload of baking soda, too."

"Think it's safe to leave it on?"

"We'll watch it. Now, let's go upstairs and choose our bedrooms."

Shelly grinned. "Race you." She charged up the stairs,

taking the steps two at a time, while Ivy took her time, admiring the wooden steps that had hand-painted tile risers in between each step. The attention to detail in the house was impressive.

When Ivy was halfway up the staircase, a melodic doorbell chime sounded in the hallway, though it sounded a bit garbled. "Wait up, Shelly. I think we have company."

Ivy hurried down to the front door and opened it.

Bennett stood on the steps with their luggage. Blinking, he took in Ivy's new style. Then, raising his eyebrows, he swirled his hand around by his head. "Hi. You have…something…in your hair."

"I do?" She touched her hair, remembering the cobwebs. "Oh no, are there any spiders?"

"Spiders? I don't see any," he said.

Ivy began shaking her hands. "Please check. I was behind the refrigerator." Her breathing quickened, and it was all she could do to keep from screaming. "Hurry! I hate spiders more than anything else in the world." And of all people to see her like this…

"Well, okay," Bennett said, cautiously taking a step toward her. "I'm not too fond of them myself."

"Oh, come on. Just look, will you?" Ivy shook her head and fluffed her hair. "Do you see anything?" She bent lower so he could get a better look.

Gingerly, Bennett lifted strand after strand, peeling off stray webs. "You've got a lot of cobwebs in your hair."

Ivy shivered. "Please get it all out," she pleaded. She couldn't believe this was actually happening.

"Hold still, I'm working on it."

"Any spiders yet?"

"No. Oh, yuck." He plucked something out and flicked it.

"What was that? Why didn't you let me see what it was?" She shook her hands in despair.

"It was some sort of insect that was caught in the web. Don't worry. It was long dead. Kind of crunchy."

"No details, please." She shuddered again.

"Hold still," he said.

Shelly appeared in the foyer. "What's going on here?"

"I got into a spider's web behind the refrigerator. Bennett's picking out the cobwebs."

"Among other things," Bennett added.

"Oh no, anything in my hair?" Shelly asked.

"Let me see." Bennett peered at her hair.

Still bent over, Ivy glanced up. "Hey, remember me down here?"

"Oh, yeah. I think you're all clear," Bennett said. "But you should wash your hair as soon as you can."

Ivy whipped back up and shook her hair. "I don't need grooming tips from you."

"You asked me to—"

"I know, and thank you," Ivy replied, miffed at him for ignoring her the moment Shelly appeared. Her sister was younger and more beautiful, but for Pete's sake, Ivy had spider webs and dead creatures in her hair.

"Our luggage, thank goodness." Shelly clapped her hands.

"I got your message," Bennett said to Ivy. "When I saw a car out front, I thought it might be yours."

"Thanks," Ivy said. "It's good to have our clothes back."

Bennett cast another appreciative glance over her. "You look nice, though. Really nice."

Ivy's hand shot to her cleavage. Had she been hanging out when she was doubled over? She was filled with embarrassment.

"Courtesy of our mother's closet," Shelly said.

"Your mother has exceptional taste," Bennett said, shifting on his feet. He glanced back at Ivy, then reached toward her hair. "Wait, just one more…"

"What are you doing?" Reflexively, Ivy dodged his hand.

Bennett plucked something from her hair. "Got it. You really need to—"

"Wash my hair. I know," Ivy said, tossing it back. The way he looked at her was uncomfortable, and her heart was already pounding from the thought of spiders. "Thanks for the luggage and everything." She reached for the door.

"Wait," Shelly cried. "Bennett, do you have any extra keys to the house?"

"I might. I'll check Claire's files. I believe there were some documents—and maybe a set of plans—that went with Las Brisas."

"Guess what?" Shelly's eyes flashed with excitement. "We're calling it the Seabreeze Inn. Do you like it?"

"Inn?" Bennett asked, frowning. "You can't run this as an inn."

"And why not?" Ivy was growing perturbed with him. Why couldn't he just leave the luggage and go?

"Because it's not zoned for that. This is strictly a residential neighborhood."

Ivy put her fists on her hips. "So who should I see about having that changed?"

Bennett hesitated for a moment, staring at her before he spoke as if he were weighing something in his mind. Finally, he said, "You'll need a business license, too. Start at the treasury office and the zoning department at City Hall. It's in the village." Narrowing his eyes, he said, "I thought you planned on making this your home."

"I am, but I have to do something with all this space to pay the property taxes," Ivy said, exasperated at his inability to understand her dilemma. She spoke slowly to make her point. "If I don't run this as an inn, I'll lose the house to a tax sale."

"Unless you make improvements and list it for sale again. Now that you've finally found time to see your property, I'm sure you can understand the problem I had in trying to market it all these months."

Ivy drummed her fingers on her arms, anxious for him to leave. "I appreciate your advice, but I prefer to handle this property my way."

"The zoning is there for a reason." Bennett shook his head. "You're just like your husband, aren't you? Next you'll want to tear down the house."

"Okay, you two." Shelly cut in, touching each of their shoulders. "Bennett, we're so glad to get our bags. Hope to see you around town soon."

"Or not." Ivy held open the door and tapped her foot. What had she ever seen in him?

"Oh, you will," Bennett said. "I can guarantee that. By the way, you'll also need to transfer the utility bills into your name."

After Bennett left, Ivy blew out a breath. "The nerve of that guy, thinking he should stick his nose into my business. That sounded like a threat, and I sure don't need his uninformed opinion. Hope I never have to see him again."

Shelly watched Bennett get into his SUV. "Think he's right? About the zoning, I mean?"

Ivy slammed the door. That man was as full of himself as he had been when he was younger. "We'll see about that. There are plenty of seaside inns up and down the coast of California. When I tell the zoning department about my plans, I'm sure they will approve the use."

Chapter 7

FIRST THING IN the morning, Bennett strode into the Summer Beach City Hall and pushed through a door marked Planning and Zoning Department. A trim man with a thick thatch of silver hair and a fit, ramrod-straight physique even Bennett envied stood behind the desk tapping on a computer keyboard. Bennett rapped his knuckles on the counter.

"Hey Boz, I've got a heads-up for you."

"Yeah, boss?" Boz finished typing and turned toward him, peering over his half glasses.

"Jeremy Marin's widow just moved into Las Brisas."

"About time. You'd been trying to reach her forever.

Imagine having enough money that you don't even care about a place like that." Boz chuckled. "What's her story?"

Bennett glanced around and lowered his voice. He didn't want to be seen as gossiping, but the Las Brisas estate was a serious issue in the town. "She's planning on running it as an inn."

Boz shook his head. "Not zoned for that. Didn't you tell her?"

"Like speaking to a rock. Couldn't get through to her. Thought you should be ready for the hot-headed Mrs. Marin. She's argumentative and opinionated. Expect a scene."

"No worries, boss. I'll set her straight. So, no luck on a potential buyer?"

"The place is dated, and with the historic designation, it takes a special person who's dedicated to its preservation."

"Someone will turn up," Boz said. "Sure would help if she did something with the landscaping. That's been a real eyesore ever since her husband bought it and let it go. That lady's got no one to blame but herself for that."

Bennett nodded, though he still wondered why Jeremy Marin hadn't told his wife about the house. At least, that's the story he got from his real estate sales partner Claire, who was meticulous with details. She was undergoing chemotherapy, and he didn't want to disturb her with this mess.

"Good luck with her," Bennett said, grinning. "Alert security if you have a problem." He could just imagine how that scene would play out.

"Will do, boss." Chuckling, Boz turned around and went back to work.

After leaving the Planning and Zoning Department, Bennett made his way to his office down the hall and opened the door marked *Bennett Dylan, Mayor.*

He hadn't planned on continuing his real estate practice while he was in office, but neither of them could have foreseen Claire's illness. His days were divided between his mayoral duties during the day, and his evening and weekend work in real estate. He used to sit in and jam with a local band that played around town, but he hadn't done that in months. With hardly a moment of free time, he was planning to bring on another partner in the real estate practice to handle Claire's book of business, though it had been difficult to find the right person.

Ivy Marin. He sat at his desk and ran his hands over his face. As far as he was concerned, she was a toxic woman taking up space in his head. Just another rich lady thinking the world revolved around her, even though she was pleading poverty. While owning a valuable property like Las Brisas. Figure that one out.

He leaned back in his chair and stared through the plate glass window from the City Hall perched on a hill. Tyler and Celia, his neighbors on the ridgetop, were easing their boat out of the marina for a sail. The line out the door at Java Beach told him Mitch was doing brisk business today. Once summer started, Mitch would hire local high school students to help him manage the summer crowd.

Many Summer Beach residents found work at the nearby horse racing track—a world famous, seaside race track that attracted affluent visitors from the middle of July to the beginning of September, and again during November. The Summer Beach population would surge when the wealthy second—or third or fourth—homeowners arrived for the meet. No doubt Ivy Marin was bent on attracting part of that crowd.

Ivy Marin. He had to get that infuriating woman out of his mind. Women like her were why he'd retired from dating.

It was hard to believe she was any relation to Flint Bay—who was a great guy—but she'd said they were relatives. Definitely distant relations. He hadn't known Flint long, but they'd connected on a bike ride for charity, and Flint had referred a real estate client to him, among other things. They'd connected on social media, too, and that's when he'd seen a post about Ivy attending a party Flint's parents were giving.

He'd jumped at the opportunity to get Ivy to see her property. Now he almost wished he hadn't. But with Claire's medical treatment, she could use the commission, so he'd tried to do everything in his power to sell it.

Heaving a deep sigh, Bennett thought about how much he loved Summer Beach. As mayor, he'd pledged to represent all residents. Unfortunately, now that Ivy was a resident, she was included in the population, too. But with any luck, one of the real estate agents, Hollywood moguls, or racehorse owners he'd pitched Las Brisas to before would come back with an offer to buy the property. And that would be the end of Ivy Marin.

-100-

Chapter 8

"YOU MIGHT AS well have all the linens in this closet for your new inn," Carlotta said, motioning to high stacks of neatly folded sheets and towels. "I haven't used most of them since you all left home."

Ivy gazed up at the linens that reached to the top of the linen closet. The scent of lavender from neatly tied bundles of dried lavender stalks harvested from her mother's garden wafted out. The herbal aroma reminded her of her childhood when she'd slept on similarly scented sheets. She still found it comforting. "Don't you need these linens anymore for when friends or grandchildren come to visit?"

Her mother drew a breath to speak but stopped short.

The small movement caught Ivy's eye. "Mom, what is it?"

Carlotta waved her hand. "We have far too much of everything. Whatever you want, please take, *mija*. And keep the dress and shoes you borrowed, too. They look better on you than me."

Ivy knew that was an outright lie. "Mom, that was a new dress, and the shoes were barely worn."

Carlotta lifted a shoulder and let it fall. "I bought those last year. Take them. Tell Shelly to keep hers, too. Maybe I have other things you can wear."

"Mom, this isn't like you. Next, you'll be offering me your jewelry."

"As a matter of fact, if there are any pieces you want, I'd rather see you enjoy them. I won't wear most of what I have anymore."

Anymore? What did that mean? Dreading the worst, Ivy placed her hands on her mother's shoulders.

"Please tell me what's going on. Are you ill?" Ivy's words felt thick in her throat. All her life, her mother and father had been active and vital. Now she realized she'd often taken for granted that her parents would always be there. How she wished she'd visited more often. Was she too late to make up for her self-centered adulthood?

Carlotta pursed her lips. "I promised your father that we would wait until everyone is together to make our announcement. Sterling would be livid if I said anything before then."

"Mom, please. I'm worried about you."

"I'm a strong woman. I'll be fine."

Ivy's hand flew to her mouth. "You *are* ill."

"*Mija*, stop. Please."

"Is it Dad?"

Carlotta hugged her. "You're only worrying yourself, and there's no cause for it. None of us live forever anyway." She nodded toward the sheets and towels. "Now take whatever you need. I'm going to the kitchen for a wheatgrass juice drink before Zumba."

"Wheatgrass? Has Shelly influenced you?"

"Dear me, no. But if the two of you would like a glass—"

"No, thanks." Ivy liked to think of her diet as healthy, but clearly, she hadn't gone as far down that path as her mother had. Why was her mother suddenly embracing wheatgrass?

Shelly was in her old bedroom. Ivy made her way there and poked her head in the doorway, just as she used to do years ago. Photos of ballet recitals, old toe shoes, gardening gloves, and horticulture books were still strewn around the sunny yellow bedroom. "Hey, I have to talk to you."

"Sure," Shelly said. She had propped herself against a stack of ruffled pillows and was texting on her phone. "Can you believe Mom kept everything we left here? Except for Honey's room. She converted that to a fancy guest room."

Ivy eased onto the bed next to her sister. "Did you know Mom's drinking wheatgrass juice?"

Shelly stopped texting. "What's wrong with that?"

"A lot of people with serious illnesses drink that stuff."

Shelly turned on her side to face Ivy, propping herself up on one arm. "A lot of healthy people drink it, too."

Ivy stared at her sister, desperate to make her understand. "She offered me all the linens in the linen closet."

"So? It's not like she needs that much anymore. Some of those sheets and towels must be twenty or thirty years old."

"Plus the new dress and shoes she lent me." When Shelly failed to look impressed, she added, "And any of her jewelry."

Shelly shot up in bed. "What? Which pieces?"

"Anything I wanted. Shelly, she'll give us anything she owns if we want it. You know what that means."

Finally, her words sunk in.

"Like Grams did before she died," Shelly said, nodding solemnly.

Ivy flopped back against the bed. "She won't tell me anything—even though I confronted her. Said she has to wait for all of us to be together. Dad insisted."

Shelly's eyes widened. "Could it be Dad?"

Ivy didn't like that idea either. "Something is wrong. But I'm glad we're back now. We can help them."

"We've been away a long time," Shelly said quietly. "I

never came back as often as I should have."

"And Honey is in Sydney. Even farther away than we were."

"Flint and Forrest are here," Shelly said. "Maybe they know something."

Ivy thought about their brothers who lived not far away in another small coastal town. "I don't think so. They never could keep secrets."

Shelly sighed. "They definitely would have told us. So what should we do?"

Ivy chewed on her lip. "Wait for the party, I guess. Doubt if Dad would give it up before then." Carlotta and Sterling Bay were the sort of married couple that finished each other's sentences and had each other's back. They'd go to their grave with their secrets, not that they had any, Ivy thought.

Except for right now.

The next morning, Ivy and Shelly brought necessities that Carlotta had insisted they take to the Summer Beach house. They each cleaned the bedroom they'd chosen—Ivy, the master bedroom, and Shelly, one on the other side that was almost as large. Each one had magnificent ocean views, along with a fireplace, deep claw-footed tub, and antique furnishings. After dusting their bedrooms, Ivy and Shelly helped each other make their beds.

Ivy stepped back from her bed. The room was cool,

and all morning she'd imagined Amelia Erickson's presence. She could hardly describe the feeling she had, but she sensed a sort of welcome. Almost as if Amelia had been waiting for her.

Placing a pillow on the bed, Ivy said, "Life is strange, isn't it? A month ago, I never would have thought I'd be moving in here."

"Me neither." Shelly grinned. "After I told Ezzra I wasn't returning, he had a melt-down."

"And?"

"And nothing. Totally over."

They planned to fly back to Boston soon—Ivy to move out of her rented room at the professor's home, and Shelly to collect her things from the tiny apartment she shared with a friend from college. Ezzra had been so demanding that she hadn't spent much time there.

Ivy surveyed the bedroom. She loved the mahogany armoire with cherrywood inlays that stood near a fainting couch—a good place for reading, she imagined. An antique Chinese dressing screen partly obscured the entry to an entire dressing room filled with shelves and mirrored closets with beveled mirrors—more than she would ever use. "You know what this room needs?"

"Your artwork," Shelly said.

Ivy walked to the window and pushed back the old navy drapes that covered white shutters. With care, she folded the shutters back and gazed through the old glass panes that were a little wavy. "I'd like to sketch this beach soon." This vantage point was perfect.

"You will."

Ivy turned back to Shelly. "But before I start that, we have to get this place ready for guests."

"Let's get the kitchen set up," Shelly said.

After they brought in more supplies their mother had packed—coffeemaker and coffee, toaster, and an assortment of citrus fruit from the trees in the yard—they placed it all on the kitchen counter.

Ivy flicked a switch. "Lights work." The windows were large and flooded the room with sunshine. They'd have little need for lights during the day. She opened the turquoise refrigerator they had plugged in. "Wow, it's cold. Amazing that it still works."

"Like I said. Built to last." Shelly put a few supplies inside the old unit.

Ivy emptied another bag. "I need to change the utilities and stop by City Hall to get the business license. Want to come?"

Shelly pushed aside a curtain and peered outside. "I'll stay here. I want to inspect the landscaping to see what we can salvage and what we need to make it presentable. If I need anything, I can walk into the village."

Ivy climbed the steps to the Summer Beach City Hall and Civic Center, which was a small building on a hill overlooking the sea. Mounds of blazing pink bougainvillea and other flowering desert-scape plants surrounded the mid-century modern structure.

Inside, sunshine spilled through clerestory windows in the high-ceilinged room. Mature, fiddle-leaf fig trees stretched broad leaves toward the light, and glossy-leafed philodendron thrived beneath their shady canopy. Ivy scanned the entry area.

A voice rang out from the reception desk, where a vase of garden-cut roses filled the air with their soothing aroma. "Good morning, it's a glorious day in Summer Beach. May I help you, hon?"

Ivy turned toward the kind voice, which belonged to a sweet-looking woman with a halo of red curls who looked to be in her fifties.

"I need to get a new business license."

"Opening a new business here, are you? Wouldn't be the old ice cream shop next to Mitch's Java Beach, would it?" She chuckled. "I'm Nan. Welcome to Summer Beach. I've heard about you."

"Not the ice cream shop. The Seabreeze Inn."

When the women looked nonplussed, Ivy said, "The old Erickson home. I'm the new owner," she added quickly. She was learning to distance herself from her unpopular husband in Summer Beach.

"Ah, yes. We've all been watching that mighty closely." A shadow crossed her face. "The city spent a lot of our taxpayer's money defending Las Brisas. You're not tearing it down, are you?"

"Not at all. I think it's a beautiful old home, and I want others to experience it, too."

"Good. That Jeremy Marin was a devil, I tell you. What nerve, coming in here with his fancy LA girlfriend and thinking he could do whatever he wanted in Summer Beach." She shook her head. "I don't know how you came by the old place, but I'm happy you did. You look like a nice sort. Awfully pleased to meet you." Nan whipped out her hand and gave Ivy a hearty handshake. "What's your name, hon?"

"Ivy, uh, Bay," she said, giving her maiden name. Numbly, Ivy shook Nan's hand. Girlfriend? She felt like she'd just been slammed with a bucket of ice cubes.

"Ivy Bay, what a sweet name. Any relation to Carlotta and Sterling Bay?"

"My parents," Ivy managed to say, despite the crushing heartache that was making it hard to breathe. "They had a lot of fun naming me and my brothers and sisters." She wasn't surprised; her parents were quite social and well known in San Diego County.

"Glad to have you in Summer Beach." Nan pointed toward an open door. "Business permits right over there," Nan chirped, clearly oblivious to Ivy's distress. "Hope to see you around town. My husband and I own Antique Times on Main Street if there's anything you need or want to sell."

"I may, thanks." Ivy stumbled toward a water fountain to compose herself. LA girlfriend? This was all so out of character for Jeremy. Or was it? She ran his business trips through her mind, trying to recall any details she should have noticed. He'd been so upbeat about those trips, but so tired when he returned. He always said they were exhausting. Another thought struck her. Did Bennett know about this?

A young woman with a toddler waited for her to finish at the water fountain. Ivy tried to pull herself together. It wasn't as if she hadn't suspected something, but to be faced with Jeremy's betrayal was shattering. Yet, nothing in the past would change her situation now. She drank from the stream of cold water to calm her feverish thoughts.

She still had a job to do here.

Once she had composed herself, she marched through the doorway that Nan had directed her toward and stepped to the counter, summoning her strength. "Hi, I'm new here, and I'd like a business license for a new business I'm opening."

"Welcome to Summer Beach," the young woman said with a smile. "I'm Tracy. Here's a form to fill out. What kind of business are you opening?"

"An inn."

"We sure need more of those. Here's a pen, too." Tracy handed her a yellow and orange pen with the Summer Beach logo emblazoned on it in blue script.

Ivy wondered if everyone was this friendly in Summer Beach. She'd been used to the impersonal, bureaucratic nature of Boston city government. Much as she loved Boston and all the city's museums and universities and restaurants, that was simply the big city way.

Ivy filled out the form and slid it back.

"Okay, I'll check that for you." Tracy typed in the address on her computer. Frowning, she said, "One moment, I'll be right back. You can keep the pen. Won't you have a seat?" She pushed away from the counter and disappeared into an adjoining office.

Ivy eased onto a bright orange, modern-looking chair. To keep her mind off Jeremy, she pulled out her notepad and added a few household items to her shopping list. Staying organized and focusing on details helped calm her mind.

Holding her sunny new pen poised in mid-air, Ivy paused, suddenly aware.

Or, had she used that method as a crutch to ignore the truth about her marriage she couldn't face?

She closed her eyes in thought, trying to maintain her equilibrium. Just when she thought she was getting used to functioning without her husband, now she had to process this disturbing news. She wanted to run screaming from the building, but she had to take care of business first.

Breathe. Just breathe.

A few minutes later, Tracy returned with a youngish-looking man with a thick head of silver hair.

He stuck out his hand. "Jim Boz, head of Planning and Zoning. Tracy tells me you want to run an inn at the Erickson house."

Ivy stood up. "That's right. A bed and breakfast." She recalled Nan's comment. "I understand there's a real need here for that."

"True, but your house is zoned for residential use."

"Can you make an exception?"

"I'm sorry. I can't."

At his words, Ivy felt her world crumble. Unless she could generate income from the property, she would surely lose it. She lowered her eyes and blinked, trying to clear the hot tears of anger and frustration that threatened to spill from her eyes.

A second blow inside of five minutes was almost too much to handle. Her world seemed to flash before her, and her knees wobbled. She'd have to return to Boston and live out her years alone in the professor's extra bedroom.

Or she could stay and fight.

She pressed her hands on the counter. "I've heard zoning laws can be changed. How can I do that?"

"There's a process for that, Mrs. Marin. You can file a request."

Tracy interjected. "Her name is Bay," she said, consulting the form Ivy had filled out. "You're thinking of Jeremy Marin, the former owner."

"He was my husband." A chill snaked through Ivy.

How had this man known who she was?

"Oh." Tracy backed out of the office as if Ivy were contagious.

"Mr. Boz, I'm nothing like my husband was," Ivy said, her voice rising. "I only want to rent out rooms. I need to run it as an inn. If I can't, I'll surely lose the property."

"Wasn't it listed for sale?"

"It was, but that didn't work out—" Ivy stopped at the sight of Bennett. Tracy trailed behind him.

Bennett approached her. "I understand there's a problem here?"

"What are you doing here?" Ivy asked, her pulse ratcheting up another notch. Of all the people to show up at City Hall. Had he been waiting to trap her here? Anger burned her cheeks.

Boz turned to him. "No problem. I was explaining to Mrs. Marin—"

"Bay. I'm Ms. Bay now, if you don't mind." She'd had enough of her husband. She tamped down a twinge of guilt, though she couldn't deny the facts about Jeremy that were coming out.

Boz cleared his throat and continued. "As I was saying, Mayor Dylan, I told Ms. Bay—"

Turning on Bennett, Ivy spat out, "Mayor? Why didn't you tell me you were the mayor?"

"I didn't think it was relevant," Bennett said. "Now, as Boz said, you're welcome to file a zoning change." He took the official form from Boz and handed it to her.

"You bet I will." Ivy snatched the paper from his hand. "This inn is going forward." Mayor Dylan? And as far as she was concerned, Bennett was just another man keeping secrets from her. Just as he had before.

"If you run an illegal inn, you'll be fined," Boz said. "The city can also shut down the operation."

Livid, Ivy clutched the counter. That was the third knife in her gut today. She slammed the pen down on the counter.

"This is your doing, isn't it, Bennett?" Without waiting for a reply, Ivy charged from the office. She had to get out of there before she broke down.

As Ivy rushed through the lobby, Nan touched her shoulder. "I'm so sorry. I couldn't help but overhear. I know you're crushed."

Nan's kind face and the greenery around them blurred before her. "It was my last hope," Ivy said, choking back a sob. She wasn't the type of woman to cry in public, but the last year had proven so difficult. At random times, she'd found herself tearing up over apples in the produce department, or blinking back tears on the T, surrounded by stony-faced subway riders. And now that her suspicions of Jeremy were proving well-founded after all, it was almost more than she could take. And then there was Bennett.

Nan put an arm around her. "Come to our shop for tea. My husband is there during the day, and I'm there from five to seven every evening."

Nodding, Ivy thanked her and stumbled outside into the bright, unrelenting sunshine. What on earth was she going to do now?

Chapter 9

IVY SAT IN her parents' Jeep outside the house, watching Shelly digging in the yard with her earphones in, swaying to some music only she could hear. How was she going to break the bad news about the zoning to her sister, who'd bought into the whole idea of moving here and working with her in this venture?

With the windows down, the ocean breeze was cool on her hot face. Ivy was limp from stress and the surge of adrenaline that had coursed through her at City Hall. She heard Shelly singing; her sister looked so happy. Shelly had a whole new purpose outside of Ezzra of the double Z. And Ivy had this house to salvage from the mess her husband had left behind.

She chewed her lip. She had to figure out a way to save what they had.

A thought suddenly occurred to her. Her daughter Misty had once said something about rentals. She fished her phone from her purse and pressed the screen for her number.

"Hey Mom, what's up?"

Ivy was pleased that Misty had answered the phone. Both of her children preferred texting, but since Jeremy's death, Misty often picked up when she called now. "Hi Misty. How's the rehearsal for the new show?"

"Great. You sound funny. Kind of stopped up. Are you okay?"

"Okay enough. Probably allergens in the air." Ivy wasn't used to confiding her troubles in her children. She had always been the one to provide emotional support in the family. "Remember when you were telling me about some website that hooks up people to stay with other people?"

Misty erupted with an awkward giggle. "Mom, I told you not to use the term hook up anymore. It doesn't mean what it used to."

"What does it mean again?"

"You know when two people don't really want to date, but they're into each other. They want to be intimate, but not—"

"Oops, I remember." Was she that out of touch? Ivy asked, "What was that website?"

"I hope you mean the one for home stays and vacation rentals—not the other one. Hang on. There, I just texted it to you. Mom, I'm being called onstage. Gotta run, loves you, babe."

"I loves you, too, babe," Ivy said, smiling at the term she'd cooed to the girls when they were babies. Even though Misty always seemed to be in a hurry, she took a little time to talk. Ivy hung up and clicked on the website link.

Ivy hadn't yet told her daughters that she'd decided to remain in Summer Beach. The girls had their own lives now, especially Sunny. She'd hardly heard from her in weeks. Of her two daughters, Misty was the solid one who always had a plan. Sunny took more after her father with her mercurial personality.

Shelly spotted her and ambled toward the Jeep. She had dirt smudged on her cheek, and she looked happier than Ivy had seen her in years.

Ivy pocketed her phone and stepped out. "How's it going?"

Shelly swept wisps of hair from her forehead with the back of her garden-gloved hand, leaving another streak of dirt across her skin. "These grounds are fascinating. Overgrown and untended, but I can see that it was once a fine garden. Wait until you see what I'm planning. Did you get the business license?"

"Tough morning."

Shelly peered at her. "You okay? You look upset."

"Jeremy's quite the gossip topic around town." Ivy blinked back the tears that threatened to spill from her eyes. "Seems he was seen around town with another woman."

Shelly drew up her brow in compassion. "I'm really sorry to hear that." She opened her arms to Ivy.

"Me, too." Ivy let her sister envelop her. There was little else to say.

After a few moments, Shelly pulled back and said, "Lemonade would taste good right now. Luckily for us, there's a Meyer lemon tree around back that's laden with fruit. Found an old herb garden, too. Mint, oregano, and sage are still growing wild. The rosemary has morphed into a giant shrub. Come, I'll show you." Shelly took her by the hand.

Ivy followed her sister. While they picked lemons, she told her more about what had happened at City Hall with the zoning issue and Bennett.

Shelly gaped at her. "Bennett's the mayor?"

"Just my luck," Ivy said, tugging at a large yellow lemon.

They lugged the fruit into the kitchen and washed it in the oversized sink. Ivy squeezed juice from the lemons with a vengeance the poor lemons didn't deserve. Still, the juice was sweet.

Shelly reached into the refrigerator's freezer section.

"We even have ice." She brought out a dulled silver ice tray with a lever on top.

Ivy stared at the relic from the past. "I haven't seen one of those in forever."

Shelly used the edge of her shirt to lift the lever, but it barely budged. "It's really stuck. Wonder how people got the ice out?"

"Try running the bottom under hot water. I think I saw Grams do that when we were kids."

Shelly followed her direction. "Ah, voilà. Ice cubes." She turned the cracked cubes into a stainless pan she'd rinsed out. "I feel like a pioneer woman here."

Ivy managed a smile. "You've lived too long in the city."

A few minutes later, Ivy sat nursing mint-infused lemonade on an old stool at the counter, grateful for the cool drink. She pressed the cold glass to her still fevered cheeks.

Shelly eased onto another rickety stool. "So if we can't run it as an inn, what do we do now?"

"I had an idea and called Misty. Here's what she sent me." Ivy showed Shelly the website. "People rent out rooms in their homes through this site, iBnB. It says to check your area to see if local laws allow the renting out of rooms. I wonder if this is different from operating a business."

"Let's find out. Call the city."

"I didn't leave them with a great impression of me." Ivy slid the phone across the counter. "You call."

Shelly found the telephone number and called. After explaining what she needed to know, a grin spread across her face. "You're absolutely certain?" She flashed a thumbs up sign. "That's wonderful, thank you, Nan." She ended the call. "We're good to go for iBnB."

Ivy gave Shelly a high five. "What about hosting events like weddings?"

Shelly sipped her lemonade. "I'm sure we can figure out something."

Tapping her temple, Ivy said, "People could also pay us for our wedding planning services."

"Our *what?*"

"I'm sure we could manage," Ivy said.

Shelly grinned. "My floral arrangements will blow them away."

"See? That's fantastic," Ivy said, falling into Shelly's arms. "We're back in business." She was so relieved that she did a little dance, twirling around the kitchen.

"Dance party!" Shelly tapped her music app on her phone and joined in. Soon they were singing to Adele and Sara Bareilles songs and swinging each other around the kitchen as they had when they were kids.

"Anyone home?" The back door edged open.

Ivy spun across the kitchen and stopped just short of Bennett Dylan, the last man in the world she wanted to see. "Don't you knock?" she asked, pressing her hand to her chest to catch her breath.

"Saw a Jeep out front, but no one answered the door. Now I see why." Bennett grinned at her. "Glad you're not upset anymore."

Ivy folded her arms and glared at him. "I'm still angry at you. What do you want?"

Reaching into his sports jacket, he pulled out a ring of old keys. "These go with the house." He laid them on the counter, along with a yellowed tube and a folder. "As well as architect's blueprints and other documents pertaining to the house that Claire had in her files."

Shelly picked up the keys. "Sure appreciate that. And it's nice to meet the mayor."

Ivy didn't respond. An infuriating smile was still plastered on Bennett's face, just as when they were teenagers. He thought he'd trashed her plan to run an inn, but she was just beginning.

"Guess I'll see you two around town." He shut the door beyond him.

Rolling her eyes, Ivy turned back to Shelly. "I could live a life of happiness without ever seeing that man again."

"Don't let him get to you," Shelly said. "Besides, he's kind of hot."

"Now I know you're kidding." Though she loathed to admit it to Shelly, she'd often had the same thought. "You have no idea how persistent and persnickety he can be."

"Persnickety?" Shelly laughed. "I haven't heard that word since Grams was alive."

"I'm older than you, remember? Now, let's check the cabinets in the butler's pantry."

After trying half a dozen keys in the lock, Ivy slipped in another one and turned it. The cabinet creaked open.

Ivy and Shelly peered inside.

Empty.

"Well, we tried," Shelly said. "Wonder what the rest of these go to?"

Ivy shook her head and glanced in the folder Bennett had left. She thumbed through old receipts and letters from the trustee of Amelia Erickson's testamentary trust. She was just about to close the folder when an old letter slipped from the back of the file. She picked it up and eased open the crinkly paper.

Sliding onto a stool, Ivy said, "Listen to this. It's a letter from Lausanne, Switzerland. I think it's to Mrs. Erickson's trustee."

Dear Mr. Atkins,

I hope this letter finds you well. Mrs. Erickson's condition remains largely unchanged; however, she has become quite agitated over the disposition of her art collection and insisted I write this letter to you. This worry interferes with her sleep and general well-being. I wish I could be more specific, but you must understand her difficult decidedcondition.

It is my understanding that the Amelia and Gustav Er-

ickson art collection was donated to several museums, but she remains adamant that there are other important paintings at her home in Summer Beach. Would you be so kind as to send a brief letter to reassure her that all paintings have been distributed as per instructions? We feel it would put her mind at ease. Thank you for your attention to this matter.

Dr. Carl Stager

"That poor woman," Shelly said. "I wonder what was wrong with her."

"Maybe someone in Summer Beach remembers." Ivy's heart went out to Amelia. "For her physician to have been so concerned that he asked her trustee to reassure her, Amelia must have been distraught enough that her emotional condition threatened her health."

And Ivy could understand why. Paintings were more than mere wall decorations. Art was a reflection of the artist's soul and the world around them. To paint was to create impressions that brought joy or shed light on humankind's shared journey.

"She must have really loved the artwork in her collection," Shelly said.

"And the artists." Ivy looked at Shelly. "Every work of art carries with it a piece of the artist's soul. Paintings are windows to our human experience."

"No wonder Amelia was so upset."

Ivy wondered which paintings Amelia was worried about and if her concerns had ever been addressed.

Ivy folded up the letter. If Amelia's questions had been resolved, she'd think this letter would not have been saved.

And yet, here it was. Ivy returned the letter to the folder, which she placed in a drawer for safekeeping.

Two days later, stifling a yawn, Ivy watched as the ballroom filled up with Bay family relatives, hugging and chatting and laughing despite the early morning hour.

Ivy greeted her father as he arrived with an armload of drop cloths for painting. "Thanks for rallying the family, Dad."

Her father deposited the paint-spattered cloths on the kitchen counter and stopped to hug her. "Actually, it was your mother."

Her mother was a force of nature. Carlotta could mobilize an army of volunteers when she wanted to. And today, that army consisted of Ivy's brothers and their children—her nieces and nephews. The extended Bay family gathered in the ballroom, ready to be deployed on a clean-and-repair mission. Ivy had bought plenty of supplies, and her Dad and Forrest had promised a lot more, but she still needed paint.

"I'm surprised Forrest came. Is Flint around?"

"He'll be back shortly," her dad said. "Said he's bringing a local buddy to help."

Ivy greeted her brother Forrest, who was a couple of years older than her, with his children. Forrest and Flint were twins. Flint's wife Tabitha was there with their four twenty-something children: Skyler, Blue, Jewel, and Sierra. Forrest and his wife Angela had arrived with their five children: Poppy, Coral, Summer, Rocky, and Reed, who were similar ages.

The brothers had stayed in San Diego, though Ivy and her sisters, Shelly and Honey, had moved away. It was great to see them all again. The last time had been at Jeremy's funeral, and she'd been far too distressed to spend much time catching up with their lives.

As Ivy moved among the spirited clan, she realized the camaraderie she had missed by living in Boston. Her daughters, Misty and Sunny, had plenty of friends, but they'd never had an extended family like this surrounding them.

Watching the younger generation reminded her of when she and her siblings had been that age. It didn't seem that long ago, and it surprised her to see the amount of gray in her brothers' hair. The years had sped by like a bullet train; she'd jumped on, unaware what changes the destinations would bring in her life.

Listening to their laughter, Ivy recalled how much fun it had been growing up here. For the first time in years, she wondered why she'd ever left. Being back here felt right to her at this time in her life, but she didn't know how Misty and Sunny would take the news that she intended to stay.

Her daughters still thought she was selling the house and returning to Boston. She'd talk to Misty when she returned to Boston and connect Sunny on a call. Or she could text. *Hi, it's Mom. Decided to move to Summer Beach. Visit when you can!* She shook her head. Definitely a call—if she could put her daughters together at the same time.

Shelly bounded downstairs. She'd been on her phone when Ivy had passed her bedroom. With rooms on the same floor, it was almost like being kids again.

"This is complete chaos," Ivy called out over the incessant chatter. Her nieces and nephews were a high-spirited group, and she hoped this day wouldn't dissolve into a disaster of family squabbles and careless work. They didn't have much choice, though.

"This job would have taken us weeks or cost a fortune," Ivy said. "But we have to manage them well, or things will spiral completely out of control."

"And feed them." Shelly nudged Ivy. "Once they're finished with the inside, I have an outside list to start on." She glanced out the window, and her face lit up. "Oh, good. Breakfast is here." Shelly raced to the door.

"Good morning," Mitch said, looking like he'd just come in from a morning surf. His hair was spiky and damp, and he wore an old T-shirt and shorts with flip-flops. "You call, Java Beach delivers." He had several boxes filled with coffee, pastries, and yogurt-granola parfaits, along with bananas, apples, and oranges.

Ivy smiled. So that's who Shelly was on the phone with so early this morning.

A couple of their nephews, Skyler and Reed, jumped up to help. Shelly led Mitch into the kitchen, and everyone followed, swarming around the aroma of coffee and food.

"Good to know Java Beach delivers." Ivy helped Shelly arrange the food on the counter while their younger nieces and nephews helped themselves.

"I figured Mitch would be up early, and he offered to bring everything over," Shelly said. "He's a sweet guy."

"I think he likes you," Ivy whispered, arching an eyebrow. She wasn't surprised. With her natural beauty and easy-going ways, Shelly drew men with hardly any effort.

Shelly shook her head. "He's too young for me. But he's awfully nice."

Their father insisted on paying Mitch, who gave Shelly a broad smile before he ducked out the back door. "See you around," he called out to Shelly.

Ivy poked Shelly in the side. "See? You definitely have an admirer."

Their older brother Forrest, a rugged outdoorsman who owned a construction company, gave a sharp whistle. "Attention everyone. You've all volunteered—or were goaded, shamed, or tricked—into being here."

Laughter bubbled across the room as everyone grabbed pastries and coffee.

Forrest went on. "But we're all here to help our sisters—your aunts—get this mess under control," he said with a wink. "And let's show them how glad we are that they've decided to move back here with us."

When the cousins broke out in a cheer, Ivy and Shelly gave a few high-fives. It did feel good to be back among family.

"The Seabreeze Inn opens June first," Forrest said.

"If not before," Ivy added.

Forrest stretched his arm around Ivy. "I expect there will be an opening party, sis?"

"I can promise a party," she replied. "Though we can't officially operate as an inn until the zoning is changed. Still, your friends can find us on the iBnB website once we get this place spruced up and take photos."

Her niece, Poppy, shot up her hand. "I can do that. And create your social media pages."

"You're on," Ivy said, relieved. She'd offer to pay her, of course. Ivy hadn't had time to think about the social media they'd need. Poppy had graduated from the University of Southern California in Los Angeles and was building her marketing business. She'd done a fantastic job helping their sister Honey's daughter, Elena, promote her jewelry business in Beverly Hills.

Ivy unfolded her list. "Okay, here's what we need to do. I'm going to divide you into teams with captains, and each team will have a section of the house to clean. If you see something that needs to be repaired, tell the captain, who will keep a list and call the repair team—that's our engineer graduates and fix-it folks—Dad, Forrest, Reed, and Sierra." Sierra had just graduated as an electrical engineer, and Reed had studied construction management.

Ivy caught an approving look from her mother. Carlotta had settled onto one of the stools, and Ivy hoped she would leave the hard work to the grandchildren. Her mother had aged, though she still looked vital and energetic— and easily a decade younger than her years. Sterling looked healthy, too.

A wave of guilt overtook Ivy. Having been wrapped up with the needs of Jeremy and the girls for so many years, she had often neglected to visit her parents, though they frequently spoke by phone. The thought that her mother or father might be concealing an illness terrified her. After losing Jeremy, she would be devastated to lose one of her parents.

Ivy shook off the thought and returned her attention to the other family members before her. "All right, team number one."

She went on, separating her siblings and nieces and nephews into teams. "The first team to finish with a job well done—no sloppy shortcuts—gets a surprise."

Ivy motioned to the long center counters filled with spray bottle and rags, brooms and mops. "Shelly will tell you what you need to use. Now, get your supplies and start work."

"Woo-hoo!" Shelly banged a pot with a spoon and let out a rallying cry. Cheers went up, and everyone gathered around her.

Ivy made her way to her mother's side. "Thanks for gathering everyone, Mom. I guess this old ship has set sail."

"This is how we finished our home before we moved in." Carlotta clasped Ivy's hand. "We had a fix-up party, and my brothers helped your father hang cabinets, while my sisters helped me paint and hang wallpaper. Family pulls together, *mija*, even though we sometimes disagree."

"I'm determined to see this through," Ivy said, her hands on her hips. "The house is all I have. Since it hasn't sold, I've got to do this, or face losing it to a tax sale."

Ivy's father hitched on a tool belt and joined them. "I didn't know you were in such a dire situation," he said frowning.

"I can manage, Dad." Her parents had helped them all through college, though she and her siblings had also worked, earned scholarships and grants, and took out loans. Five children were a lot to support, and Sterling and Carlotta had supported their own parents, too.

"You were always responsible," Sterling said, beaming at her. "Good to see you making sound decisions."

Carlotta turned to her. "What do you plan to do about furnishing it?"

Ivy had been dreading this topic. Only two of the bedrooms upstairs had adequate furniture, which were the ones that she and Shelly had moved into. "I thought I'd visit some antique stores and yard sales."

Carlotta threw a swift glance at Sterling, who nodded his assent. "Take what you need from the house."

"I can't do that," Ivy said. She wouldn't strip her mother's lovingly curated home, especially if Carlotta were ill.

"Of course you can. We're—" Carlotta began.

"Planning to make a few changes at the house," Sterling finished.

Ivy detected something amiss. Before she could quiz them on it, Shelly waved for her attention. "I couldn't do that," she said, making a note to try to find out more.

Her father was in on the secret her mother was keeping. *Whatever that is.*

Chapter 10

THE SQUAWKING OF shorebirds through an open window woke Bennett from a sound sleep, just when he'd been planning to sleep in this Saturday morning. Usually, he woke before dawn to start his day with a run on the beach or attend a city event, but today he was relishing a chance to catch up on sleep. Closing his eyes, he burrowed his head back into his pillow just as his phone rang.

"Go away," he mumbled, pulling a pillow over his head. Then, remembering his civic duty, he slid out a hand. It could be something important. When he glanced at the screen, he saw it was his friend Flint. Bennett groaned and rolled over.

"Hey, Flint."

"Where are you, buddy? Thought we were meeting at Java Beach this morning?"

Bennett yanked the pillow off his face and pummeled it against the wall. His assistant kept his mayoral schedule, but he'd forgotten about the promise he'd made to Flint, to whom he owed several favors. Flint had hosted a party for him with friends in Summer Beach during his election campaign, and he'd referred him to a local radio station who'd interviewed him on the air. They'd also gone for a few runs and gotten coffee together. Flint was a good guy, and he hated to let him down.

"Oh, yeah," Bennett said, trying to sound awake. "Your sister's place, right? Can I meet you there?"

"It's just a few blocks away, but I'm ashamed to say I don't know the address. How quick can you get here?"

"Give me a few minutes."

"Hurry up. I finished my coffee. Meet me at the hardware store next door."

Bennett rolled out of bed and eased into his jeans. He pulled on a T-shirt and cap, ran a toothbrush over his teeth, and headed out the front door.

He still lived in the same ridgetop home that he and Jackie had bought after they'd married. It wasn't one of the new mansions that were sprouting up along some of the beach communities, but the view was incredible—from Catalina Island and Long Beach all the way to Tijuana. And he couldn't ask for better neighbors.

As he walked to his SUV, a couple of his neighbors called out. "Morning, Ben."

He waved at them. "Good morning."

Celia and Tyler had retired in their late thirties after selling their tech start-up in Silicon Valley. Now they spent their time sailing and investing in other young companies along the California coast. Tyler had told him they were anxious to stay relevant, a term Bennett usually heard from older residents, but that he supposed reflected the rapid pace of change in the technology sector. "Getting an early start on the gardening? Thought you'd be out on the boat."

"Nah." Tyler motioned to his towering palm trees where a couple of young guys with special equipment were scaling the trees. "Getting rid of the dead fronds. Heard that Santa Ana winds will be blowing through here soon. Want them to trim yours?"

"Sure, thanks."

One of the workers shook his head and spoke to Harvey. "They're booked for a couple of weeks. That okay?"

"Sure, give them my number. See you around."

When Bennett arrived at Nailed It, he strolled inside and grinned at the owner. "Hey George, be careful waiting on that guy." He jerked a thumb toward his buddy Flint, who was wearing a navy blue Padres baseball cap. "I hear he's been banned from home repairs."

Flint gave him a bear hug. "Woke you, didn't I?"

JAN MORAN

"First time I've been able to sleep past five in the morning, and you have to call," Bennett said, giving him a punch on his muscular arm. "Ow. Pretty buff for an old guy."

"Look who's talking." Flint paid for some wood adhesive and other supplies. "Take my truck?"

"Sure. How's your work going?" Flint was a marine biologist, or more specifically, a marine mammologist. He was as likely to don scuba gear for underwater research as he was to be teaching at the university or writing an academic journal paper.

"I'm taking a team of PhD students out next week to follow an interesting pod of dolphins."

They were still talking when Flint pulled up in front of a 1950s beach bungalow shrouded by eucalyptus trees.

Bennett was surprised. "Your sister bought this one? Didn't even know Darla had it for sale."

They stepped from the truck.

"It's the one next door. Come on." Flint started off.

"Wait right there." Bennett clamped a hand on his friend's shoulder. "What's your sister's name?"

Flint laughed. "I've got three, didn't you know that? This house belongs to my sister Ivy. She's recently widowed, and—hey, you might like her. She's—"

"Look, buddy," Bennett cut in. "I don't know how to say this, but your sister Ivy and I aren't exactly—"

"What's *he* doing here?" Behind him, Ivy's voice was knife's edge sharp.

"Told you I was bringing a buddy to help," Flint said, looking perplexed. "You two know each other?"

Bennett took a step back. "Hey bud, I'd like to help, but this isn't such a good idea. I should leave."

Ivy's green eyes blazed. "That's the most considerate thing you've said so far." Ivy spun on her heel and charged back inside the house.

"What happened between you guys?"

Bennett jerked his thumb toward the house. "I had the listing on her house. You can see the condition it's in now. When I got the listing, it was even worse. I did what I could, but your sister wouldn't approve any expenses. I tried to be straight with her, but she wouldn't communicate with me."

"She was pretty broken up about her husband's death, plus he left a mountain of debts for her to sort out," Flint said with a trace of anger in his voice. "They had two children just out of college, and my sister was forced to sell their home in Boston and rent a room in someone else's house. They'd had that home for years, but he'd mortgaged it to the hilt. I tell you, I never thought much of the guy. Jeremy might have been a tech genius, but he was flashy. Always spent a lot of money. You know the type. He left her in pretty bad shape."

Bennett hadn't known about Ivy's children or that she'd had to sell her primary home and rent a room. That explained a lot about her attitude and her blow-up at the zoning department. "This house is worth a lot of money, but it needs work. Think she could get a loan on it?"

"Doubt it," Flint said. "Ivy's been a stay-at-home mom and a freelance art teacher. That's why we're all pitching in. It should do well on iBnB." A look of concern shadowed Flint's eyes. "Hey, that's allowed here, right?"

Bennett nodded. "It's not zoned for an inn, but we do have a lot of Summer Beach residents who post their extra bedrooms and guesthouses on iBnB, especially during horse racing season. What with prices going up as they are, many of our elderly residents use that money to supplement their income."

Now he felt guilty. He should have thought to mention that to Ivy when she'd inquired about turning Las Brisas into an inn. But once her luminous eyes had locked onto his—furious though she was—he'd found it hard to think straight.

Unnerving, that's what she was.

The picture Bennett had of Ivy shifted. He'd pegged her as a wealthy, selfish woman, but now he understood why she wanted to operate the house as an inn. He shot a sideways look at Flint. "I met Jeremy, you know."

Flint hitched up his jeans and put his hands on his hips. "Yeah? What'd you think of him? And you can be honest. He was never my favorite."

"My real estate partner, Claire, represented the Erickson estate and sold this property—Las Brisas—to him. He wanted to tear it down and build a resort monstrosity, but Las Brisas has a historic designation. The residents like Summer Beach the way it is. His lawsuit cost the city a lot of money, but we prevailed."

Flint looked perplexed. "We still can't figure out why he drained his retirement and stock accounts to buy this place." He glanced behind him and lowered his voice. "When you met him, was there anyone else with him? A man doesn't just buy a place like this out of the blue. I wouldn't mention it to Ivy, but do you think there was another woman?"

Bennett rocked on his heels, weighing his friend's question. Should he answer that? Now wasn't the time to get into that story, and besides, what good would it do?

"I'll take that silence as a yes," Flint said, shaking his head.

Just then, the front door of the house slammed, and Ivy stalked outside toward the Jeep. As she passed, she said to Flint, "Your crew is making good time without you. I'm off to buy more paint."

"Relax, Ivy. I'll be there in a minute," Flint said.

She slipped on her sunglasses and glared at Bennett. "Why are you still here?"

Bennett held his hands up. "I was told you needed more hands on deck."

"Nope. We've got this." She slid into the Jeep, slammed the door, and took off.

Flint chuckled. "She's got it in for you. But we really could use your help."

Looking up, Bennett shaded his eyes against the morning sun and considered the old house. Most of the neglect had occurred after Jeremy had bought it. The exterior had suffered the most; an exterior paint job was long overdue. "So you're painting the house, too?"

"Only the interior," said Flint, following his gaze. "The exterior is a job for professionals. Will need scaffolding to reach that height, and I can't imagine that's in the budget. Forrest can give her a deal through his company, but he's still got to pay his employees. And she has to furnish the place before she's ready."

Bennett thought about that. If only Ivy had shared her troubles with him in the zoning office, he could have been more helpful. That's what he had vowed to do when he was sworn in as the Summer Beach mayor. Irritated with himself, he kicked the ground and sent up a puff of sand. She had every right to be angry—on several levels. But Ivy was resourceful, and he admired that.

Flint adjusted his Padres baseball cap. "I've got to lend a hand inside. Are you coming or not?"

"Ivy's upset with me, and she's got enough to deal with without worrying about me being underfoot," Bennett said.

Flint chuckled. "You're probably right. When my sister gets an idea in her mind, it's hard to change it."

"You stay here. I'll walk back to the hardware store and

pick up my vehicle." Bennett slapped Flint on the back and promised to see him again soon.

Bennett walked back, stopping first at Java Beach to get his favorite coffee from Mitch before continuing past Antique Times. Nan and her husband had a shop full of customers, so he didn't stop but waved and went on.

He took his coffee and sat on the pier watching folks who were fishing reel in their morning catch. As he watched, he thought about what he could do to help Ivy. Strictly as a mayor for a constituent, of course.

If she ever spoke to him again, that is. The only problem he could see was that Ivy—stubborn as she seemed to be—might not accept his help.

Chapter 11

"HELLO," SAID THE man languishing behind the counter at the hardware store with the clever name of Nailed It. He had a straw fedora hat pushed back on his cropped hair and wore a Burning Man T-shirt. "What will it be today?"

"I need some interior paint," Ivy said. "Quite a lot, probably." Summer Beach didn't have giant big-box stores or fast-food drive-thrus, or even chain restaurants, which added to the charm of the small coastal town. Every shop and restaurant in town was family owned and splashed in sunny shades that gave Summer Beach a sherbet-hued color palette that Ivy loved.

The color palette reminded Ivy of the Amalfi coast,

where she'd once visited as a foreign exchange student. She imagined painting a village scene here, along with an expanse of beach and endless ocean in the background. Soon, she promised herself.

"Happy to help you. My wife is better at paint than I am." He called out to the back of the hardware shop. "Jen, you have a customer. I'm George, by the way."

"Nice meeting you, George. Ivy Bay."

"Bay…I had a Flint Bay in earlier this morning. Your husband?"

"My brother."

George snapped his fingers. "You're the new owner of the old Erickson estate, aren't you? Nan at the antique store was talking about you yesterday."

"I am," Ivy replied, surprised at how quickly word got around here.

"You didn't tell me Flint was in this morning." Jen emerged from the stock room, tossing her long, straight hair over her shoulder. She moved with vitality and self-assurance, and with her faded blue jeans and T-shirt, she looked as youthful as her husband.

"Is this your shop?" Ivy asked.

"It's ours," Jen said. "I inherited this shop from my father. Worked here when I was a kid."

"I've been living in Boston for nearly three decades." Ivy's words stuck in her mind. Thirty years. It seemed as if she'd woken from a long slumber and found herself back on the west coast.

"The old Erickson house." Jen's eyes lit up. "Glad it's got a new owner. That last one—Jeremy Marin—was a piece of work. But then, you've probably heard all about that ratbag."

"I'm beginning to." Ivy tried to maintain a pleasant expression, but inside, she felt like screaming.

Jen leaned conspiratorially across the counter. "That guy was smooth, I'll give him that. Not my style, though." She gave George a peck on the cheek.

"I can just imagine." Ivy's pulse quickened. The more she learned about her husband, the more her old life seemed like a facade. She crumpled the list she'd made into a tight ball in her fist.

Anxious to change the conversation, Ivy reached into her purse and drew out a blue washcloth from her mother's linen closet. "Can you match this, but go a few shades lighter? I'm planning a blue-and-white nautical theme—mostly white, but with accent walls of blue—and adding pops of orange, pink, and yellow. I'll use antiques and white-washed pieces throughout the house."

Although the house had been more formal, Ivy envisioned an airy, casual style since the house was so close to the ocean. She imagined opening the windows and filling the house with fresh sea breezes.

Jen studied the color. "I know just what you need. Come with me." She pulled three paint cans from the shelves, opened them, and dipped a stick inside each one.

Ivy hadn't chosen interior paint colors since her daughters were young and she'd repainted their rooms, but as an artist, she could envision the shade on a broad swath of wall. "The one in the middle, the nautical blue."

"Good eye," Jen said. "It's on trend, but will work well with the age of the house. How much will you need?"

Ivy spread out the list she'd crumpled and tallied the wrinkled figures for Jen.

"You got it." Jen counted out the number of cans.

Soon, Ivy had everything on her list. And she'd made two new friends.

George and Jen helped Ivy load everything into the back of the Jeep, and soon Ivy was driving the short distance back to the house. The entire trip had taken her a fraction of the time she would have spent in Boston driving to a giant home store, circling for a parking place, walking miles through the store, searching for an employee to help her, and waiting in a long check-out line. And no one would have helped her put her purchases in her car.

Ivy rolled down her window and breathed in the fresh morning air. Summer Beach was certainly a less complicated lifestyle. And despite Jeremy's lingering presence here, she was finding herself very much at home.

Except for Bennett Dylan. She could still remember the evening so many years ago that he sang to her, strumming his guitar and seated around a fire with her and her friends.

She'd fallen utterly, absolutely, unquestioningly, in love. All summer she'd been in love and dreamed of seeing him alone again.

Not anymore.

After arriving home, Ivy slid out two cans of paint.

Skyler and Blue, Flint's two lanky sons, bounded outside when they saw her taking paint cans from the back of the Jeep. "We'll get that for you," Skyler said.

"Thanks," Ivy said, surprised. "I'll take these." Her daughter Sunny seldom lifted a hand to help, and Misty hadn't been around much to offer, though she supported her frequent rehearsals and lessons. At least Misty was dedicated to her craft. She sighed, hoping that her relationship with Sunny would improve.

When Ivy walked back up the front steps to the house, music was blaring from speakers Shelly had set up and her nieces Poppy and Coral were belting out songs while they cleaned the front windows. They were having fun, and Ivy couldn't believe how fast they'd worked—or the difference clean windows made. Already the house looked more inviting.

"Looks great, you two," Ivy said, and the girls beamed at her. A warm feeling gathered in her chest. She was so grateful for their help. Living in Boston, she'd missed the closeness of family.

Continuing inside, Ivy saw her nephews Reed and Sierra inspecting a chandelier in the dining room.

Sierra called out, "Okay, Gramps, flip the switch."

Ivy heard Sterling confirm, and a moment later, light flooded the wainscoted dining room. Poppy and Coral had cleaned the windows here, too.

Sierra turned to her. "What do you think?"

"It's gorgeous," Ivy said.

"Took Coral half an hour to clean it," Sierra said. "She found loose wiring, so we tightened it up. Good as new now."

Flint and Forrest walked in, and Ivy turned to her brothers. "Are my painting teams ready? I had planned for them to follow the cleaning teams. Here's the paint for the dining room."

Forrest's deep laugh rumbled in his chest. "Same as you always were, Ivy. The most organized of any of us." He threw an arm around her. "I'm not surprised you're taking this on. You're a natural leader, Ivy. If you don't mind my saying so, Jeremy—may he rest in peace—often held you down."

Ivy loved having her brothers there. She'd always looked up to them. "I don't have any choice, Forrest. This has got to work, or I'm broke."

Forrest shook his head. "Flint filled me in. Awfully sorry to hear the financial condition that Jeremy left you in. Wish there was more we could do to help. You let me know when you need the outside painted. My crew can do it at cost. But a little touchup, and you can make another season."

"You're doing plenty," Ivy said quickly. "You can't imagine how thankful I am that you came and brought the kids."

Though Ivy's parents and siblings were successful, they all had family responsibilities. Flint and Forrest had put most of their children through college, and she knew they were still paying off education loans, even though their children had worked, too. Everyone was resourceful, but none of them were in a position to help her—nor would she ask.

Ivy pointed to the paint cans. "The blue goes on the bottom of the wall, and above that, white. Skyler and Blue are organizing paint supplies."

"I'll get the team started," Forrest said.

Shelly ducked her head in the doorway. "Wow, look at this. What a difference."

"Wait until you see it with a fresh coat of paint." Ivy already had ideas for artwork that she wanted to create to fill the wall space. All her work would be for sale, too.

"I'm going outside to work on the landscaping plan with Tabitha." Shelly had always been good friends with Flint's wife, and Tabitha loved plants as much as Shelly did.

Ivy turned back to the dining room. She could just imagine the family dinners and holiday celebrations this room must have hosted over the decades. This is where she would put out the dishes for the opening day celebration, once she had a table and chairs to fill the space, that is. Furnishings would be expensive, although she would keep to her strict budget. The most expensive items would be high-quality mattresses and pillows for the guest rooms.

Later that afternoon after everyone had gathered for an enormous lunch spread of lasagna and salad that Forrest's wife Angela had brought over, Ivy pulled Poppy to one side.

"Poppy, I have to start renting rooms here by June the first. Do you think you can create a website and drive reservations by then?"

Poppy studied the calendar on her phone. "I'll create your profile on iBnB as soon as we have some photos. Then I'll set up your social media accounts, and I have a few friends who are bloggers in LA. They can help spread the word. Everyone knows how expensive hotels are here in the summer." Poppy nodded toward the window. "Get some deck chairs and beach umbrellas for the beachfront lawn, and I can take photos there. That's a great view."

Ivy followed her gaze. "Loungers and beach umbrellas in bright colors would be perfect there."

"I'm up for that," Poppy said, grinning. "The most important thing will be to get positive reviews right away. If you don't mind, I can invite some bloggers to stay. Comp them, and they'll write reviews and share with their fans."

Ivy agreed. "The horse racing crowd is also important to reach."

"I'll be sure to use the right keywords," Poppy said.

"I'd like to put a gazebo or arch near the pool that we can use for wedding parties." Ivy's mind was whirring with thoughts as to the services they could offer.

After leaving Poppy, Ivy made her way to the music room, where the piano was now gleaming under a coat of restorative furniture oil. She made a mental note to call a piano tuning service. Next, she checked the library, where the shelves had received the same treatment. Admiring the fine fixtures, Ivy opened a cabinet door to reveal a row of letter slots and a series of small drawers in an old-fashioned built-in desk.

She picked up a cloth that had been left behind and ran it over the compact drawers. Every stroke brought out the wood grain and added a satin sheen. She pulled out the drawers. Inside of one, she found old receipts dating back decades. Most of them looked like they were for household repairs. Yet another one held rusted paper clips and a dried-up ink pad. Swiping her rag under the desk, she peered into the space and found a pull-out piece that served as a writing surface. Pale ink stains dotted the leather surface.

She imagined Amelia Erickson seated here, settling her accounts and writing checks. What did the woman look like? She'd love to find a photo of her. Maybe she could search online, although it had been an awfully long time ago.

Ivy smoothed her polishing rag over the surface, then slid the writing surface back. She figured it should have a support of some sort under it, so she bent down and looked up under the area. Unable to see well, she flicked on the light from her phone and shone it under the desk. Sure enough, there was a support arm that could swing out for the writing top.

A ledge at the back caught her eye.

Edging farther in, she spied a small leather-bound book on the ledge. Ivy reached for it. Easing herself into a cross-legged position on the floor, she opened the yellowed pages. Bits of paper cracked off and slipped onto the floor, so she turned the pages with care. It was some sort of ledger with pages of numbers. Farther back in the slim volume was a receipt. She lowered it to read it better. *Building supplies. January 15, 1942.*

The feathery writing on one page composed a list of furnishings. Each one had a check mark beside it as if someone had been taking inventory. For what purpose, she wondered?

Deciphering the old script, she read a few lines. Was this a list of furnishings for this house or for another home? Bennett said the couple had owned another home in San Francisco and had later returned to Europe. Maybe this was a shopping list, or more likely, these were the furnishings that had been sold.

Ivy looked around the vacant room. *Because they're sure not here.* She'd have to figure out some way to bring the house to life.

She turned the pages to the front of the ledger, which had rows and rows of numbers. She couldn't imagine what they meant.

Later that afternoon, Ivy walked back through the house. With windows cleaned, wooden trim polished, light fixtures cleaned, and most rooms painted, Ivy was pleased that the old house looked much cheerier. The paint colors had been a success.

"Wish I had furnishings for the photos we need to take for iBnB," Ivy said. They were just weeks before the high summer season for rentals began in Summer Beach.

Standing beside her, Poppy snapped her fingers. "Why not take the photos, and I'll Photoshop furniture in place?"

Ivy laughed at the thought, although she had to give Poppy credit for creativity. "Wish we could, but when people arrive, they'd wonder what happened to the room they thought they were reserving."

Poppy giggled. "Guess you're right. But I can get started on the iBnB site right away. We can upload interior photos later."

"That sounds like a plan," Ivy said. They set a date for Poppy to come by the house and take exterior photos. Ivy was worried that her funds were dwindling fast, and she had to be ready for the summer season. A delay of a couple of weeks might be more than she could afford.

Chapter 12

"CAN YOU BELIEVE how much they accomplished?" Ivy and Shelly had seen the last of their family off, and now they were walking through the mostly empty rooms. Clean windows framed the ocean view, and every surface and light fixture gleamed. The long weekend had been worth it, though every muscle in her body ached and her jeans and T-shirt were covered in paint splatters. "I can almost feel the house smiling again."

"Funny, I know exactly what you mean," Shelly said. "Time to tackle the landscaping."

Ivy groaned. "Isn't that your department?"

"Sure, but I have a landscaping plan I want you to see."

They made their way into the kitchen, where even the turquoise appliances sparkled with retro brilliance. Pulling up two stools, they sat at the counter. Shelly went through her plan.

"We'll start with cleaning up the palm tree skirts a little. It's kind of trendy to leave the skirts on now, and that will save a fortune in trimming off those stubborn suckers."

Ivy nodded. She liked that shabby chic look. "I'm all for that."

"The coast live oak in the back is in good condition, too. Again, just light trimming for now. We can trim more in the winter when the trees are dormant. Next, drought-resistant plantings will reduce your water requirements, but you can still have a lush look, almost tropical, in fact." Shelly rattled off a list of plants that Ivy hardly recognized.

"Can you add some gardenia and jasmine near the patios? Guests will love the scent."

"Sure," Shelly said, adding that to her list. When she had finished, she gave Ivy a cost figure. "We can follow this plan in phases so that it's not as expensive up front." She tapped a number. "I can get started with this."

"Okay, but try to hold it to that." Ivy chewed on her lip. The faster they could open their doors, the better.

Ivy reached for a calendar her mother had given her. It was one of Carlotta's calendars that she received every year from the animal shelter for her donation but never used. Ivy flipped it open to June. "Hey, cutie." An adorable rescue puppy that looked like a Labrador mix gazed out at her as though ready to scamper around. She'd always wanted a dog, but Jeremy had been highly allergic to pet dander.

Ivy drew a circle around the first day of June. "That's our opening date. Even sooner if we can." As she stared at it, she realized this was the first positive goal she'd had since before Jeremy had died. A goal that meant expansion in her life, not forced contraction.

They both stared at it.

"Think we'll be ready?" Shelly asked. "Still a lot to do."

"I don't have a choice." She leaned on the counter and touched Shelly's shoulder. "We must get bookings as soon as we can. Poppy will take photos when we have furniture in place."

"I'll handle the floral arrangements. And I've got some great before-and-after shots that I took for the blog. Poppy took a video of me describing the before shots, as well as the work-in-progress. We can use that to tell the story. People love that. They might want to see it in person."

"Great idea." Ivy loved having Shelly and Poppy in-volved. "We can do this. We just have to get creative and think of all possibilities to further rentals, no matter how crazy."

"Our rooms are furnished. We could rent out those first."

Ivy grinned at her sister. "Sleeping bags in the maid's quarters out back?"

"It would be almost like camping at the beach. Remember doing that?"

"My back is aching just thinking about it. But that's a good idea." Ivy stared out the window. She was determined that whatever it took to keep the house, that's what they would do.

Shelly slid a hand over hers. "It wouldn't be forever."

"As it turns out, nothing is." Ivy blinked back the tears that always seemed ready to spring out. How long would it be until her nerves weren't on edge? She thought about another friend whose husband had died, and someone who had commented on her sadness. *It's been a year already.* As if grief adhered to a time schedule. She swallowed and pushed through her feelings.

"Now is not the time to give up. Now is the time to take action." Shelly tapped on the calendar. "Look at this sweet-faced puppy. Doesn't that make you smile? We need to hang this calendar so we can both see it every morning." She stood up and began looking for a suitable place.

Ivy saw a slightly inset wall. "That's a good spot." She picked up the hammer Flint had left behind for them. Even though she kept appointments on her phone calendar, she also liked to have something tangible to write on. This way, they could both see it. She found a nail and Shelly positioned the calendar on the wall.

"Here we go." Ivy gave the nail a tap, but it hit something hard and bent to an angle. "Ouch."

"You okay?"

"I hit something. Hope I didn't put a hole in a pipe behind the wall." She tapped her knuckles on the painted wall. *Solid.* The sound was muted, which told her there was something behind it. She continued tapping on the wall, expecting to hit a hollow spot, but whatever was behind the wall was entirely solid. She stepped back and looked at the wall, perplexed.

"What's up?" Shelly asked.

"This wall. Something is behind it."

"No telling what. Old houses often have generations of renovations."

"We just want to hang a calendar." Ivy stared at the wall and the space surrounding it. "Looks like it could have been a doorway, doesn't it?"

Shelly ran her fingers around the corners and tapped it. "Could be."

"Maybe it's a secret passageway. Some old houses have those."

"But it's solid. And it's in the middle of the house. What's behind here?"

The two of them walked out of the kitchen to explore the other side of the wall, which seemed awfully wide to Ivy.

Shelly circled the area. "Looks like there's dead space here. Could it be an old closet?"

"Who would go to all that trouble to board up a closet and leave the other walls exposed?" She circled the area.

Something was amiss.

They returned to the kitchen and stood in front of the blank wall, gazing at it.

"It's definitely not original," Shelly said. "I can't imagine a famous architect would waste space like that."

"This house has a secret," Ivy said slowly. "I felt it the moment I stepped inside. I can't articulate why, but I feel like it's been waiting for me, wanting me to discover its secrets."

"The house?" Shelly stared at her. "Now you're worrying me. You were always the sane one."

"I know what I'm saying sounds strange, but I feel like there's something we're meant to discover." Ivy hefted the hammer in her hand, weighing the chance of what they might find versus the damage they would do. She might regret it, but she had to know why someone had gone to the trouble of putting up a fortified wall where once there had been none. With a sudden swing, she brought the hammer down across the wall with a dull thud. Chips of old paint and crackled wallpaper flew everywhere.

"Hey! What are you doing?" Shelly stepped out of the way of flying particles.

"Someone put this up to hide something." Ivy brought the hammer down again. "Look! Bricks." Ivy gripped a large piece of old painted wallpaper and tore it off. "It's all bricks."

"A fireplace?"

Ivy gazed up and then strode out the back door.

"What are you doing?" Shelly called out.

Ivy peered up at the roofline. She raced back inside.

"There's no chimney above it. No reason to have bricks here. Come on, give me a hand. If there's a brick wall, I bet there's something behind it." Feeling excited, she gripped a corner of the old fabric-backed wallpaper and tugged.

"There goes the clean kitchen floor." Shelly chuckled. "We could just look at the architectural plans Bennett brought over."

Her mouth agape, Ivy whirled around. "You're a genius. Where are they?"

Shelly opened a cupboard. "I put them here for safe-keeping." She removed the long tube that held the rolled up paper.

Ivy smoothed out the architectural plans on the counter, which bore yellowed traces of time and the architect's name. *Julia Morgan*. She ran a finger over the woman's name in reverence. "She was a real trailblazer." She lifted a large sheet of paper.

Shelly peered over her shoulder. "First level."

Ivy turned another page. "Second level."

When she flipped another page, an ample space stared up at her. She looked up in awe. "Lower level. Looks like a basement of some sort, though it couldn't be. We're too close to the water."

"Maybe it was in the plans, but not built," Shelly said.

"That's why there's a brick wall."

"Still, that wall looks like it was added. It's not original." Ivy studied the drawing. "Maybe it was bricked up for safety."

"In which case, you just destroyed the wall covering for nothing."

Ivy gazed back at the damaged wall. "Bennett said Amelia closed up the house during the war."

"And then reopened it for military housing. What if they buried people down there?"

"It was housing, Shelly. Not a morgue."

"I don't know…" Shelly shuddered. "Someone never wanted that opened again. Maybe the creature from the black lagoon was captured down there. Or zombies."

Ivy chuckled at the thought. "You've been watching too much horror."

"Dad and Bennett both said the place was haunted," Shelly said, her eyes widening. "You should think about this. What if you're disturbing old graves?"

"And why would you care?"

"Duh. Because I have to sleep here." Shelly tapped on the plans. "Aren't you afraid of what's down there?"

"I doubt there are any graves," Ivy said, laughing at her sister.

"Bomb shelter? Those were popular during the 1950s."

"Could be." Ivy returned to the wall and peeled off a thick piece of paint. Inspecting it, she slid her fingernail under it to separate the pieces. When she'd renovated her condo in Boston, she'd found a lot of older material. "Look, this is paint over fabric backed wallpaper. This material is older than the Cold War era. After the war and in the 1950s, builders started using drywall. It would have been easy to slap that over a frame. I'll bet this dates back to the 1940s or before. That might correlate with what Bennett told us."

"About using it for military housing?"

"Maybe. He said Amelia Erickson closed the house right after Pearl Harbor." Running her hand over the wall, Ivy turned the thought over in her mind. "She was frightened that the war would reach the west coast."

"The brick wall doesn't match anything else in the house, and Mrs. Erickson sounds like she had an appreciation for design."

"They probably would have used lathe and plaster back then." Ivy ran her hand over the exposed bricks. "But bricks are solid. You'd have to really work to get behind this."

"We can do that. Give me another hammer." Shelly flicked on the radio, and Ivy passed a second hammer to her.

Shelly took aim and pummeled the wall. Tiny brick chip projectiles shot back at them.

"Hold up," Ivy cried.

Shelly stared at the hammer in her hand. "It's not working."

"I think we're going to need a bigger hammer."

The two women looked at each other and spoke in unison. "Sledgehammer."

Chapter 13

"LOOK TO STARBOARD at two-o'clock," Mitch called out, planting his feet on the upper deck of his boat for balance. "We've got a friendly fin whale checking us out." He pointed toward a wave where a giant whale was arching gracefully through the water.

"Wow!" Bennett's tow-headed nephew, ten-year-old Logan, jumped up and down.

"Hang on, buddy." Bennett drew his arm around the boy, bracing them against the starboard side of the vessel while they marveled at the magnificent creature. He was pleased that Mitch had found a whale for Logan to see.

Bennett was taking care of Logan while his sister and

her husband had a short trip to Phoenix for a golf tournament. After the morning rush at Java Beach, Mitch often took out private charters in the afternoon for whale watching on his vessel, which was a sport fishing boat that he'd equipped with long benches and inside seating to accommodate charters.

"Fin, or finback, whales are the second largest whale in the world," Mitch said to Logan. "That one's about 65 or 70 feet."

"Whoa, for real?" Logan's big blue eyes widened.

Bennett laughed. "For real." Being out on the water, feeling the sun on his shoulders, and breathing in the fresh salty air was a balm to his soul. From childhood, his life had been centered on the ocean, and he couldn't imagine ever living too far away from it.

Mitch eased back on the throttle to get a better view. "There's another one, just below the birds." He pointed to a spot beneath a flock of birds that were following the whales.

"Pretty smart birds," Bennett said to Logan. "They know the whales are in search of plentiful fish, so they follow to scoop up their leftovers."

"This is awesome," Logan said.

Bennett tousled his hair. He loved spending time with his nephew and felt as close to him as if he'd been his own son. He and Jackie had been trying to have their first baby when she had become ill. Just as they were becoming excited about the baby, she'd lost the child, and they were plunged into the fight for her life against choricarcinoma, a rare cancer that had developed in the abnormal pregnancy. And then he'd lost Jackie, too.

Logan turned his face up to Bennett's. "Do you know everything about the ocean, Uncle Bennett?"

"No one does. Did you know marine biologists are still finding new forms of life?"

"That's cool. I'd like to do that someday."

"Maybe you will," Bennett said. "I have a buddy who studies dolphins. That means you have to keep up the grades, buddy." His child would've been about Logan's age now. He and his sister had been excited that their children would grow up together, but life had a different, devastating plan for him. To compensate, Bennett had been putting money aside to help with Logan's education, or whatever he wanted to do.

The fin whales crested along beside them, matching their speed and observing them. After a while, the two great mammals disappeared into the blue. As Mitch turned for home, a small pod of dolphins joined them.

"Bottlenose dolphins, port side at nine o'clock," Mitch pointed out. "Looks like ten, no twenty."

Logan's excitement ratcheted up again.

Laughing, Bennett pulled out his phone and snapped a photo for his sister, Kendra, and her husband. They'd love that.

Mitch cruised along while the dolphins kept pace.

"Hey Bennett, I met the two sisters who are converting the old Las Brisas estate into a bed-and-breakfast. Didn't know you'd found a buyer for the place."

"I didn't. That's Jeremy Marin's widow."

"Yeah? Which one?"

"Ivy." As much as he tried, he couldn't get that woman out of his mind. Maybe it was because she reminded him of a girl he'd once had a crush on so many years ago. Her name was Ivy, too, and she had those same bone-chilling eyes that this Ivy had. Eyes you couldn't look away from. He guessed that must have been a popular name for green-eyed baby girls. He'd seen that girl on the beach a few times when he'd been surfing, and at a beach bonfire. He'd even written a song about her and played it on his guitar for her in front of her friends, but she had to know it was for her. When he'd finally mustered the courage to ask her out, she'd suddenly vanished. It wasn't the first time he'd been ditched, but it had hurt.

Bennett took off his sunglasses to clean the saltwater spray from them, and as he did, he wondered about that girl and Ivy. He shook his head and shoved on his sunglasses.

"She can't run that house as an inn without a zoning change," Bennett said. "And I doubt that's going to happen soon enough for her. But she can still rent out rooms on iBnB. "

"Sure had a crowd of people over this weekend to help her fix it up." Mitch paused. "Her sister's nice looking, too.

Shelly called, and I delivered coffee and pastries for the crew."

Bennett slid on his sunglasses and peered over the rim. "Sounds like you're interested in her."

Mitch gazed toward the horizon. "Maybe I am."

"Be careful. With a sister like Ivy, you don't know what she's like. Could be lying in wait like a rattlesnake."

Mitch let out a hearty chuckle. "And just when have you seen a rattlesnake lie in wait?"

Logan swiveled his head between them with interest. "Have you, Uncle Bennett?"

"As a matter of fact, I have." Bennett pushed his hat back on his head. "Sometime back, one of my clients cleared out an old date palm grove near Palm Springs to build a golf course. The rattlesnakes that had been growing fat on field mice in search of sweet dates for decades were suddenly displaced. They slithered out to the nearest food sources they could find, which had the neighboring community up in arms." Bennett glanced at Logan, who was making a face. "Well, you can just imagine."

"Geez, don't gross out the kid." Mitch screwed up his face. "Besides, I don't know how you can equate that story to Shelly."

"She and her sister have been displaced, too. For all you know, they're lying in wait. Looking for husbands."

"Huh." Mitch rotated his shoulder and shook his head. "When did you get this cynical?"

"I'm not cynical." Bennett stole a sideways glance at Mitch. Or was he? He'd been through so much with Jackie, but he was hurt, not cynical. "Do I come off that way?"

"Not usually," Mitch replied. "Relax. Ivy's got you upset is all. Can't blame her for wanting to earn some money in this economy. My mom was like that after my dad died. Did anything she could to keep us afloat."

Mitch pointed ahead. "Sea lion straight ahead off the bow."

Logan let out a yelp and scrambled to the front deck to get a closer look.

Bennett laced his hands behind his neck and lifted his face to the sun. "Sure appreciate you taking Logan out. Means a lot to him. But we probably need to get back. Tomorrow's a school day."

"For all of us," Mitch said.

After Logan got a good look at the whiskered sea lion frolicking among the waves, they were back underway toward Summer Beach.

Bennett's sister and her husband had a cottage near the beach. After he and Mitch had dropped off the tired little boy, Bennett took the beach road back, which led past Las Brisas. As they neared the property, he slowed and peered from the window. The yard had been cleaned up.

Loud music filtered from the house. He glanced at Mitch beside him. "I see what you mean. The place is looking better, especially since—"

A scream ripped through the night, piercing the loud music coming from the kitchen.

Mitch whipped around. "What the heck? Turn around."

Bennett already had the SUV in reverse. Through the open windows, a chilling scene was playing out in the kitchen.

A shadowy figure had what looked like an ax raised and ready to strike. Bennett's heart hammered with outrage.

Screeching to a halt, Bennett bolted from the car with Mitch at his side. The two men raced across the sandy lawn and burst into the kitchen before skidding to a stop.

"What's going on here?" Bennett roared. He'd been ready to pounce on an intruder, but it was only Ivy and Shelly. He strode across to Ivy and grabbed a sledgehammer from her hands, furious that whatever these two were up to had scared the daylights out of him.

"What are you doing?" Ivy yelled, pushing safety glasses up over her head.

Mitch caught Shelly's hand. "We heard a scream. Are you okay?"

Shelly burst into a cascade of laughter. "We're taking down that brick wall." She tapped her phone and turned off the blaring music that was coming from a set of speakers.

"At this time of night?" Bennett felt Ivy's chilling glare on him.

Jutting out her chin, Ivy took a step toward Bennett. "Mr. Mayor, is there a rule against that, too, in your town?"

"There's a law against disturbing the peace, which the police assiduously enforce," Bennett said as evenly as he could. "This is a quiet community. Why all the screaming?"

"We were just having fun," Shelly said with a mischievous glance at Mitch. Her eyes lit as she gestured toward an old blueprint spread out on the counter. "Look what we found."

Mitch followed Shelly, and she tapped her finger on the drawing. "There's a lower level down there. It's been bricked up, and we're about to find out why."

"Know anything about this?" Ivy stood before him, irate.

"Can't be a basement because this house is too close to the shore." A flush crawled up Bennett's neck. Claire hadn't included any such information in the listing description, and he'd never thought to look at the plans. Had he been negligent?

He leaned the sledgehammer against the wall and looked over the plans on the counter. An idea dawned on him. "The house looks like it's built on a hill. It's possible that dirt was mounded up over that lower level to create a sort of cellar."

"Doesn't that strike you as odd?" Ivy jabbed her fists to her waist. "And shouldn't you have told me about this?"

"I didn't know, and I don't think Claire knew either."

Bennett felt himself grow warm under Ivy's intense gaze. Why did she have this effect on him?

Ivy pressed her lips together. "This isn't a spectator sport. Helps us out or get out."

Bennett jerked his chin toward the brick wall. "That's a big job for you to handle."

"I've got this," Ivy said, hefting the large hammer.

"Please, let me." Bennett rested his hand on hers. After a moment of hesitation, she released her grip, letting Bennett take the sledgehammer from her. He had no doubt that she could handle this job, but what kind of a man would he be to sit by and watch?

She slipped off her protective eye goggles. "You should wear these."

Bennett adjusted the safety glasses and lined up the large hammer on the wall. "Right about here?"

Ivy raised a shoulder. "Go ahead."

"That's perfect," Shelly said, hopping from one foot to another with excitement. "Do it!"

Bennett reared back and brought the sledgehammer down hard against the brick wall. The old wall shuddered from the shock, spewing dust and crumbling brick.

"Hit it again," Shelly cried out, clapping.

Once again, Bennett brought the hammer down, making a small hole in the center of the wall.

Waving the dust away, Ivy stepped closer. Flicking on the light on her phone, she held it to the opening and peered through. "There *is* something in there," she said, her voice rising. A fine layer of dust settled on her hair.

Ivy sounded excited, and it was all Bennett could do to keep from brushing the dust from her hair. She was easily the most vexing woman he'd come across in all his years in real estate and as mayor of Summer Beach.

"Step back, and I'll make an opening for you to get through." Bennett was curious to see what was behind the wall as well.

What had Mrs. Erickson kept concealed here, and why? Bennett knew that local residents often speculated on the long-vacant house, conjuring stories. At the annual graduation bonfire on the beach, teenagers told stories of ghostly inhabitants, but to his knowledge, there wasn't any truth to them.

Or was there? What could Mrs. Erickson have been hiding?

Chapter 14

IVY STEPPED THROUGH the jagged entryway that Bennett had smashed and chiseled from the brick enclosure. "There's a staircase leading down."

She paused on the landing to adjust to the darkness and the dank, musty odor. Mitch had raced to the truck for flashlights, which Bennett had told him he kept in an earthquake preparedness kit. She glanced back.

"Are you coming?" She'd rather not do this alone, even if it meant having Bennett by her side.

"Wait up, Ivy." Bennett gulped a long drink from a water bottle Shelly had given him.

Perspiration beaded on his brow and upper lip, not that

Ivy had intended to notice. His virility was overwhelming. She caught her breath and shifted her gaze. Yet, seeing how much effort Bennett put forth made her grateful for his help, though she and Shelly could have managed without him, even if it had taken them all night.

Still, he and Mitch had been so concerned about them when they'd heard Shelly's scream. Surprisingly, Ivy found that comforting. As long as she'd lived in Boston, she hardly knew her neighbors. Turnover was frequent, and they kept to themselves. Not here. Summer Beach seemed like a close community. She wouldn't have guessed that Bennett and Mitch were such good friends.

"What do you see?" Shelly poked her head through the opening.

"I'm not sure." Gingerly, she slid her foot forward, fearing rats or traps. Her pulse quickened. Sweeping the space with the flashlight from her phone illuminated a landscape of tented mounds below. An involuntary shudder gripped her, and she wondered what they would find.

She could understand why someone might store items in a basement—that was normal—but why brick up the opening? And not open it for decades? The more that Ivy came to know of Amelia Erickson, the more of an enigma the woman became. Who was she, and what was she hiding?

She heard the kitchen door bang and retreated into the safety of the well-lit kitchen. Mitch bounded in with an armload of equipment.

Bennett pulled straps with a mounted light over his head. "Here, you should have one of these, too." Bennett whipped one of the contraptions over Ivy's head and showed her how to turn it on.

"Thanks, but I can do it." Ivy adjusted the straps, though her headlamp seemed to slip on her forehead. "Do you always take control of situations like this?"

"That's why he's the mayor." Mitch nudged Bennett. "He rallied this community back after the last earthquake."

"I just serve where I can," Bennett said, tossing off the praise. He tightened the side of Ivy's headlamp strap. "Better?"

Ivy wrinkled her nose at his closeness. "Yeah, but why do you smell like fish?"

Bennett looked amused. "We were out on Mitch's boat this afternoon. Saw some incredible fin whales and bottlenose dolphins, and my nephew caught a few fish."

"And released them," Mitch added.

Bennett divided up the gear on the table. "Each of you will need a flashlight, gloves, and a dust mask. Get your gear on and let's go."

While Shelly and Mitch followed his instructions, Ivy put a paper mask over her mouth and nose. She pulled on a pair of large work gloves and waggled her fingers at her sister.

Shelly burst out laughing. "You look like Indiana Jones."

"We're on a mission." Ivy wasn't going to let Bennett take over. With a wave of her hand, she said, "Follow me, everyone."

Ivy stepped through the brick entry and flicked on her flashlight to swing it around, although her headlamp was quite bright. Sucking in a breath, she made her way down the wooden stairs, which creaked with every step as if the old bones of the house were complaining of stiff joints.

The others joined her. With their lighting gear, the spacious room was soon illuminated with beams of light zooming around like a laser show.

"Wow," Shelly breathed. "Look at all this."

Ivy lifted the edge of a long swath of canvas, disturbing decades of dust, which took flight in the still air. She closed her eyes against the cloud, grateful for the face masks Bennett had supplied.

"Careful there," Bennett said. "I'll give you a hand."

Bennett took the other edge, and together they folded back the old canvas fabric to reveal an antique dining room table with a rich wood grain. Ivy swept her flashlight over ornate carvings. With awe, she ran her fingers over an exquisitely carved ram's head that joined the leg to the table top.

"There's your dining room table," Shelly announced.

Ivy shook her head. "Could be a Chippendale piece," she said, recalling a university class she'd taken on the history of art and material culture. "Thomas Chippendale was the Shakespeare of English furniture."

If the table were one of his make, it belonged in a museum, not in a seaside inn where coffee cups could mar the surface or vacuum cleaners could nick the legs. The wood seemed alive under her touch as if the artisan's care was imbued in the grain.

"I've never seen anything like this," Ivy said. At least, not this close. It could be a reproduction, but it still took her breath away.

"Hey, look at this." Mitch flashed his light on rows of bare-wood shelves that looked like they'd been hastily constructed to hold long, rolled-up rugs covered with sheets.

Ivy hurried over. Running her fingers along the rug backs, she noted the exceptional work and high knot density, which were hallmarks of quality. She flipped over a corner to reveal brilliant shades in an ornate design.

"Persian," Ivy guessed, although she was no expert. "They're made of wool and silk. She touched each one with reverence and imagined how the chandeliers upstairs must have once cast their glows on these works of art. That explained the darker borders on the wooden floors she'd seen in some rooms. These would be stunning in the library and music room.

"This place is a treasure trove." Ivy's heart pounded at the discovery. Recalling the letter from Amelia Erickson's trustee, she wondered if the paintings the former owner was so worried about might be here.

Another thought brought shivers to Ivy. Perhaps Amelia's spirit still inhabited the house and had influenced her decision to move in. Was that even possible? As she thought of Jeremy's intended wrecking ball, she couldn't help but imagine how these treasures might have been damaged in the process.

"Jeremy's plans to raze the house could have ruined all this," Ivy murmured.

Bennett caught her comment. "I'm incredibly glad you found this instead."

She swung around to face him in the light of their headgear. His hazel eyes shone like glittering embers and drew her in like a warm fire on a winter's night. Her pulse thudded at the thought. "Do you understand the value of these pieces?"

He nodded solemnly, holding her gaze. "I've helped several clients value property they inherited from family estates. What they thought of as old rugs and outdated antiques fetched quite a lot at auction."

Breaking the spell that seemed to bind them, he turned to sweep his flashlight over the crowded room. "If the rest of this is like what we've seen so far, this is an astounding discovery."

"I studied art history, and I've never seen anything like this." Catching her breath, Ivy flicked her flashlight and gazed around the spacious room. More roughly crafted shelves held books, and beyond that, cartons concealed more treasures. One was scrawled with the word *Waterford*. Another, *Sèvres*.

"It's like Aladdin's cave," Bennett said. "Filled with artifacts."

Ivy liked his analogy. "Was Amelia Erickson the genie?"

"A collector," Bennett said. "She donated her art pieces during her life and upon her death to several west coast museums."

"I wonder which museums," Ivy said.

"Nan and Arthur at Antique Times might be able to answer that question," Bennett said.

Slowly, Ivy spun around. "I'm overwhelmed," she said. By what she saw, and by the nearness of him—even if a trace of fishy odor still clung to his clothes. "This was more than mere redecorating," she added. Something had prompted the gutting and concealment of a collection of such treasures.

At once, Ivy recalled the ledger she had found and wondered if there was a connection. *1942*. Not long after Pearl Harbor had been attacked. Was that an inventory of the items downstairs?

Bennett touched her arm. "It's late. Have a fresh look in the morning."

Ivy nodded numbly and let him guide her back up the stairs to the airy kitchen.

Once upstairs, Shelly brought out bottles of ice cold

water from the antique refrigerators and passed them around. They all drank and wiped dust from their eyes.

"I'm in shock," Ivy said. "Some of that is priceless, I'll bet."

Bennett glanced at Mitch. "We should keep this discovery between us."

"Why?" Shelly said.

"Here in Summer Beach, robberies aren't uncommon," Bennett said, glancing at Mitch. "Especially in second homes left vacant for part of the year. There wasn't much of value in this home that someone could steal, though police caught a couple of drifters who'd broken in a few years ago. Most of the expensive homes here have alarm systems, which I highly recommend."

Ivy nodded, fully comprehending his meaning, although that was one more expense. She regarded the gaping hole they'd made. "We should finish the demolition and install a door with a lock until we get this sorted out."

"That's what I'd advise," Bennett said.

"I can do that for you," Mitch said. "I'm pretty handy."

Ivy flicked a glance at Shelly. They didn't really know Mitch, and she hoped they could trust him.

After Bennett and Mitch left, Ivy plopped onto a stool, exhausted from their effort and discovery.

Shelly joined her, a wide grin stretching across her face. "At least we don't have to worry about how to furnish the house now. We can be up and running in a couple of weeks."

"I need to get an appraiser in here first," Ivy said. "I suspect some of that could be worth a lot." Already her mind was at work. If she could sell some pieces, she could pay for other needed repairs. But getting appraisals would cost money, too.

Another sobering thought occurred to her. "If the seller—that is, Mrs. Erickson's heirs—didn't know about that lower level, then those items might not be a legal part of the sale."

Shelly made a face.

"Still, if I can sell some of the pieces—if they're what I think they are—that could pay for the taxes and maybe exterior painting. And your landscaping plan. Maybe some new appliances."

Shelly shot a look at the turquoise refrigerators. "Nah. I kind of like Gert and Gertie. Why retire them?"

Ivy burst out laughing. "You've named the refrigerators?"

"They're like kitchen staff. Look at them standing guard over us. Gertie's the one doing all the work right now. Gert's the one on the left. We should see if he works as hard as his spouse, too. Why should Gertie have all the fun?"

"Because he might be high maintenance, as some men can be." Ivy glanced back at the second refrigerator. "But we should test him. Maybe he'll be useful when we have a full house." She smiled and reached across for her sister's hand. "We're going to get through this, aren't we?"

"You better believe it." Shelly gave her one of her quirky grins. "More water? Hydration is important." She pushed off the stool to get more water from the refrigerator now known as Gertie.

Ivy rested her chin in her hand. "You know, it feels good to take control of our own destiny."

"I'll say," Shelly said. "Even though I sort of miss Ezzra." She stuck out her lower lip in a pout.

"Don't you dare." Ivy crumpled a piece of paper and threw it at her sister. "That means you're not busy enough. Besides, we just had an extraordinary day, from our family pitching in to help us, to finding Aladdin's cave down there."

"Long day," Shelly said, tossing Ivy another bottle of water.

"We have to get one of those water purification thingies." Ivy gathered several empty bottles and tucked them into a bag they'd designated for recycling. "Too many plastics."

As exhilarating as the lower level discovery was, Ivy couldn't get Bennett's eyes out of her mind. He'd been different tonight, racing in like a hero when he thought she was in danger. Being so helpful—though she didn't *really* need his help, he didn't need to offer, either. More than that, he understood what this discovery meant.

Most of all, when her headlamp had illuminated his eyes, she saw a flicker of recognition and interest. She felt equally drawn to him and shocked at her feelings.

Ivy shifted back onto the stool. Was she ready for that? Passing a hand over her forehead, she decided she was just tired.

So tired that she imagined a connection with Bennett Dylan, which was completely out of the realm of possibilities.

She still hadn't forgotten what had happened between them that summer so long ago.

Chapter 15

"FOUND THE SILVERWARE," Shelly called out, waving a soup ladle.

Ivy made her way through the furniture, rugs, and books and knelt beside her sister. "What an unusual pattern." Ivy turned over an ornate cake server and studied the hallmark. "It's not silver plated either. This is sterling silver."

"I'm more of an Ikea person. What's the difference?"

"Cost and quality." During the early years of her marriage to Jeremy, Ivy had enjoyed visiting antique shops and finding unusual pieces for their brownstone condominium. With her artist's training, she had developed her eye for quality craftsmanship. Everything she saw here was so far beyond what she'd ever been able to afford.

Idly, she wondered if the paintings Amelia Erickson had lost sleep over were tucked away here.

As near as Ivy could tell, the former owner had virtually emptied her home at one point and moved practically everything to the lower level. Even what was remaining in the house—in the two bedrooms she and Shelly were now occupying—was modest in comparison.

"Bennett told us that the Ericksons had closed the house after the bombing of Pearl Harbor," Ivy said. "Many people feared attacks on the military bases in San Diego."

Shelly handled the silver pieces that were wrapped in dark felt cloth with care. "He said they had lived through the Great War in Europe. That's what we know as the First World War, right?"

"That's right." Ivy gazed around the vast room. "They must have moved everything down here and concealed the entry. It was unusual for a home to be built like this then. Could be they commissioned it and made special design requests, like hiding places, based on what they'd lived through." A shudder coursed through Ivy. What had this house witnessed, and what secrets did it hold?

While Shelly returned items to the carton and shifted to inspect another box, Ivy wedged a path through the furnishings to the rear of the room. She and Shelly hadn't made their way back here yet. Ivy spied several rough crates that looked like they might hold artwork.

Thinking about the Swiss physician's letter that had dropped out of the old file Bennett had given them, Ivy reached out to a crate.

As she touched it, a feeling of wonderment shot through her.

"This is odd," Ivy said.

"What?"

"The Erickson's donated their entire art collection, right?"

"That's what the letter said," Shelly called out, knee deep in boxes.

If that were so, this didn't make sense, Ivy thought, unless this artwork was of a lesser quality work. But why would the Erickson's even bother with inferior art? They'd had the money to acquire the best.

Sliding out a covered painting, Ivy held her breath. Were these the artworks that Amelia Erickson had lost sleep over?

Using extreme care, Ivy unwrapped the first painting and leaned it upright to inspect it.

Vibrant hues of manganese violet, emerald green, cerulean blue, and cobalt yellow leapt from the canvas, even in the dim light.

When she stepped back to view the painting, a chill spiraled down her spine, and she grew light-headed. Blinking, she rubbed her eyes, as if to clear the image that her mind must have imprinted over the canvas that stood before her.

Ivy reached out to touch the painting to make sure it was real, and yet, even as her fingers neared the crackled oil paint, she drew back, unable to touch the revered work. Her heart pounded, and she pressed a hand against her chest.

She slid out another painting. A towering charge of three—no, maybe four—vibrant cobalt blue horses seemed to come alive on the canvas. The fine hairs on her arms bristled as she recalled a lecture one of her professors had once given. Could this be the painting they had studied? Franz Marc was the artist, she recalled. *But there was something else about it…something important…*

Trying not to hyperventilate, she found her voice and called out. "Shelly, come quickly. You need to see this."

Dusting her hands on her jeans, Shelly made her way through the canvas-covered furnishings. "What is it?"

Awe-stricken, Ivy stepped back from the painting. "I think these are the paintings Amelia was concerned about. Look at this one…expressionism, that one, Fauvism, and here—" She touched the edge of another one. "An abstract."

Suddenly, Ivy remembered what her professor had said. *The painting had disappeared.*

"These must be worth a fortune," Shelly said with awe.

"No, priceless." Ivy's head swam as details of the story came back to her.

"What do you think we could get for these?"

"No, you don't understand." As it dawned on Ivy why these paintings might be here, Ivy felt sick to her stomach. She pointed to the horses. "That one was stolen during the Second World War." She pointed to the first one she'd uncovered. "And that one, too, I think. Maybe all of them."

Shelly let out a whistle. "Then what are they doing here?"

"Amelia Erickson was an art collector," Ivy said, although that didn't really explain anything.

"We have to find out more about this art," Shelly said. "Wasn't there a movie about something like this?"

"*Monuments Men.* That was based on actual events." Glancing around, Ivy noticed another crate. "A group of American and British museum directors, art historians, and curators were organized into a special force to find and save art treasures after WWII."

"Why not Monuments Women?"

Ivy let out a sigh. "Actually, there were hundreds of men *and* women involved in the effort. They still have an organization." She touched Shelly's arm. "This is serious. The provenance of all these must be established."

"There must be fifty paintings here." Shelly lifted a canvas from another painting. "These are remarkable. Could they be forgeries?"

"It's possible," Ivy said. "I'm no expert on forgeries, but the artists—or artist—behind these works was a master."

She spied another old cabinet nearby. "Look. A flat file case."

She slid open each drawer one at a time. Inside were unframed canvases. Her head was spinning at the thought of what this artwork represented.

"Something doesn't make sense," Ivy said, frowning. "Maybe Amelia Erickson was safeguarding these from the threat of war here."

Shelly's lips curved into a smirk. "Or maybe she had a greedy, avaricious appetite for art—wherever it came from—and a disregard for ownership."

"That's what I'm afraid of. We have to sort this out." Ivy chewed her lip, thinking about the letter they'd found. "These might be the paintings Amelia was so worried about."

With solemn faces, Ivy and Shelly covered the magnificent paintings and returned them to their original resting places.

Ivy looked up at the gaping opening at the top of the stair. "We have to secure this room."

"Mitch offered last night," Shelly said. "Seems the fewer people who know about this right now, the better."

"Good idea. Give him a call."

"Do we need to report this to the police?"

"I think we have to. But dispatch might think it was a prank call." Ivy slid a hand over her forehead. "I'll ask Bennett. As mayor, he must know the chief of police." Bennett would be the most direct conduit.

After lunch, Mitch showed up at the front door with a toolkit at his side and supplies in his truck. Ivy held the door open for him.

"Shelly called. Said you need help with that gaping hole."

"Sure appreciate it. How much do you think it might be?" He doesn't waste any time, Ivy thought. She liked that.

"No charge." He grinned and ran a hand over his spiky, sun-bleached hair.

"At least let me pay for supplies."

He just shook his head. "Is Shelly around?"

"She was working in the yard when I left." Maybe that was the reason he was refusing to take any money, but he seemed like a good guy. Quite a bit younger than Shelly, though. She hoped he wouldn't break his heart—or Shelly's—when he found out how much older she was. Realizing how hopeful he seemed, Ivy added, "I'll find her."

She didn't have to look, though. Shelly trotted around the corner of the house.

"Hi, Mitch. Saw your truck."

A smile that Ivy hadn't seen on Shelly's face in a long time lit her eyes. With her long hair pulled back in a ponytail and wearing a T-shirt and cut-offs, her sister could easily pass for Mitch's age.

Looking self-conscious, Mitch shoved his hands into

his pockets and rocked on his feet. "Came by to help you clean up that mess in the kitchen. Did you guys go through the stuff downstairs?"

"A lot of it," Shelly said. "There's so much. It will take time to—"

Ivy shook her head and interrupted with a little wave to get Shelly's attention, which was focused on Mitch. "I'm going to take care of that business with Bennett. See you later."

Ivy left them and made her way to the Jeep. As she turned the ignition and steered toward City Hall, conflicted feelings swirled within her. She knew what she must do. And then there was Bennett to contend with, although last night he'd acted differently.

After arriving at City Hall, she walked inside.

Nan popped up from the reception desk. Her face flushed when she saw Ivy.

"W-welcome," Nan stammered.

"Hi, Nan. Is Bennett—the mayor—available? I'd like to have a word with him."

"I'll check. Do you have an appointment?"

"Do I need one?"

Nan shook her head. "I'll make sure he has time for you." She glanced around and lowered her voice. "I'm so embarrassed. I didn't mean to say—well, you probably remember what I said—about your husband. I could have been mistaken." Her face reddened, nearly matching the

Welcome to Summer Beach sunset poster behind her. "My husband tells me I talk too much—gossip is what he calls it." Nan blinked back tears.

Ivy took the older woman's hand. Nan was so upset she was trembling. "It *was* a shock, but that's what I needed to know." Even after his death, Jeremy was still inflicting pain on others.

"I haven't told anyone else that story." Frowning, Nan gnawed on her lip. "At least, not since the Mayor told me who you were. I was shooting off my mouth again. I'm really sorry."

"It's okay." Ivy patted Nan's shoulder. "You know, I could use a friend around here."

Nan's face brightened, and her eyebrows shot up. "I'd like that. My husband would be happy to meet you, too. I told you about our antique shop, didn't I?"

"You sure did." Ivy had a thought. "My house has a stunning chandelier in the foyer. It's beautiful, but honestly, it's overpowering for a beach inn. I was wondering if there might be a market for it here."

"Is there ever," Nan gushed. "I sell to a lot of interior designers who work on mighty fancy houses." Her face flushed again. "I mean, not that yours isn't. Oh dear, sometimes my brain isn't connected to my mouth."

"It's okay." Ivy laughed. Nan meant well, and Ivy really did want to get to know some of the local residents in Summer Beach. "Here's my number. My sister and I are there most of the time. There's so much work to be done before we start renting rooms."

"As an inn?" Nan's forehead creased with worry. "Boz told you about the zoning."

"Relax," Ivy said with a wink. "We're using iBnB. No law against that, I understand."

A smile spread across Nan's face. "You're a smart one, aren't you?"

Ivy inclined her head. *Smart.* Jeremy had been the brains in their family, but look at the mess trusting him had landed her in. No, it had been a long time since anyone had given her credit for being smart, even if it was Nan, the dear woman. "I guess I am."

She gave Nan a hug, and as she did, Bennett emerged from his office. He stopped short when he saw her, and his eyes lit with an unexpected smile.

"Mrs. Marin," he said. "May I help you?"

The sound of his rich, gravelly voice still sent tingles through her. "You'd better call me Ivy Bay. I think that's safer around Summer Beach. Got a minute?"

Bennett gestured for her to follow him into his office.

"Have a seat," he said. "I've been thinking about last night." He winced. "I didn't mean it to sound like that."

"I know." Ivy eased into a marine blue chair in front of a desk that looked pleasantly busy, but not chaotic. As she gathered her thoughts, she stared through an expansive window, where she could see the ocean curling toward the beach and couples walking along the shoreline. Farther out, boats maneuvered out of slips in the marina.

"Quite a view, isn't it?" Bennett followed her line of sight. "I can't imagine being anywhere else."

Drawing her attention back to Bennett, Ivy caught sight of photographs behind him.

Bennett swiveled in his chair. "That was Jackie, my wife, who died ten years ago last week. And there's my nephew, Logan, who's like a son to me."

The woman in the photo was laughing, her head thrown back and the sun on her face. "She was beautiful."

"Inside and out." Bennett touched the frame, and a corner of his mouth tugged up before he turned back to Ivy. "What can I help you with?"

"Shelly and I have been going through the furniture and boxes we found last night. So much to take in. But we found something else, and I think I have to report it to someone. The police, I guess. We found so many...you can't imagine..."

Alarmed, Bennett leaned forward, his hands tightly clasped. "Bodies?"

"What? No, paintings."

Bennett blew out a breath. "That's a relief."

Concerned, Ivy stared at him. "Have you found bodies in Summer Beach before?"

"Bodies?" Bennett ran a hand over his chin. "No, but not much surprises me anymore. Though Summer Beach isn't exactly a hotbed of crime. Back to what you were saying. Paintings?"

"Extremely fine European paintings. Do you have any idea why they might have been stored there?"

"Mrs. Erickson *was* a collector, so it doesn't surprise me. Why does this alarm you?"

Ivy jiggled her foot. "The paintings—they're exceptional. I mean, *masterpieces.* I looked up a few of them online and found that they've been missing for years." She paused. "Since World War II."

Studying her, Bennett pressed his fingertips together. "That's when the house was closed up. The first time, that is. Isn't it possible that Mrs. Erickson stored the paintings then?"

Ivy shook her head. "They could be forgeries, but my guess is that the paintings were acquired on the black market. Or at an auction."

"Isn't that how paintings are often sold?"

"These were reported stolen years ago."

Bennett drew his dark eyebrows together. "That's a lot of conjecture."

"I majored in fine art and art history." Ivy's words tumbled out. "In the late 1930s, Hitler tried to censor art and deemed a lot of works degenerate—which only meant they were modern styles he didn't approve of. Impressionism, Fauvism, and abstract art. Or they were created by people he didn't like. Thousands of works of art—maybe

20,000—were confiscated. Collections were gutted and museums treated like shopping malls. Many collectors and artists lost their most treasured works of art."

"Wait, slow down." Bennett picked up a pen to make notes. "What happened to the art?"

"There was an auction in 1937. At the time, many artworks were sold or diverted into private collections. But the fact remains—that art was stolen from the original owners." Ivy paused for a breath. "I don't know if Amelia Erickson was sheltering these works, if she bought stolen property, or if they're forgeries." Pressing her hands to her temples, Ivy said, "Whichever it is, those paintings don't belong to me. I have to report them."

Bennett tapped his pen on the desk. Finally, he said, "The property was sold 'as is' with all its contents. Like the Chevrolet in the garage."

Ivy watched his little movements. "If those paintings are real, they never would have been sold with the house. They're too valuable. They belong in museums. Besides, if those paintings are real, they should have a provenance, or ownership history, that can be traced. I want to turn them over so they can be properly investigated."

"This is way beyond our police force, but we'll start there." Bennett picked up the phone on the desk and tapped a button. "Chief Clarkson, I have someone in my office who needs to speak to you about an urgent matter." He said a few more words, then hung up. "He'll be right over."

Ivy expelled a breath. Most likely, she was turning over a fortune, but she'd never forgive herself if she didn't.

Chapter 16

"CHIEF CLARKSON, MEET Ivy Marin." Bennett introduced the police chief and gestured to a table in his office where they could all sit. Since she'd come to him about the paintings, he had new respect for her. Not everyone would have reported such a find.

Because of this, he felt protective of Ivy, though he knew she could certainly take care of herself. No, he would be like this with any Summer Beach resident, he told himself. And she had been his client, too.

"Pleased to meet you," Chief Clarkson said. "The mayor tells me you don't agree with what your husband planned to do with Las Brisas."

"That's right," Ivy said. "Word sure gets around here."

"You have no idea," Bennett said. "Mrs. Marin—"

"Call me Ivy, please."

"Ivy has encountered an unusual situation," Bennett said. "As her real estate agent, I was completely unaware of it as well."

"And just what is this situation?"

Ivy leaned forward and clasped her hands on the table. "We discovered a lower level in the house that had been concealed. It's full of antiques—and art."

Chief Clarkson flipped open a small notepad. "And who discovered this?"

Ivy relayed the story about the four of them and how they'd stumbled across the bricked-up entry to the lower level. "I had a good look at everything this morning."

"And what did you find that's concerning you?"

She drew a breath. "Paintings—masterpieces, I believe. Maybe stolen, maybe forgeries."

"Mrs. Erickson was a known art collector. Maybe she stored them and forgot about them."

"I don't see how anyone could forget about these."

"So what makes you think they could be stolen? Or forged?"

Bennett cut in. "Ivy is an art expert. A fine painter and historian, right?"

When Ivy nodded, Bennett noticed she sat up a little straighter. He caught himself musing about what type of artist she was, and his gaze fell to her hands. Her nails were neat and short, though her fingers were delicate and tapered. He could just imagine...

"Did you recognize any paintings?" the chief asked.

"I recognized the artists' style." She told the chief about thousands of paintings and other art pieces that the Nazi leader had confiscated in an attempt to censor art, and how these were sold, destroyed, or hidden. "Even today, discoveries are still being made. Some museums in Germany have acquired found works—from their rightful owners—and have them on display again. Their modern art collections were ravaged, too. And those of private collectors and artists."

The chief made another note on his notepad. "Based on what you've told me, we're going to need to take photographs. Front and back."

"And you'll share those with other law enforcement agencies, right?" Ivy asked. "Can you contact the FBI? See, while I was living in Boston, I followed the theft of paintings at the Isabella Stewart Gardner Museum and the FBI's investigation of the case."

The chief was studying Ivy as she spoke. "Do you think these might be related?"

"I don't think so," Ivy said. "The wallpaper covering the brick wall is much older than that case, and it looks like it's been painted quite a few times. But I'm certain the FBI's Art Crime Team needs to be on this case. These paintings might be valuable."

Chief Clarkson slid a finger around his collar as he considered this. "It's possible the paintings are copies."

"I'm no expert on forgeries," Ivy allowed, though her eyes flashed with conviction. "But the paintings are of exceptional quality. And if they're forgeries, they should not be in circulation."

"You have a point." Chief Clarkson made a note and underlined it. "I'll send an officer to photograph the paintings, and I'll make sure to forward those to the FBI."

Ivy sighed in relief and smiled at Bennett. He was glad that Chief Clarkson was taking her claim seriously.

"Will you put the art in storage?" Ivy asked.

"She's right to be concerned about safety," Bennett added.

"At this time," the chief said with measured words. "Those are just paintings you found in the basement of a house you own. Until we get a hit that they might be stolen property, there's no reason for us to confiscate them. I would, however, suggest that you keep the area secured."

"That's exactly what we're doing," Ivy said.

"If there's anything else you need, call my office." Chief Clarkson slid a card toward Ivy and got up. "I'll go to work on this right away."

After the police chief left, Bennett offered to walk Ivy to her car. He didn't want to alarm her, but he wondered if she realized the impact this discovery could have on Summer Beach. A high profile murder case had occurred in a beach community a few miles south of Summer Beach, and the media had swarmed the area for months. Residents had grown weary of the spectacle, and tourists avoided the area. Even today, that community was still trying to overcome the stigma.

If the paintings were really lost masterpieces, the media would be all over the story—and descending on Summer Beach right at the beginning of their high summer season.

As Bennett ushered Ivy from City Hall, he wondered if the community's revered Mrs. Erickson had been involved in art theft and if Ivy was up to handling the stress of such news coverage.

'

Chapter 17

AFTER GIVING HER statement about the paintings to the chief of police, questions regarding other items on the lower level still swirled in Ivy's mind. She wondered if any of the other items, besides the paintings, would be considered evidence, too.

As Bennett walked her to her car, she asked, "Bennett, does Summer Beach have a historical society?" She unlocked the door, and Bennett opened it for her. His small gesture did not go unnoticed. *Good manners,* Ivy thought.

"It does," he replied, holding the door for her. "The community is proud of its heritage."

Ivy hesitated beside her open door and turned to face

Bennett, who caught her direct gaze and held it, sending an unexpected connection through her. "I'd like to find older photos of the house, and I thought they might have some." Bennett seemed to know a lot of residents. "Do you know how I can get in touch with the society?"

A smile shadowed his face, and again she thought how attractive he was.

"You've already met the president," he said. "That would be Nan, the receptionist. She and her husband run it."

Nan. Of course. She thought about Nan's change of attitude and the details she'd conveyed to her about Jeremy. The breeze whipped her hair across her face, and Ivy swept it back with impatience. "You told her who I was, didn't you?"

"I hope you don't mind." Bennett hooked a thumb into his pocket and tilted his head. "Nan likes to talk. She doesn't mean any harm, but I reminded her that story could be hurtful."

"I appreciate it." Ivy fell silent. One point had been bothering her. Since they were alone in the parking lot, she decided to ask him. "All the time you had the listing on my house, you never said a word about Jeremy being here with another woman."

Bennett's gaze veered off toward the ocean. "That was awkward. I wasn't sure if you knew about that, or would want to know." He blew out a long breath and brought his gaze back to her. "I wish I could say your husband had been discreet here. But that story won't go any farther, I assure you. And I'm sorry it had to happen to you. I don't know you well, but no woman deserves that kind of treatment." He paused. "I'm sorry I didn't tell you. I feel bad about that."

Ivy touched his sleeve. "It's okay. Don't let Jeremy's actions weigh on you."

"You deserved better."

"Yes, I did," she said, raising her chin to Bennett. She had been a good wife to Jeremy. That much she was sure of. "I didn't know about an affair, but if I'm truthful with myself, there were small signs. If I called him late at night from the east coast, he wouldn't answer. He always said he turned off his phone for client dinners. Finally, I stopped calling."

Ivy paused. "I know people will talk, but I can't let that bother me. My identity wasn't wrapped up in Jeremy then, and his actions don't reflect who I am now."

A slow smile spread across his face. "I can see that. I wasn't sure about you at first."

"His death was so unexpected. For a while, I moved through each day, doing only what I had to do to survive. My mind was a jumbled, grieving mess. When I found out that he had drained his retirement to buy this house, I was even more devastated. And to top that off, I received a demand letter from the tax authority. He hadn't even paid the property taxes." She hesitated. "I was under a lot of stress, and I know I wasn't very responsive to you back then. I'm sorry." There, she'd said it.

"I understand."

As Bennett touched her shoulder, Ivy felt his compassion emanating through her thin sleeve. From the warmth of his hand, a shiver coursed through her.

"What I felt was complicated." She looked down and saw her keys jiggling in her hand, aware of the nervousness she felt at being so close to Bennett. The unkind memories she had about him receded.

She shook her head, returning her thoughts to Jeremy. The man Ivy had known as her husband acted differently from the one who'd wreaked havoc among Summer Beach residents. How she wished she'd been able to confront Jeremy. She'd even thought about what she would have said about his financial mismanagement and had imaginary arguments with him.

And that was before she'd discovered his Summer Beach behavior.

One night in Boston, she'd even wondered if she were having a nervous breakdown, and she might have, too, if it hadn't been for her daughters. Sunny and Misty needed her to be strong; they needed her to guide them through their grief. Her stomach tightened. *Should I tell them about their father's indiscretions?* She pursed her lips with resolve. This, too, she would handle—when and if the time were ever right.

Bennett kept his hand on her shoulder. "Were you very much in love with him?"

"I thought I was, but now…" She swallowed hard against her new reality. "I'm no longer devoted to maintaining Jeremy's reputation, though my daughters know nothing of this. I don't expect that they'll visit any time soon, though."

She wished her daughters would come to see her, but they had their own lives now. Remembering what she had been like at that age—feeling impatient to get on with life and leave her parents—she felt a pang of guilt. Her parents must have felt that loss, too.

She sighed. "Jeremy didn't seem concerned about his reputation."

"Not here, anyway."

At this moment, alone in the parking lot under a clear sky, Ivy's trust in Bennett was growing. It felt good to talk to someone about what had happened with Jeremy. And the fact that it was Bennett Dylan? She couldn't be more surprised. She inched closer to him.

"The Summer Beach house was the first clue," she said, pouring out her words. "Jeremy was fastidious in covering up details, after all, computer security was his specialty. But I'm glad I know now."

She gritted her teeth. Inwardly, she blanched at her own words. *Glad.* What a meek term. What she really felt inside was like a volcano erupting, spewing molten lava of anger in every direction. Her dreams had been like that ever since she'd found out about the house. No more hiding behind words like *glad*, or *nice*, or remembering him with kindness.

"Correction." Fuming, Ivy squared her shoulders. "Actually, I'm furious. In having an affair, my husband compromised my trust, my faith in him, and my health. Jeremy denied me proper closure and left questions that will probably never be answered, including who *she* was, and were there any others?"

"You have every right to be upset." Bennett didn't flinch, didn't look away. His hand remained on her shoulder.

"Furthermore, when someone dies, why do they become a saint and suddenly blameless? Because no one wants to hear what he was *really* like," she said, answering her own question. "So who do I tell? What can I do about it now?" Frustrated, she wiped hot tears from her eyes with her fingertips, but she didn't care. Being angry felt good.

"Exactly what you're doing. Telling me." Bennett was patient with her, and let her get her emotions out, which took a minute or two. Spying a tissue box in the back seat of her car, he reached inside and pulled out a couple of tissues for her.

When the worst of her breakdown had passed, he said, "Write him a letter. Tell him how enraged and betrayed you feel. Write a hundred of them if you need to."

"And do what with them?"

"Keep them, rip them up, burn them. Throw the ashes into the sea. Tell somehow else how you feel. Start with your sister or mother, a friend, a therapist. Even your dog."

"I don't have a dog." She sniffed. "Is that what you did?"

"I don't have a dog either." Bennett let out a soft chuckle. "Believe me, no one is perfect, even after they die. Jackie was pretty close to perfect for me, but we'd had an argument the night before she died. She was being stubborn, and I wasn't listening. It was a stupid disagreement about something meaningless, and I know she didn't feel well. We were both under stress."

"So you wrote her a letter after she died?"

"Quite a few."

"I'll try that." Feeling spent, Ivy slid into the Jeep and turned back to him. "I appreciate your help today." She paused, sure that her cheeks were flushed and her eyes swollen. "And thanks for listening to me."

"Anytime," he said, curving up one side of his mouth. "As mayor, I'm here to serve." He shut her door and turned back to City Hall.

Ivy watched him go, realizing she'd read him wrong in the beginning. She was grateful for his help today—and for his advice. It felt good to have someone she could talk to in Summer Beach.

After Ivy left Bennett's office and returned to the house, she stepped out of her shoes by the door and dropped her purse on the floor. A table by the door would be a nice addition, she thought. She'd seen something like that downstairs.

In the library, she found Poppy waiting for her. Her niece was sitting cross-legged on the floor in the library and tapping on the computer she'd brought with her. She had set up her equipment on the floor.

"Shelly let me in," Poppy said, tucking her long blond hair behind her ears and tapping a button to lower the volume of music playing on her laptop. "I've already got a lot of the property information filled in on these iBnB forms."

Ivy padded across the wooden floor to see what Poppy had done. Peering over Poppy's shoulder, Ivy said, "I'm impressed. You're on time and organized, which is more than I am."

"I came in here because of all the racket in the kitchen."

Over Poppy's music on her laptop, Ivy could hear muffled thuds coming from the kitchen. "Before we go on, I need to check on that. I'll be right back."

Ivy hurried into the kitchen, which had turned into a full-scale construction zone. Mitch had finished the demolition and was framing a wide doorway in the empty space. Shelly was sweeping up debris and filling a trashcan. The scent of fresh-cut wood filled the air.

"Hey, how was your meeting?" Shelly asked.

Ivy stepped over a long board. "Chief Clarkson is sending an officer to take pictures."

"That's good. You did the right thing." Shelly jerked a thumb outside. "We stacked the bricks by the side of the house. I can use them for a pathway."

Hoisting a hammer, Mitch raised up. "What do you think?"

"Looks good," Ivy said. She appreciated his efforts, though she figured he just wanted to hang out with Shelly any way he could. "We need that to be secure."

"It will be," Mitch said. "I can sheetrock around it and paint later. I made the opening wide enough for double doors so you can easily move large things through it."

Shelly motioned to Ivy to join her. "You'll be happy with this." She flicked a light switch on the wall inside the door. "Mitch changed the light bulbs."

The lower level lit up, and Ivy stared in amazement at the amount of furnishings she could see now. "More work than I thought."

"We'll get it done," Shelly said. "Mitch offered to help."

Ivy glanced at Mitch. "Shelly, can I talk to you?"

"Sure." Shelly followed her into another room.

"The chief of police is sending an officer out to photograph the paintings. I don't think it's a good idea to share the paintings we found with Mitch."

Shelly's eyes darted to one side.

"You told him?" Ivy was nervous enough without this getting out.

"We left a couple of paintings out. It was so dark down there that we didn't notice. Mitch saw them when he was changing the light bulbs. But I'm sure we can trust him."

"I hope so. Tell him not to share this with anyone."

After leaving Shelly, Ivy made her way back to Poppy, who was typing on her laptop.

"I've already entered your address, features, and keywords," Poppy said. "What would you like to say in your description?"

Ivy grinned. "How about...please stay here and save us from financial disaster?"

Poppy laughed as her fingers flew over the keyboard. "Spacious, charming home just steps from the beach. Gather around the fire pit—"

"We don't have a fire pit."

Poppy furrowed her brow. "Can you get one? People love fire pits." She scrolled through some romantic-looking photos of couples lingering beside fire pits. "They're so atmospheric, and they encourage guests to mingle. I promise you'll get your money back on the first rental, and the reviews will be worth it."

"Well...as long as they're truly *atmospheric*." Ivy nudged her with good humor. "Okay, fire pit it is." *Cha-ching*. One more cost.

Poppy continued. "And sleep to the sound of gentle waves. Enjoy one of Southern California's most pristine beaches. Indulge in the grandeur of this rare historic home designed by California's first female architect." Poppy looked up. "This will appeal to those who love antiques and history. How's that for a start?"

"Sounds grand. You're a marketing genius." Poppy had helped her niece Elena manage publicity in her Los Angeles jewelry business during a particularly disastrous time. "Keep going."

"Can you give lectures on the history of this home?"

Just then, Ivy's phone buzzed. "Hold that thought." Though she didn't recognize the number, she tapped the screen. "Hello?"

Nan's voice floated through the phone. "The mayor tells me you want to know more about Las Brisas."

"Hi Nan," Ivy said. "I'd love to find old pictures of the house, especially the interior."

"We have a book about Las Brisas that we created. We'd put it together to demonstrate the significance of the house to maintaining Summer Beach's local history. Not only was your house built by a noted architect, but it was also used in the military effort during WWII. Mrs. Erickson was quite a character."

"So it seems." Ivy didn't mention what they'd found on the concealed lower level. "Could I get that today?"

"Come by the shop. We have a copy in the office. And

you can meet my husband."

Ivy promised she'd visit and hung up. She turned back to Poppy. "What else do we have to do?"

"Number of rooms, price per night, availability." Poppy motioned to a form on the iBnB website. "I'll survey the competition. Hang on a minute." She pulled up a map with nearby nightly rates displayed.

They discussed a pricing strategy, and Ivy gave her a date that was now four weeks away. "We'll be ready." And in that time, she'd have to squeeze in her mother's party, a quick return trip to Boston to settle her affairs there and ship a few belongings back, furnish the entire house...

And talk to the FBI.

Poppy arched an eyebrow. "Are you sure? Because once people book their stay, if you cancel, they'll scorch you with bad reviews."

"No problem." Ivy lifted her chin and gave her niece a confident smile, though the butterflies raging in her stomach were more like a hoard of bats now. "One way or another, we're opening on the first day of June. Have to run now, though."

Ivy parked the Jeep in front of the address Nan had given her. Located near Java Beach and on the block across from the ocean, Antique Times was a charming shop with an arched stucco façade. Flaming pink bougainvillea bracelets curved around the doorway. A sign proclaimed: *Treas-*

ures of Yesteryear. Ivy stepped inside, and a bell attached to the door announced her arrival.

The scent of peach potpourri welcomed her to the serene shop. A polished craftsman-style settee rested next to a bookshelf of vintage, leather-bound books. Illuminating the area was a Victorian lamp, which brought to life a Persian rug woven of deep shades of burgundy and navy. As a still life, Ivy thought, this would be an intriguing grouping to paint.

A professorial man in his fifties with a shiny shaved head and a Hawaiian shirt and flip-flops greeted her. "I'll bet you're Ivy."

"You'd win that bet. Ivy Bay."

"Arthur Ainsworth. Nan's my better half. I understand you've come to rescue the grand dame."

Ivy detected a trace of a British accent. "My husband didn't leave me much choice."

"Better you than him."

Before she went off again on her dear departed, she changed the subject. "Nan tells me that the two of you had put together a history of my property."

"I have it right here." Arthur lifted an over-sized, bound copy with *Las Brisas del Mar* printed on the front. "We also created a website to educate residents on the property's cultural importance. The site is still live, so you can capture photos there."

"That's exactly what I need." A thought occurred to

her. "How long has this shop been here?"

"Built in 1949, though the original owner had lived in Summer Beach before the war. Served in it, too."

"Did Amelia Erickson ever bring in pieces to sell here? Art pieces, paintings?"

"That was a long time ago, but I can check the records if it's important."

"It might be. Did you ever meet her?"

"No, she left before I arrived, but at the time, most everyone in town knew her. That's why her illness was so sad. So many people loved her, but she didn't know them anymore, and she thought she was all alone."

"Why was that?"

Arthur tapped the book. "We found some writings about her. They say her memory began slipping. She was just forgetful at first, sometimes a little confused, and then it became increasingly apparent that she was mired in a fog of dementia more often than not. Alzheimer's, most likely. Evidently, it had been coming on for a long time. She went to stay at a care facility in Switzerland, where she eventually died."

"I wonder why she didn't stay here," Ivy said.

"When she discovered her encroaching illness could be not be reversed, Mrs. Erickson enlisted a friend there who helped her make arrangements."

Ivy admired that. She could just imagine how difficult such planning must have been for a once-vibrant woman to face. "What about her family?"

"Sadly, she had no one left." Arthur flipped open the book and pointed out a black-and-white photograph of a handsome man. "This was her husband. He died while they were in residence at their primary house in San Francisco. Before that, she'd lost her entire family in the first war between France and Germany."

"I heard that's why she closed the house."

"After the bombing of Pearl Harbor, I could hardly blame her. The entire west coast was on alert, especially after a Japanese submarine bombarded targets off the coast of Santa Barbara, just a couple hours north of here. But when she realized the need for civilian assistance, she reopened her home and pitched in to help. She overcame her fears to help others, and I'm sure she wasn't entirely well then."

Arthur paused to put on reading glasses. "There's a photo in here of that time." He turned a few pages, then stopped. "Here it is. The ballroom was turned in to a gymnasium of sorts."

Ivy peered at the photo. Sure enough, old exercise equipment and dumbbells rested under the chandeliers. A healthcare worker was helping a man on what looked like rehabilitation equipment. "That's fascinating."

"Many young naval recruits and nurses lived there and received physical therapy for injuries they'd sustained. Heard some carved their names in the cedar closets." He chuckled. "She was none too happy about that, but she left them that way because she said it helped her remember them. They were the sons and daughters she never had."

Ivy wished she could have known Amelia Erickson. She turned a page to a photo of the foyer. "I'm thinking of changing light fixtures. Do you know what this chandelier might be worth?"

"Nan mentioned that, but I'd have to examine it."

"You can come by anytime," Ivy said. "My sister and I are working hard to open the doors to iBnB guests. We'd like to host community events, too."

Arthur nodded in thoughtful agreement. "Mrs. Erickson would've liked that, and I know our neighbors will. I think you're going to fit right in at Summer Beach."

"I already feel at home," Ivy said, thinking about her conversation with Bennett.

After thanking Arthur, she tucked the large volume under her arm and left. The old-fashioned bell on the door tinkled behind her. As Ivy walked to her car, she wondered if the photocopied clipping and interviews in the book might shed light on Amelia's actions surrounding the artwork they'd found.

Ivy hoped that she might find clues to absolve Amelia, but she had to face the fact that the woman might have been complicit in the theft by receiving stolen art.

Before Ivy got into the Jeep, she paused on Main Street to take in the town around her. Couples strolled the beach and children raced along the shoreline. Boat owners were puttering around their craft in the marina. A few people sat outside at Java Beach, just as she and Shelly had done on their first day here. Others strolled into a quaint, independent bookstore or one of the beach boutiques, while still others nodded to her or said hello as they passed.

Ivy lifted her face to the sun's warm rays.

A month ago, moving here and putting down roots had been the farthest thing from her mind. But now, besides wanting to be close to her mother in case she was ill, she was feeling more at home here than she'd ever been in Boston, even though she had loved living on the east coast for years.

With Boston's history, culture, educational offerings—not to mention the New England clam chowder she loved so much, especially from Legal Sea Foods or Turner's Seafood—few cities could compare. She would always feel as though she had left a piece of her heart there.

Still, Summer Beach felt like home. The beach community offered the peace and calm she craved. Her creativity was awakening, and she planned to set up her easel in the sun porch where the light poured through vast windows.

She'd just have to learn how to make clam chowder

After Ivy swung into the Jeep, she placed the large volume on the seat beside her and ran her hand over the cover. She couldn't wait to delve into the story of the mysterious Amelia Erickson.

Chapter 18

POPPY WAS STILL sitting on the floor in the library, tapping on her laptop, when Ivy returned.

"You haven't moved," Ivy said, clutching the historical volume on Las Brisas that Nan's husband had given her.

Poppy tore her focus from her screen and looked up. Her eyes sparkled with excitement. "I've reached out to a lifestyle blogger in Los Angeles. She has a huge following, and she wants to visit and post about the historic Las Brisas del Mar—now the Seabreeze Inn. She loves the historical angle. And the fire pit on the beach."

"Of course she does," Ivy said, laughing. "I'll buy one right away."

"Do you know of any local businesses we can chat up? The best place for brunch or coffee. A cute boutique. Oh, and I need to create a website for you, too."

"Poppy, you're a dream. You can mention Java Beach and Antique Times." Ivy marveled at Poppy's organizational and computer skills and knew she'd have to dust off her skills, too. "I'll buy a domain right away."

"And look at this." Poppy spun the laptop around. "I took exterior photos of the house and used an app to paste flowers into the garden. I hope you don't mind. Shelly said she's planting them anyway. When do you think we can have interior photos?"

"Maybe sooner than we think." Ivy tapped the historical volume she held. "This is the key."

Poppy's eyes grew wide. "What's that?"

"Shelly and I were poking around and found some furniture on a lower level. I just need to verify what is original, and what might be...on loan."

"Wow, what incredible luck. Shelly wouldn't let me go down there."

"We wanted it to be a surprise." Ivy felt a little bad about not bringing Poppy into the secret, but she'd promised the chief to keep it quiet.

"Do you need help bringing things up?" Poppy pushed to her knees.

Ivy hugged her. "I'd love your help."

"I'll call my brothers. They have friends, too. Get a

bunch of strong guys, and bam, the job is done."

Shelly sauntered in. "Bam, what's done?"

"Bringing up things from downstairs," Ivy said. She held up the historical book. "I met the president of the Summer Beach Historical Society at City Hall. This volume is chock full of old photos that can help us separate the original furnishings from the other…later pieces."

"Good idea," Shelly said. "Mitch is just finishing. You should see the kitchen now."

"And Mitch. He's awfully hot," Poppy said, suppressing a giggle.

"Are you interested in him?" Ivy asked. She guessed Mitch was maybe five years older than Poppy, if that.

Poppy flashed a grin at Shelly. "Wouldn't matter if I were. He's been checking out Shelly all day."

"Not all day," Shelly shot back. "He's been working hard."

"Every time I went in the kitchen for a glass of water," Poppy said. "He would've been done in half the time if you weren't there."

Ivy wasn't surprised. Guys had always been drawn to Shelly. She just hoped her sister would choose well this time around. Mitch seemed more reliable than Ezzra, but then, they didn't really know much about him other than he owned Java Beach and a boat. "Eyes wide open this time, Shelly. Remember Ezzra."

Her sister's mouth gaped open. "You think I'm already

replacing Ezzra?"

"I just don't want you to make the same mistake."

"Like you did?"

Ivy couldn't reply. Jeremy was far from perfect.

Her anger rising, Shelly folded her arms. "So what kind of mistake might I be making?"

Ivy didn't like where this was going, but she knew Shelly well enough to know that if her sister was becoming defensive about Mitch, then she was definitely interested in him. "Getting involved with someone emotionally unavailable or afraid of commitment."

"Who said I'm getting involved with anyone?" Shelly threw up her hands. "When you're ready to see the fine job that the commitment-phobic Mitch has done—for free, I might add—be my guest." Shelly whirled around and marched from the room.

Poppy widened her eyes. "Aunt Ivy, she's really sensitive about that issue."

"You think?" Yet if the situation were reversed, Ivy would expect Shelly to look out for her best interests, too. As far as Ivy was concerned, that's what family was for, like it or not.

"I have to see another client soon." Poppy powered off her laptop. "What are you wearing to Nana's big bash on Saturday night?"

Ivy shook her head. With so much going on, the dates had slipped past her. "I have no idea. I had planned to ask

Shelly to go shopping and help me choose a new outfit, that is, once she starts speaking to me again."

"If you want, I'll go shopping with you." Poppy slipped her computer into its case.

"That would be fun," Ivy said. The next few weeks would be a blur, but the most critical task was to find out what her mother had been concealing from them. She prayed that Carlotta was in good health, but both of her parents were of an age where they needed their children to look after them more. After hearing about Mrs. Erickson's battle with Alzheimer's, Ivy was even more concerned about her mother's health.

That evening after a tense supper with Shelly, Ivy tucked herself into bed early and armed herself with a notepad, sticky notes, the historical house volume, the ledger, and a glass of red wine. At last, she could relax and try to sort out this mystery.

Cool evening breezes lifted the sheer curtains at the open window, and moonlight spilled across the room like a heavenly balm for her aching muscles and fevered thoughts. All the lifting and sorting and cleaning that she'd been doing around the house had awakened every dormant muscle in her body.

She picked up her new reading glasses, which were indigo blue with cadmium-yellow, the exact shade that Monet had used for his Water-Lilies after 1916. She'd had black frames before, but she was feeling more daring. Shelly liked them, too.

As she slipped on her glasses and sipped her wine, she began to read about Las Brisas, the architect Julia Morgan, and Amelia Erickson. Studying the photos taken in the 1920s and 1930s, she recognized much of the furniture that was stored on the lower level.

She opened the ledger to the page she'd seen. January 1942. The receipt tucked between the pages might have been for the bricks and building supplies. Deciphering the flowing cursive script, she found that the descriptions matched the furnishings downstairs, as well as those she saw in the book. Amelia might have been keeping a record of the furnishings she'd moved downstairs.

Hidden from potential invaders.

Ivy reached for a magnifying glass to look at the photos again. Peering closer, she didn't see the paintings that she'd seen in the crates or flat files, although Amelia's taste had been unerring.

Even though Ivy hadn't finished exploring the treasure trove down below, she'd seen enough to know that if Mrs. Erickson had purchased the paintings Ivy had seen before WWII, she would have proudly displayed them in the most visible places in the house. The artistry was that impressive.

Unless she couldn't.

Ivy removed her glasses, thinking about how frightened Amelia must have been. Running her hand across the old ledger, she wondered if she might find other items Amelia had tucked away in the house. Where might she have hidden other writings or treasures?

The painted Chinese screen caught her eye. Behind it were mirrored closets, shelves, and cubbyholes, but she was too tired to investigate tonight.

By the time Ivy turned off the crystal lamp next to the antique walnut bed she slept in, she had a good idea about which pieces were safe to bring upstairs to furnish the bedrooms. In the morning, she would ask Arthur to come by the house and inspect the chandelier in the foyer. If she could get a good price for that, she could afford the new mattresses, linens, and pillows that every guestroom would need.

As she punched her pillow and snuggled under the thin blanket, she thought about Shelly and hoped her sister would be in better spirits in the morning. She sighed and stared at the ceiling. Maybe she owed her an apology.

As much as Ivy had once loved Jeremy, he hadn't turned out to be the stellar catch either, even though he had been a good father to the girls. When he was around Sunny and Misty, he had spoiled them by lavishing them with shopping sprees while she was the one who was stuck with the mundane discipline when he left on his business trips to Florida or the west coast. Had she but known then what she knew now…

She wondered if she could ever forgive Jeremy his behavior and his flaws.

Or did it even matter now?

Dead tired but restless, she punched the pillow again, trying to make sense of the strange predicament in which she now found herself.

What she needed was a good night's sleep.

She blew out a breath of exasperation. Tomorrow was, indeed, another day.

Thank you, Scarlett O'Hara. She closed her eyes.

Ivy and Nan peered up at the sparkling chandelier in the foyer, while Arthur balanced on a ladder above them inspecting the vintage crystal. It was quite the statement piece, but to Ivy's eye, it overwhelmed the area.

With a frown of doubt etched on her face, Nan asked, "Are you sure you want to let this go?"

"I'd like a more casual beach vibe," Ivy said. "And I really need the money."

"Gilt-bronze and rock crystal," Arthur pronounced, his shaved head and half-glasses gleaming against the crystal. "Circa 1800, I'd say, and definitely Italian. This is a collector-quality piece and should go to auction at one of the large auction houses."

"I don't have time for that," Ivy said.

Nan caught her husband's eye. "What about you-know-who in Beverly Hills?"

Arthur looked perplexed for a moment before his eyes brightened. "Ah. That's a distinct possibility."

Nan turned to Ivy. "I have a friend who's an interior designer to the stars, and she has a shop in Beverly Hills. One of her former clients—a mega superstar known for her over-the-top style—just bought a home that she wants to renovate. This might be perfect for her. It's certainly large enough."

"That would work," Ivy said with hope.

Fumbling in her vintage designer handbag, Nan said, "Let's find out." She pulled out her phone, snapped a photo, and tapped a text to her friend.

A knock sounded at the door behind them. When Ivy opened it, she was surprised to see Chief Clarkson. One of his officers had arrived at eight o'clock sharp this morning to take photographs. Having just put on a pot of coffee then, Ivy and Shelly quickly changed clothes and helped the officer unwrap each painting for her to photograph. Including the canvases in the flat files, they found more than a hundred paintings—a staggering number that Ivy still couldn't believe. Each new discovery had touched her heart. And nearly all were museum quality.

"Afternoon, Ivy. Is now a convenient time to talk?" the chief asked, raising his eyes to Arthur, who was still perched on the ladder. "Hello Arthur, Nan," he said, his deep voice booming in the empty room. "Always nice to see you two."

Arthur descended the ladder to shake the chief's hand. "How did that gift for the missus work out?"

"My wife loves antiques, so it was perfect. Thanks for

your help." Chief Clarkson turned back to Ivy. "May we have word in private?"

Clearly interested in why the police chief was visiting Ivy, Arthur nevertheless folded the ladder and nodded to his wife. "We'd better be off, Nan."

"Oh, of course," Nan said, her eyes wide with curiosity. "We'll let you know if we hear back from you-know-who."

"I sure appreciate it," Ivy said and closed the door behind them.

Chief Clarkson was a barrel-chested man who looked like a former Marine. His tight, curly black hair was closely cropped. He towered above her, and Ivy hadn't realized how tall he was when they were sitting in Bennett's office. He ducked to avoid grazing the tip of the chandelier.

After the door closed behind the Ainsworths, the chief began. "We transmitted the photographs to the FBI's Art Crime Team. Two agents on the team are on their way."

Ivy hadn't expected such a rapid response, which made her all the more convinced that the paintings were indeed lost masterpieces. "That's good news."

"They'll need a statement from you and others who were present."

"Just my sister, Shelly."

"Good. You should expect the team of Cecile Dupont and Ari Steinberg tomorrow."

"Tomorrow?"

"Any problem with that?"

"No, of course not." Only that her parents' party was this weekend, and she'd hoped to go shopping in the afternoon.

After Chief Clarkson left, Ivy sat on the first step of the grand staircase and thought about the weekend ahead.

The more she thought of what her mother's announcement might entail, the less festive she felt.

Earlier today, Carlotta had called Ivy to say that the family—and only the family—should be there an hour before other guests were due to arrive.

Once again, Carlotta had asked, "Are there any pieces of my jewelry that you would like?"

A chill crept over Ivy. "Mom, we discussed this when I was there. I'd like for you to continue enjoying your things." She paused. "Why do you keep asking?"

"We'll go over that tomorrow," Carlotta replied, her tone pleasant, but firm. "We're simply trimming our belongings."

Ivy's heart thudded with anxiety. Whatever Carlotta had to say, she would tell her family first. Ivy had to brace herself for the worst.

Between her mother's possible illness, the hovering tax collector, and now the FBI, Ivy was afraid this summer was shaping up to be truly unforgettable.

Chapter 19

IVY FLICKED THE lights on and led the FBI team to the lower level. Agents Cecile Dupont and Ari Steinberg were decidedly low key. Dark suits, plain black pumps for her, and black dress shoes for him. Which meant they stuck out like the plainclothes FBI agents they were here in Summer Beach.

Eyeing a coffee cup in Cecile's hand that bore a Java Beach imprint, Ivy wondered how long it would take for gossip to ricochet around the small town.

The FBI agents had arrived a half hour early, before Bennett and Chief Clarkson had promised to meet them at the house. From their line of questioning, she suspected that might have been intentional.

As they made their way down the stairs, Cecile asked, "When was the first time you saw these paintings?" Her tone was pleasant but brisk.

"Just a couple of days ago," Ivy said as she descended. "Watch your step."

"So the doorway we walked through was bricked over, but do you know for how long?" Ari asked, mirroring Cecile's tone. He carried a black, hard plastic case, which Ivy guessed held the tools of their trade.

"I inherited the house from my late husband's estate a year ago. I'm sure it was like that when he bought it."

Ari continued. "But if the first time you saw the house was two weeks ago, as you stated, then you can't be sure the entry was bricked up when your husband acquired the house."

"You're right. I don't know." Ivy realized she needed to listen to their questions and give precise answers.

"So it's possible that your husband might have stored the artwork there and put the bricks in place," Cecile added.

Did they suspect Jeremy? Or her? A cloud of nerves enveloped her. "We kept the bricks to reuse. They're stacked near the house if you want to inspect them. The wallpaper that covered the bricks is in the trashcan."

"We appreciate that," Ari said. "Did your husband tell you about the bricked entryway?"

"No," Ivy answered. Was that a trick question? "He

didn't even tell me he'd bought the house."

Cecile's left eyebrow twitched slightly at that, but she said nothing.

Ivy led them to the artwork. "The framed paintings are in the crates standing upright. The unframed canvases are in the flat files." She tapped the top of the sturdy wooden file case.

"Have you removed any paintings?" Cecile asked.

"Only with the police officer to photograph them, but we put everything back."

The two agents traded a look. Cecile said, "We'll be here for some time. We need to catalog and inspect every painting."

Ivy knew she was being dismissed. "If there's anything you need—coffee, or—"

"We're good," Cecile said, holding up her Java Beach cup.

"Right." Ivy pointed upstairs. "I'll be up there if you need me."

"You've been very helpful," Ari said.

Ivy climbed the stairs, and just before she reached the entry to the kitchen, she pulled up short to avoid running into Bennett. Teetering on the top step, she let out a little cry, and he caught her by the forearms to steady her. "I didn't see you," she said.

"That was close," Bennett said. "You could've fallen backward down the stairs." Behind him stood Chief Clarkson.

Bennett held her arms a little longer than seemed necessary. As she stared back at him, she felt a shift inside of her, a tug on her heart that she hadn't felt in...years. *What's happening to me?*

Bennett led her into the kitchen, his hand lightly touching her elbow. When he finally let go, he moved his hand protectively around to the small of her back. It was all Ivy could do to catch her breath. The feelings that he'd nudged from dormancy during their conversation by her car now notched up another level.

"Shelly let us in," Bennett said, his voice sounding deeper in the sparsely furnished room. "I saw a rental car out front. The FBI team is already here?"

"Downstairs," Ivy managed to say, tilting her head toward the staircase. "They're through with me for now."

"We'll check in with them," Bennett said. "You can stay up here."

Ivy nodded, fighting to process the powerful feelings that were surging through her.

Bennett and Chief Clarkson made their way downstairs, and Ivy slid onto a stool next to Shelly.

"I'm in desperate need of more coffee," Ivy said.

"Just put on a fresh pot. Figured we could use it." Shelly shifted on the stool. "About the other day. What you said about Mitch."

Ivy waved Shelly's comment away. "That wasn't my

place."

"No, it is." Shelly swiveled to face her. "Sisters look out for each other. We should always be honest with each other, even if it hurts. This is the rest of our lives, and we can't mess up anymore." Shelly took Ivy's hand. "I'm sorry I got so upset."

"I shouldn't have been so direct."

"You had to be to cut through my infatuation fog."

Ivy grinned. "Mitch is cute."

"Isn't he?" Shelly sighed. "And ten years younger than I am. He's probably not even ready for children. But I'm a ticking time bomb."

"No, you're not."

"Don't back off now. If I ever want a family, I have to be practical." Shelly got up to pour coffee and brought two cups back. When she returned, she said, "So how about you? You've already had your kids. I know it's only been a year, but do you ever look at a man and think you might marry again?"

Ivy was sipping her coffee as Shelly spoke, and she gulped too fast at her last comment. "Why would you ask that?" she managed to say between coughing fits.

"You okay?"

Ivy shook her head. She was definitely not okay. And Bennett Dylan had everything to do with it. Once she stopped choking, she managed a weak grin.

"Was it something I said?" Shelly asked with an innocent grin.

"Not funny." *Not. At. All.*

Cradling her coffee, Shelly leaned forward over the counter. "I mean, how do you know when a relationship is right? How did you know with Jeremy?"

"Let's leave Jeremy out of this."

"Right." Shelly tapped on her cup. "We can ask Mom or Honey. They seem to have gotten it right." Shelly clutched Ivy's arm. "Honey! She and Gabe are flying in tonight. I wonder what she's wearing to Mom's big bash?"

Ivy dropped her face into her hands. "I have to go shopping."

"You don't have anything to wear yet?"

Ivy shook her head. "What with a house to clean and paint, a secret room, a hundred stolen paintings, and the FBI descending upon us, who had time?"

"Wow. That's a pretty good excuse."

"Come with me? Maybe I can carve out an hour for shopping after the agents leave."

"You know I will." Shelly paused and bit her lip. "Except I promised Mitch I'd go whale-watching with him this afternoon."

"Really? After what you just said?"

Shelly shook her hands. "I know. Look, I'll cancel."

"No, go ahead," Ivy said. "We can go in the morning."

"Really?"

"Yes, really."

"Hey, maybe we'll meet some nice guys at the party."

Ivy raised a brow. "Like you want a nice guy." She'd say anything to keep Shelly off that line of questioning again.

"No, I do. I really do this time. And you should, too."

Ivy started to reply, but Bennett appeared in the doorway, saving her.

"Got a minute?" he asked.

I have a lifetime, she wanted to say. Where did *that* come from? Instead, she rose and said, "Sure," as stoically as she could manage.

What on earth was wrong with her?

As she walked toward him, Ivy glanced back at Shelly, who was staring at them quizzically.

Following Bennett downstairs, she asked, "Find anything new?"

"You'll see."

Shelly appeared at the top of the stairs. "May I listen, too?"

"Sure." Bennett motioned for Shelly to join them.

The FBI agents and Chief Clarkson had removed the covering from a table and placed chairs around it. Bennett pulled one out for her, and she eased into it, casting her gaze around the table. Cecile wore a serious expression, while Ari had a triumphant air about him. Chief Clarkson's expression was unreadable.

Shelly perched on a bench beside them.

Cecile templed her manicured nails and began. "When we received the photographs from Chief Clarkson, we were struck by the number of works and the purported artists. A team was immediately pulled from other work to focus on this. Our colleagues have been matching the images you sent to the National Stolen Art File, an FBI database, around the clock since receipt. Many of these works were considered lost or destroyed. Of more than 20,000 works confiscated during the time period in question, thousands were burned. We fear many on our list met that fate."

Cecile paused to consult her list. "As of right now, we have an extraordinarily high match on the stolen art list. Given that the disappearance of these pieces occurred during a similar time, between 1937 and 1939, we will probably find that most can be traced to one event."

"Hitler's degenerate art sale," Ivy said, growing excited. "Paul Klee, Franz Marc, Max Ernst, Marc Chagall." And Max Beckmann, Otto Dix, Wassily Kandinsky...and so many more. A frisson of excitement passed through her as she thought of these great artists—and their work leaning against crates and boxes in her house. "They're all there, aren't they?"

Cecile flicked her gaze toward Ari.

Nodding, Ari cleared his throat. "You've seen them, and we understand you have a background in fine art and art history. You must know that this is one of the most significant finds we have encountered. For that reason, we must gather evidence and take possession of the artwork."

Shelly sucked in a breath. "Then, the paintings are genuine?"

"Most likely," Cecile said. "Chief Clarkson will provide officers to secure the area until we have our own personnel, who will arrive soon. Until we have completed this phase of the task, we ask that you not share any information or details with anyone. And please don't speak to members of the media. We'll issue a statement when we're ready."

"Not a word," Ivy said. She could feel the energy flowing from Shelly. For Shelly to keep a secret of this magnitude, especially at a party, would be the supreme test of her control. Ivy hoped she'd pass. "I can assure you that this will remain among the people in this room."

Ari looked up from his notes. "We have another person who was present at the discovery of the room. Mitch Kline. Can anyone tell me how to reach him?"

Chief Clarkson pointed toward Cecile's coffee cup. "He probably made that cup of coffee for you this morning. Mitch owns Java Beach."

Ari made a note. "We'll interview him next."

Chief Clarkson splayed his hands on the table. "Before you do, I'd like to discuss an issue about Mitch Kline with you."

"Other than the fact that he is a convicted felon?" Cecile coolly relayed this detail. "For burglary. And he installed the door and lock?"

Shelly's mouth formed an "O."

Ivy blinked.

Bennett spoke up. "Mitch is a hard-working, valued member of our community."

"Be that as it may, having him near the premises might prove compromising," Cecile said.

Ivy clutched Shelly's hand under the table. "We understand."

"Is he aware of the paintings?"

When Shelly's face turned fiery red, Ivy leaned forward. "He did see them when he was installing the door."

Cecile, Ari, Chief Clarkson, and Bennett remained stone-faced.

Finally, Ari said, "Our entire team can't thank you enough for bringing this discovery to our attention. Your honesty will benefit many people whose families owned these works."

Ivy's heart filled with gratitude. She asked, "Will the art will be returned to them, or their heirs?"

Ari replied, "Once the paintings are verified, a court order will be issued to return the works to their rightful owners." He hesitated. "One thing we don't know is how these paintings came to rest here. We have theories, but have you found any documentation, letters, or diaries that might shed light on Amelia Erickson's activities?"

"Only a small ledger, but it didn't have any notes about the paintings." Ivy had seen other numbers in the ledger, but she couldn't make out what they might pertain to. "And a letter."

"May we see these?"

"Of course."

Bennett said, "Mrs. Erickson was an avid art collector, but she was also a generous community benefactor. We can only imagine that she was sheltering these works for the owners and artists."

"Perhaps that's true, but we would appreciate any information you might have. While we cannot prosecute the dead, the truth might help us in other investigations." Ari pushed back from the table. "Thank you all again—Ivy and Shelly, Mayor, Chief—for doing the right thing and contacting us as quickly as you did."

After the meeting broke up, Shelly started up the stairs, and Ivy followed her. As Ivy climbed the steps, she thought about the joy that individuals and families would have over the return of their stolen paintings, and this suffused her with pleasure.

However, the news about Mitch was startling, and she could hear Shelly's angry sniffles just ahead of her. *Better now than later*, she thought, but she knew Shelly had developed real feelings for him. First Ezzra, now Mitch. Another broken heart for her sister.

Ivy couldn't help but wonder if she could she withstand the same.

Chapter 20

"MITCH, I'VE GOT to talk to you," Bennett said, placing his hands on the Java Beach counter. "Can you leave for a few minutes?"

"Why not here?" Mitch nodded toward the customers who were waiting for orders. "Line out the door for the early morning rush. "Can it wait?"

"Can't talk here." Bennett motioned for Mitch to lean closer. "FBI wants to talk to you," he whispered.

"Maddy, take over for me for a minute." Mitch followed Bennett out the side door.

Satisfied they were out of earshot of customers, Bennett pulled out a business card. "FBI agents are in town investigating the artwork in Ivy's basement."

"What do they want with me?"

"You helped break the wall down, and you installed a door and a lock."

"So? I was doing Shelly and Ivy a favor."

"You also know what's down there."

Mitch blew out an exasperated breath. "Look, I really like Shelly. I just wanted to help."

"Listen, Mitch, I'm trying to do you a favor here. You've gotten your life back on track. Don't mess it up now."

Mitch held up his hand. "I've got nothing to do with the art or antiques."

"Think carefully. Given your history, they may want to search your home, your boat, your business."

"Not without cause, they can't."

Bennett stared at him. "I hope you have nothing to hide."

"I swear. I might have been stupid once, but I've changed."

Bennett put a hand on his hip. For Mitch's sake, he hoped that was true. "If you were tempted in any way, there's still time to rectify your actions."

Mitch's lips separated, and his face took on a genuine look of hurt. "I haven't let you down, Ben. I've got nothing to hide."

"Word to the wise is all." Bennett bumped his fist and

left. Mitch was like a younger brother to him, and he wanted to see him make a success of his second chance.

Mitch went back to work, and Bennett paused on the sidewalk, praying that his friend hadn't been tempted.

Years ago, Bennett had found him sleeping in the back of his pickup early one morning. Mitch confided that he'd just been released from serving a year in prison for burglary, but he was trying to make an honest living. He'd been selling pastries on the beach, so Bennett had guaranteed his rent for a tiny coffee shack on the beach that was vacant. The city owned the property, and it was before Bennett had become mayor, so there was no conflict of interest.

Bennett had felt sorry for the poor kid, who'd lost both his parents in an accident. Mitch seemed smart, and he needed a break after spending a year in prison for his lapse in judgment. Since Bennett had known him, Mitch had worked tirelessly, and they'd never spoken of Mitch's past again.

Bennett prided himself on helping Mitch get a foothold on the path to rehabilitation, and he prayed Mitch hadn't messed up. Given his friend's previous crime, this was a temptation as big as the moon for him.

Chapter 21

THE NEXT MORNING, Shelly opened the door to Ivy's bedroom. "Still want to go shopping this morning?"

"Either that or I'm wearing what I have on to the party tonight," Ivy replied. She wore her usual scuffed running shoes—not that she had run in years—along with blue jeans and a plain white shirt she'd bought years ago at J. Crew or Gap. She couldn't remember which shop, except that it had probably been on clearance.

Shelly grimaced. "Can't let that happen. Twenty minutes and we're out of here."

Ivy glanced at the clock. Anxiety prickled her neck; by the end of today, they would know why her mother had summoned them here. She'd hardly slept last night, worrying about her parents.

To keep her mind off her mother while she waited for Shelly, Ivy flipped open the book, *The T-Shirt & Jeans Handbook,* her sister had given her. The feeling that Bennett was awakening in her was spilling into other parts of her life. It had been a year since Jeremy's death—a year of not caring what she looked like and reaching for the most comfortable clothes in her closet. If she managed to get out of bed.

Now, she had finally crawled out of her self-imposed exile and was rediscovering who she was without Jeremy and without their children. For the first time in her adult, post-college years, she was on her own and free to make her own decisions. It was also time she worked on her outer image. Although her dream of an inn would have to begin with iBnB room rentals, she planned to file the paperwork for the rezoning with the Summer Beach zoning department. She would need to launch a campaign to win over neighbors, too. For all that, she would need to look and feel her confident best.

Turning a page, Ivy studied the photographs. She saw how easy it looked to change from plain to pulled-together. The author had a few tips Ivy hadn't thought of. The right jacket, some fashionable jewelry, a stylish scarf. Nice shoes—maybe even a heel—and an interesting handbag. The look was comfortable and stylish. Not too intimidating, but she would have to make a conscious effort.

She dug through the meager wardrobe she'd thrown into her suitcase. Jeans, white shirts, a couple of lightweight cardigan sweaters, and loafers. On the dresser, she spied the coral and turquoise necklace her mother had given her that she'd meant to return. On impulse, she looped it over her head. The white shirt she wore framed it well, and she decided to go with it. She'd already given the coral sundress to Shelly.

Next, Ivy kicked off her running shoes and slid her feet into the jeweled kitten heel shoes her mother had let her wear. She added one of the lightweight cardigan sweaters she'd brought. Then she finished the ensemble with the right lipstick and blush, along with a touch of mascara.

Ivy was surprised at how little effort it had taken, but as she surveyed herself in the old mirror, she was surprised at the effect. A good haircut and fewer pounds would make a big difference, too, but this was a pleasing start.

Shelly sashayed in wearing the yellow sundress Carlotta had given her. "Wow," she said, taking in Ivy's new look. "You look great."

"Not too much?" Ivy wondered if the necklace was too eye-catching or the lipstick too bright.

"Not at all."

"I've been reading the book you gave me. If I'm going to be running an inn or an iBnB property and welcoming guests, I need to look presentable."

"This makeover wouldn't have anything to do with Bennett, would it?"

Ivy's heart quickened. "It's not really a makeover," she said, a little flustered at Shelly's insinuation. "Just an update."

With a smug expression, Shelly folded her arms. "If you say so. During the meeting with the FBI agents, Bennett could hardly take his eyes off you."

"I didn't see anything like that."

"Because you were avoiding him, but not exactly like you used to when you couldn't stand him. Something's changed." Shelly narrowed her eyes. "Is anything going on between you two?"

"Don't be ridiculous," Ivy said, picking up her purse. "Let's go."

When they stepped outside, Ivy noticed a dark sedan parked in front of the house. A patrol car was parked across the street. She turned to Shelly. "Coincidence?"

"Doubt it," Shelly said. "Looks like reinforcements."

"They're serious about this situation."

As they walked to the Jeep, a large SUV slowed in front of the house.

"Well, well. Looks like even more company," Shelly said with a smile dancing on her face.

Bennett stepped from the car. He wore running shorts and looked like he'd been up early for a jog. "Good morning. I was just passing by. How's it going here?"

Though he was pleasant enough, Ivy saw lines of worry around his eyes—once she lifted her gaze from his muscular legs, that is.

She nodded toward the other two cars. "Is there a meeting we didn't know about?"

"Looking out after our residents," Bennett said. "You ladies going to be gone long?"

"As long as it takes to make me presentable for my mother's big party tonight," Ivy said.

"That shouldn't take much time," he said.

Ivy arched a brow. "I beg your pardon?"

Bennett drew a hand over his stubbled chin. "I mean, you already look nice. All dressed up." Seeming self-conscious, he quickly changed the subject. "The FBI agents told me they plan to conduct the removal on Monday. Then your life should return to normal."

Ivy laughed at the thought. "I haven't known what normal is for a long time."

Hesitating for a moment, Bennett shifted on his feet. "Listen, there's something I should tell—"

"Sorry, we're running late," Ivy said, suddenly conscious of the way he was looking at her, especially after what Shelly had said before they left. Feeling a hot rush of blood to her face, she turned to hide her embarrassment over her attraction to him. Gee, she was acting like a teenager.

Composing herself, Ivy added, "Thanks for stopping by." She slid into the Jeep and shut the door, grateful for the barrier between them.

Giving her an odd look, Shelly got into the passenger side.

Bennett held up a hand for her to stop, but Ivy just waggled her fingers.

"Why did you cut him off?" Shelly asked. "Don't you think that was rude?"

"I can't think about Bennett right now." She turned the ignition and stepped on the gas pedal. Her mind was flooded with thoughts of her mother, the FBI, and finishing the house to make it suitable for renters.

Ivy set her jaw. Bennett Dylan had no business taking up headspace. Not now, not ever.

Shelly turned to her in triumph. "But you couldn't miss the looks he was giving you."

"Must have been the new outfit."

"Not those kind of looks," Shelly said. "But that didn't hurt."

After four boutiques, three hours, and countless steps, Ivy finally found a long, casual dress that was suitable for the party and in keeping with the beach theme. As she emerged from the dressing room, she held it up in triumph.

"Finally ready for tonight," she said to Shelly, who clapped her hands.

Ivy caught the sales clerk's attention, and the woman wrapped up her purchase. Ivy ran her hand across her ensemble, feeling good about it—and better about herself than she had in ages. Violet and white lilies splashed across a thin black jersey dress that skimmed her hips. A slit to the knee showed off her still-slender ankles—her best feature right now, she'd joked with Shelly. A lightweight black knit sweater covered the dress's thin straps and hid her muffin-top middle and back cleavage.

"As soon as we open our doors, and rooms are rented, I plan to join a gym, or at least start taking power walks on the beach." She had to start exercising again—if not to lose weight, at least to tone up what she had.

"Why wait until then?" Shelly asked. "Before I write my blog in the morning, I do half an hour of yoga. Join me, or we can walk on the beach. You'll be much more energized."

"Start waking me when you get up." Recalling the exercise-related adrenaline and endorphin rush she'd always enjoyed, Ivy told herself she was going to start with a morning beach walk. Maybe she'd find inspiration for her painting, too.

Ivy decided it was time she started embracing life again, and a brisk walk in the morning would lift her spirits. She used to do that when she was younger. Where had the years gone?

By the time they returned to the house, it was time to dress for the party, since Carlotta had insisted that they arrive early. Outside, the dark sedan was still at its post. As they walked inside, Ivy's nerves were on edge, and Shelly was quieter than usual.

"I'm sure all Mom's friends will come," Shelly said.

"Are you thinking what I'm thinking?" Ivy asked.

"About Mom's health?"

Ivy nodded.

"You usually worry enough for both of us, but I'm concerned, too." Shelly shut the door behind them and touched Ivy's arm. "We'll face this together, as a family."

Ivy hugged her sister, thankful that they'd made up. "I can't wait to see Honey and Gabe, too."

"Gabe's been good for Honey." Shelly blinked hard, and her gaze drifted away. "Maybe someday I'll find a good guy like him. How do you know at the beginning?"

"A feeling, I guess." Ivy knew she was thinking not about Ezzra, but about Mitch. "And maybe a background check."

Shelly rolled her eyes. "For sure. You'd think I'd know better, having lived in New York all this time."

"There'll be others."

"That's the problem," Shelly said as she started up the stairs. "There always are. But I only want The One, wherever the heck he is."

Ivy nodded. How well she understood. Brightening, she said, "Maybe he'll be at the party tonight."

Chapter 22

WHEN IVY AND Shelly arrived at their parents' home, Honey greeted them at the door. "Here we all are, together at last. It's so good to see you." Tears of happiness glistened in her eyes. "I hear the two of you are sharing the house and opening it up to guests."

"We are," Ivy said, feeling good that she had positive news to share now. Yet her concern over their mother had escalated even more on the drive over. "Before we see Mom, do you have any idea what this closed meeting is about?"

"No more than you," Honey said. Worry lines scored her usually smooth skin. "She's been quite secretive."

The three sisters sauntered inside, where their family

was gathered in the main living area. The sliding pocket doors were pushed back, opening an entire wall to the outside. Many family members had spilled outside onto the patio where the late afternoon temperature was mild.

Ivy spotted Gabe talking to their brothers Flint and Forrest, while the young cousins milled about. She could see Angela and Tabitha, the twins' wives, chatting in the kitchen. Poppy and her sisters Coral and Summer were catching up with Honey's daughter Elena, who had driven from Los Angeles. She had short, sassy hair and a blue diamond twinkling in a nose piercing. At Elena's side was an attractive man, and Ivy wondered who he was. Through the open doors, Ivy saw their brother Flint's children, Skyler, Blue, Jewel, and Sierra, who were listening to music outside and talking.

Ivy glanced around, searching for their parents. She caught sight of her mother and father on the upper deck outside of their bedroom. They were holding hands and speaking softly to each other. Ivy watched as her father cradled her mother's face, and she rested her head on his shoulder.

Ivy had seen this natural movement between her parents so many times in her life, but today, it filled her with emotion. She was pleased they were still together, though their easy companionship only reinforced her loneliness.

Beside her, Shelly watched them and sighed. "Can't say we didn't have good role models."

"All these years and they're still together," Ivy said. "Now I realize how lucky they are."

"It's not just luck," Honey said, following her gaze and slinging her arms over her sisters' shoulders.

With their arms around each other, the three sisters watched their parents from below.

Ivy let out a sigh. Their parents kissed, then Sterling draped his arm across Carlotta's shoulder. It might have been a romantic scene from a movie, or one of the great love affairs of all time. The song about Bogart and Bacall sprang to mind. "They've really had it all, haven't they?"

"A great life," Honey whispered.

Ivy had always thought that she and Jeremy would grow old together like her parents. She'd once looked forward to a time when she and her husband would have the freedom to travel together or putter about a garden. Not that they'd actually had a garden, but they might've bought a little country house. When Misty and Sunny were young, they'd talked about what they'd do after the girls had finished college.

Yet after the girls graduated, Jeremy no longer talked about the future. She was the only one talking—he would listen for a while and then change the subject. While she was dreaming of their future together, Jeremy had acted on his own dream.

Ivy pursed her lips. Now, she and Shelly were the beneficiaries of his dream, and she was determined to make it a success.

And she would. She was ready for a new phase in her life. In every way. She wondered what her daughters would think about the changes she was making. She'd left messages. *Are you okay? Call me.* Usually, she received only texts back. *Fine, Mom. Busy. Call you later.*

Sunny seldom did, though Misty made the effort.

Is that how their parents had felt about her and her sisters and brothers? A lump rose in her throat, and she swallowed against it. She desperately wanted her mother to be okay. Was that too much to ask? She resolved to spend as much time as she could with her mother. She and Shelly could work out a schedule so their parents wouldn't be alone.

Ivy blinked back the tears that threatened to spill from her eyes and turned to Honey. "What's it like for you and Gabe now that Elena is on her own?"

"We miss her, but we're happy that she's living her dream in Los Angeles." Honey's eyes crinkled at the corners as she smiled. Now almost fifty, she still had a youthful glow about her. "And we're fortunate to live near the beach where we have many friends, so we're not lonely. We didn't know just how many friends we had until Gabe's heart attack. Now, he has a second chance at life, and he's living it doing exactly what he loves, though with more exercise and a better diet."

Shelly nodded with enthusiasm. "Vegan burgers on the

barbie, I heard."

"That's right," Honey said. "As for me, my boutique keeps me busy, and we visit every few months to see Elena, check on Carlotta and Sterling, and get in some skiing at Lake Tahoe. Now that you're living on the west coast, we'll be seeing more of you both."

"And who's the guy with Elena?" Shelly asked.

"Her fiancé, Jake," Honey said. "We like him a lot."

Shelly looked intrigued. "How did they meet?"

"When the jewelry Elena had designed and loaned to a celebrity friend—Penelope Plessen, the model—for the Academy Awards was stolen, an insurance claim was filed. Jake was the insurance investigator. Their relationship was adversarial at first because he thought Elena was involved in the theft. Imagine! But love finds a way."

"I hope that's true." Shelly sounded wistful.

"So how is work on the house going?" Honey asked.

Ivy and Shelly exchanged a guarded look. Ivy was dying to tell their family about the paintings, but they had both been sworn to secrecy.

"We'll be taking in guests soon at the Seabreeze Inn," Ivy said.

"I love the name." Honey beamed. "I'm so proud of you. You're really turning around that dreadful situation. I've been awfully worried about you."

"I'm getting my life back on track," Ivy said. "Or rather, a different life this time." She tucked her arm through

Shelly's. "It feels good to have a new home."

"We're going to rock that place." Shelly grinned. "Wait until you see what we've done."

Honey smiled. "If you don't mind Elena's old room, you're both welcome in Sydney whenever you'd like."

"Maybe during the offseason," Ivy said. "We're hoping for a busy summer." She prayed that their mother was well. If not, she couldn't venture far away. "We'd love you and Gabe to visit anytime as well."

A few minutes later, their parents appeared at the top of the stairway. A murmur rippled across the room, and the three sisters traded worried glances.

Carlotta made her way down first, followed by Sterling. Their mother wore an off-the-shoulder ivory silk blouse paired with a flowing ivory skirt. Her dark hair was piled high on her head, and large hammered silver earrings and a matching necklace framed her still youthful face.

She looked and held herself like a beautiful Mayan queen.

If Mom is ill, she hides it well. Ivy braced herself for the worst.

"We're glad you all came," Sterling began. "Honey and Gabe, Flint and Tabitha, Forrest and Angela, Ivy and Shelly. Do you know this is the first time since you were children that you've all been together at the same time? And with almost all our grandchildren."

Only my children are missing, Ivy thought. Neither of

her daughters had felt it important enough to attend, even though Ivy had offered to pay for their flights.

Carlotta beamed up at her husband. Her face glimmered in the light. "This is the best birthday present ever," she said. "And I'm glad I didn't have to wait until I was on my deathbed to see you all gathered around."

The room fell quiet, and Ivy could feel each family member preparing themselves for the announcement.

"I hope that won't be for some time," Carlotta said. "Even though several of you seem to think that we have one foot in the grave."

Uneasy laughter followed.

Forrest spoke up. "It's not that, Mom. Angela and I thought you and Dad should make plans to move in with us."

"And we thought you'd be better off with us," Flint said. "We don't have stairs to navigate like Forrest and Angela do. At your age, that's important."

Ivy couldn't help but wonder if her daughters would be willing to bear such responsibility someday. Not that she ever wanted to be in that position.

Carlotta held up her hand. "Sorry to disappoint you both, but we're not going to take either of you up on your offer."

"Mom, Dad, be reasonable," Forrest said.

"We are," Carlotta said. "That's why we've decided to buy a larger boat and sail around the world instead."

"Before we buy a motorhome to see the rest of it," Sterling added, his eyes twinkling with delight.

Gasps rippled across the room.

Ivy blurted out, "Then you're not dying?" She pressed a hand against her pounding chest.

"Dying?" Carlotta clutched her silver necklace. "*Dios mio, no, mija.* Not for years and years, we hope."

"Oh, thank goodness," Ivy said as relief washed over her. Her limbs were weak from the stress she'd carried all the way from Boston. *Not dying.*

"Sailing around the world is too dangerous," Forrest said. "Anything could happen."

"And anything could happen right here," Sterling said. "All our lives, we've loved nothing more than traveling and finding artisans to help around the world. We're going to follow our passion as long as we can. We're leaving in a couple of months, and no, you can't talk us out of it."

"We wanted to have a big party to celebrate before we left," Carlotta said. "We're renting out the house to help fund our adventure. Anything you want, you're welcome to have, because everything must go."

"What about when you return?" Flint asked.

"We won't need much in the motorhome after we return," Sterling added. "We've approached each of you individually, and I must say, you're a tight-lipped group. We're pleased our children aren't as greedy as when they were youngsters," he added, chuckling.

The younger cousins exploded with laughter at that.

"Except for a few linens that Ivy took, the rest is up for grabs," Carlotta said. "So we thought we'd have a drawing."

"For whatever pieces you would like," Sterling said. "Please write down your requests and drop them in the big Talavera vase tonight. If we have multiple requests, we'll have a draw-off. The rest of it will go to auction before we leave. With all the youngsters out there, we hope to help furnish a few new apartments."

"And the house?" Flint asked.

"We received a contract for a long-term lease, so that's settled for now," Sterling said.

Carlotta and Sterling clasped hands. "We love you all," Sterling said. "But we're going to continue living life on our own terms for as long as we can."

As she gazed at her husband with love, Carlotta added, "When the time comes that we can't, we've chosen a senior community not far from here that has a fabulous view of the ocean. All arrangements have been made, and we don't want to hear another word about it—except congratulations that we're not dying yet." She cast a glance at Ivy and smiled.

"Oh, Mom, I'm so happy for you," Ivy said, her eyes brimming with tears of joy. "You have no idea how worried we were."

"You all worry too much," her mother said as she hugged her. "It's a waste of time, you'll see."

At once, Ivy felt six years old again and as vulnerable as a child. She clasped her arms around her mother. "It isn't often that our parents run away from home. I'll miss you, but I hope you'll both have a wonderful time doing what you love." Her parents deserved to follow their passions and have fun while they still could. And who better to emulate?

At that, the doorbell rang.

"Our guests are arriving now." Carlotta flung her arms wide and hugged her three daughters. "Now where's the champagne?" She motioned to a server they'd hired for the event. "I want to celebrate my birthday in style."

The server brought a platter of champagne flutes to them. Just as Ivy was holding hers up to toast her parents, Bennett walked into the room looking more handsome than she'd ever imagined he could. And by his side was a younger blond woman.

All at once, the old memory from that summer so long ago that she'd pushed aside came roaring back.

Ivy blinked and froze in place as her heart shattered like crystal. She'd never thought to ask if Bennett might be seeing anyone.

She turned to ignore them. Then, on second thought, she whirled around.

Chapter 23

AS BENNETT WATCHED Ivy cut through the crowd directly toward him, he felt the familiar tightening in his gut that he experienced every time he saw her now. How his least favorite client had become a woman he couldn't get out of his mind was beyond him.

Ivy wore a long, black dress with a splash of flowers across it. The slit up to her knees caught his attention, and he couldn't help himself. *Nice legs.*

"What are you doing here?" she demanded. Her green eyes flashed at him.

"Flint invited me. I tried to tell you this afternoon."

"You're a mayor. You have some nerve showing up.

here with—" She leaned toward him and said in a hoarse whisper, "A woman *half* your age."

Bennett nearly burst out laughing, but Ivy was serious. He bit back his laughter. That response wouldn't help his quest. "This is Sarah, one of Poppy's friends. We met just outside the door."

"Oh." Ivy flushed furiously and frowned before her manners took over. She stuck out her hand toward the young woman. "I'm Ivy. Poppy's aunt."

Sarah swung her hair over one bare shoulder and flashed a genuine smile. To her credit, she ignored Ivy's comment. "Poppy said she's helping you with your new inn. Sounds so fascinating. I'd love to do something like that someday. Could I call you and talk about it sometime?"

"I'd like that," Ivy said, awkwardly recovering her friendly demeanor.

Bennett folded his arms. He almost enjoyed seeing Ivy struggle through this conversation, though his compassion won out. "Sarah, I think I see Poppy outside."

After Sarah left, Ivy narrowed her eyes at him. "You did that on purpose."

"What? Met her at the door?" Bennett chuckled. "I'm flattered that you think a woman—what was it?—*half my age* would be interested in me. I didn't know you cared so much about my reputation. That's touching."

"I don't. I mean, why would I?" Ivy's face was turning pink.

He brushed her arm. "I didn't mean to mislead you."

She huffed and moved out of his reach. "Why didn't Flint tell me you were coming?"

"You'd have to ask him. Do you know all your brother's friends?"

"Of course not," she said. "I've been gone for a long time."

"And I'm glad you decided to return. I mean that," Bennett said, lowering his voice. He couldn't read her mind, and he had no idea how she would take what he wanted to say, but this was his chance to plunge into the deep. "I know it was pretty lousy of your husband to die and dump the house in your lap, and I wish I could have sold it for you. But I'm happy you've stayed on. You've got guts, Ivy Bay. Maybe you'd like to join me for dinner one—"

"Bennett, my man," Flint cut in. "Glad you made it. You remember Ivy."

"Indeed, I do."

As if she were weighing what he'd said before her brother interrupted them, Ivy met Bennett's gaze. "I'd like that," she said softly. "You know how to reach me."

Flint glanced from one to another, nonplussed. "Wait a minute. Ivy, didn't you throw Bennett out when he met me at your house on clean-up day?"

"A lot has happened since then," she said, turning a deeper shade of pink.

That endeared her to him. Bennett touched her fingers, and he was surprised at how soft they were. "We've put that behind us."

"Guess you guys didn't need to be rescued after all," Flint said. "I'll stick to dolphins. They're a lot less complicated." He walked away, shaking his head.

Gently, Bennett took her hand in his. "I meant what I said. Next week?"

Her face bloomed with expectation. "Before or after the FBI invades my home and empties my basement?"

He chuckled. "Guess we have a few things to work around."

"And I have to go back to Boston and give up my rental," she said with an apology in her voice. "Shelly, too."

"We'll figure it out." He could wait. He'd already waited ten years to have a woman in his life.

As Carlotta sailed through the room, resplendent and in her element with family and friends, she paused beside them. "Bennett, so nice of you to come. Flint tells me you're a beloved mayor in Summer Beach." She flicked her eyes toward her daughter and back at him. "May we tempt you with champagne and *hors d'oeurves?*"

"Yes, ma'am, thank you," Bennett said, though he didn't need much champagne. Just standing next to Ivy was intoxicating enough. He looked from mother to daughter. Now that he saw Carlotta and Ivy together, the family resemblance was clear.

"Ivy, please take good care of our guest." Her mother pressed her cheek to Ivy's in a kiss and continued toward other guests—but not before she gave Bennett a conspiratorial smile.

Ivy turned her face up to his. "You should know that my parents are foodies with eclectic taste. Unless you're a white-bread-and-potatoes kind of guy, you don't want to miss their *hors d'oeurves.*" She took his hand and led him outside.

Bennett hadn't realized how hungry he was. The Bays had engaged a caterer, and the theme was fresh California cuisine. He and Ivy scooped up a little bit of everything. Watermelon salad with basil and feta cheese, grilled vegetable bruschetta with pesto sauce, shrimp ceviche with mint. Brioche crab rolls, lobster and corn fritters, smoked cheeses with salsa, and avocado and crab rolls with caviar. Servers offered champagne, California wines, margaritas, and mint-infused sparkling water.

"This is more than *hors d'oeurves,*" Bennett remarked as they settled at a table on the patio overlooking the ocean.

"Mom believes in a generous table. Growing up, we had a garden here and learned to cook with our weekly harvest. Do you have any idea how much better home-grown tomatoes and carrots taste?"

"I do. And did you know Summer Beach has a weekly farmer's market?"

Ivy's face lit up. "I'd love to see that."

"Happy to take you." Bennett imagined strolling around the local produce stands and beach artisans. He knew if he took her there, word about them would spread through the Summer Beach gossip network like wildfire. Well-meaning people in town had been trying to match him with women for years. In the past, he'd avoided going to the market with dates, but Ivy was different.

Ivy sipped her champagne. "I have to learn everything I can about Summer Beach so I can help guests and answer questions."

"So you're going ahead with your iBnB rentals?"

"I have to, Bennett." She reached out and touched his hand. "I'm filling out the paperwork for the zoning change and will submit it next week. An inn could offer so much more to the local residents, too. Shelly and I plan to have a range of events, from author chats and book signings to painting exhibits and gardening classes."

"That might help your cause," he said. "It's not up to me, but the community and its representatives."

"Would you mind putting in a good word?"

Bennett shifted in his chair. That wasn't a good idea, not with how he felt about Ivy. People could accuse him of favoritism. "It's better if I tell you who you need to talk to."

Her smile drooped. "I thought you would help us."

"I wish I could, but I hope you understand how I need to remain impartial. Especially if we're seen out together...on a date." He savored the taste of the word in his mouth. *A date with Ivy.* How long had it been? Two years? Maybe three? The last one had been such a disaster, he'd sworn off matchmaking offers from friends. He'd plan something special for Ivy...

"What else do people like to do in Summer Beach?" Ivy asked.

"Mitch conducts whale-watching cruises, Nan and Arthur sponsor an antique weekend, and another resident offers balloon rides."

"What about art shows?"

Bennett stroked his chin. "There's an idea."

Ivy sat back in her chair, clearly pondering his suggestion. Her face lit with enthusiasm. "I would love to coordinate one. Think of how many people that could bring into the community."

"Now you're talking." Her face was shimmering with excitement, and he could hardly contain himself.

Her eyes flickered with ideas. "We could host some events in the ballroom, and spill out onto the lawn and around the pool. The money we raise could fund art classes in the schools here."

"That's the kind of thinking that will endear you to Summer Beach." *And to me.* Bennett ached to take her in his arms.

Nearby on the lawn, musicians began to play an old Jimmy Buffet tune, *Margaritaville,* and people crowded into the dance area.

"Would you like to dance?" Bennett asked, seeing an opportunity.

Ivy hesitated. "I haven't danced in a long time."

"Neither have I. That means we're both overdue." Bennett held out his hand, and she twined her fingers with his. Her touch was like an electric shock to his system, energizing every nerve in his body.

"Fair warning. I might step on your feet," she said as they got up.

"Not if I beat you to it."

Soon, Ivy and Bennett were swept into the crowd and found themselves dancing against a picturesque sunset. Although they were both awkward at first, they eased into the rhythm and into each other's arms.

"That's better," Ivy said.

"Like riding a bike, right?" He winced inwardly at his clichéd comment and hoped she wouldn't take it in the wrong way.

Despite his *faux pas*, Bennett was in heaven just holding her in his arms. Ivy fell naturally in step with him, and thankfully, he overcame his stumbling feet reasonably quickly. He hadn't enjoyed dancing with a woman this much since Jackie, who would always hold a special place in his memory.

Could Ivy be his future? The thought surprised him but didn't make him uncomfortable. She was the most mesmerizing woman he'd met in a long, long time. Smart, compassionate, beautiful, ethical. Many people he knew wouldn't have returned the paintings. *And those lovely legs...*

He twirled her around again, just to hear the music of her laughter and see the sparkle in her eyes. "Having fun?"

"Now I am," she said, laughing.

Her smile was intoxicating. As they danced, Bennett felt himself coming back to life, surging up to the water's surface and breaking free from the depths of despair he'd nearly drowned in years ago. The prospect of sharing his heart with Ivy heightened every movement, every breath. The music seemed livelier, the sunset more stunning, the scent of jasmine even sweeter.

Although he'd been in love before, his heart had known pain for so long that he'd forgotten what it was like to fall in love again. Every poet must have been in love at some time, he decided, as snippets of verses floated through his consciousness. Corny, perhaps, but the connection with Ivy was more real than anything he'd experienced in years.

The band began playing another upbeat song, and the Bay family and friends tumbled onto the dance floor, laughing and pumping their hands in the air. This family knew how to have a good time. Soon the siblings surrounded them—his friend Flint and his brother and their wives, and a slew of younger cousins.

Ivy was bumping hips and twirling around with them, introducing them as they passed. "Here's Poppy and Coral, there's Reed and Rocky." She spun around. "Honey and Gabe from Sydney." She erupted with laughter.

Bennett turned to see Sterling and Carlotta on the dance floor, leading a conga line from the dance floor through the back yard. He and Ivy joined in, and by the time it was over, he couldn't remember when he'd had a better time.

If only he didn't have to call the FBI agents early the next morning as he'd promised.

Chapter 24

IVY STRETCHED IN bed, savoring the sunshine that streamed through her windows and puddled on the floor, warming the old oak wood floor where the sandals she'd worn to the party last night lay.

The sandals she'd worn to dance with Bennett.

She pulled the white cotton duvet up to her chin and wiggled her toes with happiness. The memory of last night came rushing back to her and filled her with joy.

She couldn't believe that Bennett had turned out to be so fascinating and fun, or that he brought out emotions she'd never thought she'd feel again.

Dancing in his arms, she had felt feminine and desired,

though entirely respected. A romantic relationship was the last thing she thought she'd find in Summer Beach, but Bennett had awakened long-dormant feelings. More than that, being together seemed so natural.

The cell phone on her bedside table buzzed.

It was her daughter Misty. "Hi, you! What's up?"

"You sure sound happy." Misty paused. "Is everything okay?"

"Why? Because you haven't heard me be happy for so long?"

"Uh, yeah."

Ivy sighed. What a poor example to set for her children. Still, it had been a year of grieving. Thought it was too soon to tell her children about how excited she was over the possibility of a new man in her life. Besides, they hadn't actually been out on a date yet.

"How're you doing, sweetie?" Ivy asked.

Misty let out a little squeal. "I landed a great part in the new theater production."

"Why, that's wonderful." To make a living acting and singing was Misty's dream. She hoped it was a paid gig so that she could leave the diner she worked at during the day. "When does it open?"

"Next weekend. I was the understudy, and the actor broke a leg snow skiing in soft spring sludge, so she packed and left."

Next weekend. That might just work. "Would you like

for me and your aunt Shelly to come on opening night?"

Misty let out a squeal. "Oh, my gosh! Could you really? You'd have to get a flight right away."

"We need to return anyway."

"You sold the house?"

"Not exactly." Ivy didn't want to go into her plans over the phone. "I thought I'd stay here longer."

"So what are you doing there?"

Ivy wished she could tell her about the artwork. As a creative person, Misty would appreciate it. "Making a few house repairs."

"Sure hope it sells fast. Hey, how's Nana?"

"She's fine. You should have seen her leading a conga line last night. She and Gramps are taking off in a couple of months to sail around the world."

"Really? That's amazing. Do you think they're up to it?"

"I do." Just yesterday she'd had her doubts, but after seeing their vibrancy at the party, she'd set her concerns aside. They were both expert sailors and knew how to prepare for a long voyage. She had to trust that they were going to have a wonderful time. And as her father had said, *If not now, when?*

"Have you heard from Sunny?" Ivy had been worried, but she'd learned not to nag.

"Sure, she posts on social media all the time. Mom, you have got to check it more often."

"I will," she promised. "It's been a little busy out here."

"Oh, hey, our table is ready. Gotta run, Mom, loves you, bye."

Before Ivy could even say *loves you* in return, Misty had hung up. Ivy supposed she should be glad she got a phone call at all. She smiled. It didn't seem that long ago that she'd left home and often forgotten to call her mother.

She flipped off the covers and padded across the hall. Shelly's door was open, and she was on her computer.

"Good morning," Shelly said. "I was just posting some photos to my blog."

"What kind of photos?"

"*Before* shots of the garden here," she said, pointing to the screen. "The *After* shots will come later, but I'm sharing my landscaping plan." She grinned and stretched her arms overhead. "What a great party. You and Bennett sure danced a lot."

Ivy flung herself onto the bed next to Shelly. "I had a great time. How about you?"

"Actually, I spent a lot of time with Mom and Dad," Shelly said. "I'm really going to miss them. It's different when your parents take off. Even though they've always traveled a lot, I've always expected them to be there. In the back of my mind, I've always thought I could go home. Now *home* will be rented out to some other family."

Misty and Sunny probably thought the same thing, if they bothered to think about her much at all. "So we make our own home. That was a big place for them to keep up anyway."

"Guess they'd rather be traveling the world than dusting furniture," Shelly said, making a face. "Go figure."

Ivy laughed. She told her about Misty's call and her new part in a play. "Want to go back to Boston next weekend? We can catch opening night and pack all our belongings."

Shelly shrugged. "Sure. But I have to tell you about Ezzra."

"Just say no." Ivy had been through several of her sister's breakups and reunions with Ezzra.

"Wait a sec. Ezzra texted last night, and then he called this morning. He said he'd really like to see me again. I guess the last woman dumped him."

"Which he probably deserved. You're not seriously thinking about seeing him again."

Shelly scooted her legs up and clasped her knees. "I do have to get my things in the city."

"Please think about what you're doing. We have a real opportunity here."

"I know. It's just that Mitch…"

"You're disappointed that he didn't tell you about his past."

"I guess we weren't to that stage yet." She punched a pillow. "But I was shocked. I thought he was a good guy. An ex-con? I sure can pick them."

"Maybe he is a good guy," Ivy said. "He owns two businesses and seems responsible. Have you heard his side of the story about why he served time in prison?"

"I'm sure he has a great excuse. They all do."

"Now you're generalizing," Ivy said. "So you're thinking of going back to the devil you know? Mitch isn't the only guy in Summer Beach who's been checking you out. You should look around. We haven't been here that long."

Clutching a pillow in her lap, Shelly picked at a thread on it. "Maybe I need a dog instead," she said in a forlorn voice.

"Don't depress a poor dog." Ivy sat up in concern. "And don't be Ezzra's second choice. You choose for a change." Ivy bounced off the bed, anxious to get Shelly out of her mood. "Come on, we have a lot to do this week, and you don't have to make a decision about seeing Ezzra right now. Besides, major decisions should never be made before coffee."

Reluctantly, Shelly shoved off the bed, pulled on her yoga gear, and followed her downstairs.

Over breakfast, Ivy talked to Shelly about her ideas to decorate the house and take the photos that Poppy needed to upload to the iBnB site. When she asked Shelly what she planned to do in the yard, Shelly's eyes regained focus, and she shared her plans for drought-resistant plants that would thrive in the mild sea breezes.

"Bougainvillea, lantana, rosemary hedges," Shelly said,

ticking off a list in her mind. "And a rose garden and raised herb beds. Some native Australian plants, and so much more, but I'll take one phase at a time. The main goal is to have the place looking presentable."

Ivy drummed her fingers on the table and eyed the locked basement doors. "Poppy offered up her brothers and their friends to help us later this week, but is there any reason why we can't start bringing up a few items from downstairs?"

"I wouldn't think so. As long as we don't disturb the paintings."

"Then let's set this place up," Ivy said, giving her sister a high-five. She could see the house exactly the way she wanted it in her mind's eye. Light and airy, with orange-oil polished antiques, vivid artwork, and an abundance of flowers. *A casual luxury experience steps from the beach,* which she thought would make a good tagline on iBnB and social media posts. "I've got Mom's linens and towels, and I can ship my artwork back from Boston."

"Come on then, let's do this." Shelly got up and cranked up the volume on her Taylor Swift playlist.

Ivy and Shelly danced their way to the lower level. Pulling off sheets from furniture and opening boxes, they sorted through furnishings and gathered a group of items to take upstairs. Shelly hoisted a headboard, while Ivy picked up a footboard.

"Let's go," Ivy said. "First bedroom on the right."

"Woo-hoo! Won't need any exercise today," Shelly called out.

Ivy grinned. But she would need a hot bath with Epsom salts later. Between a week of cleaning and painting, a night of dancing, and another day of hoisting furniture and boxes, this would be the most exercise she'd had in ages. Although she was sore, she felt physically energized and mentally buoyed.

Inside the large bedroom, the two sisters shifted the bed around until they finally decided to position it at an angle to a corner.

Ivy held up her hands as if framing an *Architectural Digest* shoot or composing a canvas. "Imagine open shutters and sheer panels at the windows, a table and two chairs in front of it with a bouquet of roses. A vanity here, an armoire there. Two small bedside tables, one on either side of the bed. A bench at the end of the bed for suitcases or dressing."

Ivy moved into the *en suite* bathroom, envisioning everything. "And in here, luxury toiletries. Molten Brown, or maybe an artisan line from a local supplier. Fresh scents like mint or lemon verbena. Or unscented if they prefer."

Swept up in the excitement, Shelly jumped into the story. "A magnifying mirror, a bowl of fruit, bottled water by the bed. Slippers and robes. Bubble bath and wine flutes."

"And the all-important corkscrew," Ivy added.

"We're going to sell out these rooms." Shelly whooped

and raced back downstairs for another armload.

They brought up what they could carry, leaving the larger pieces for their nephews and their friends to bring upstairs later. "Not that we couldn't try," Ivy said, "but I'm not throwing out my back before getting on a flight to Boston."

The two women were laughing and singing like *American Idol* wannabes, so the pounding on the front door startled them.

Shelly shrieked and raced downstairs.

"Have to get those door chimes fixed," Ivy said, catching her breath. She swung open the massive door. Chief Clarkson and the two FBI agents stood in the doorway.

The chief furrowed his brow with concern. "Everything okay in here?"

"Sure, why wouldn't it be?" Ivy replied with nonchalance. "We aren't disturbing the peace, are we?"

"You're lucky your neighbor probably hasn't put on her hearing aid yet. Back door locked?" he asked.

"It is." Ivy and Shelly traded looks.

Cecile peered inside. "Anyone else here?"

"No one but us at this party." As she spoke, Shelly brushed her hair back and twisted it at the nape of her neck.

The chief pressed on. "So what are you doing in here?"

"Decorating," Ivy said, waving her hand as she stepped aside. An occasional table now stood in the foyer, and on it rested a silver platter and a cut-crystal vase and bowl. She imagined a marine blue cloth thrown over it, with the vase overflowing with pink flowers and the bowl brimming with local fruit for guests. Tangerines, apricots, plums, grapes. Strawberries in season…acquired from a farm not far from here. That's when Ivy realized she still had on her pajama bottoms and a skimpy tank top.

"We'll let you get back to it," Chief Clarkson said. "And we'll see you in the morning to begin the removal."

Ivy closed the door and fell back against it while Shelly exploded with laughter.

After they made countless trips up and down stairs, the two sisters sat on the lower level staircase and gazed across the room of antiques. Ivy rested her arms on her knees.

"Guess your masterpieces will be gone tomorrow," Shelly said.

With a measure of sadness, Ivy nodded. "You know what I would like to do before they go away?"

"What?"

"Promise you won't think I'm crazy?"

"You know that train already left the station," Shelly said, nudging her sister.

"Ditto for you." Ivy stood and brushed her hands. "I'd like to take a few paintings upstairs tonight. When else will I ever have the opportunity to sleep with and wake to a Chagall, Kandinsky, Klee, or Beckmann?" She strolled across the room to one of the standing crates where the agents had returned the paintings. Easing one painting from its place, she sighed in awe. *The towering blue horses.* "Franz Marc was killed in the First World War," she said with reverence. "More than a hundred years ago now."

Shelly joined her and placed her hand on her shoulder. "I'll help you."

"We have to be careful," Ivy said, her hand quivering as she touched a frame. "What if we dropped one?"

"We won't, I promise."

"Maybe I shouldn't."

"I think Amelia Erickson would've approved. You once told me that art is to be enjoyed."

"You know who else would enjoy seeing this?"

Shelly nodded. "Mom and Dad."

"Do you think we could get them past our guards?"

"Why not just ask them?"

Ivy drew her lower lip over her teeth in thought. Did she dare? Her mother's advice rang in her ears. *If you don't ask, you don't get.* She fished her phone from her pocket and was surprised when a call from Bennett came in just as she was about to dial.

Chapter 25

BENNETT'S VOICE FLOATED through her phone, sounding even deeper and sexier than ever. "It was great seeing you last night, Ivy. I've been trying to reach you all day."

"Shelly and I have had the music up fairly loud. We've been bringing pieces up from the lower level and arranging furniture and accessories around the house."

"Are the protective services still there?"

"Sticking like Velcro and just as prickly." She hesitated. "Bennett, I have a favor to ask, and I'd like your advice on it." She quickly explained how much it would mean to her parents to see the artwork before the FBI agents removed it.

"They've spent their lives traveling to find artisans around the world to help them sell their work here. They inspired my love of art, and I would love to honor them with this."

"You could ask Chief Clarkson, but the FBI will make the decision."

"Of course," she said. She doubted that she could persuade them, but she would try. They spoke a little more before Ivy hung up to call her parents. She talked to them for a while, and Ivy invited them to meet her and Shelly in Summer Beach for supper. If the FBI didn't approve them, the four of them could go to a café in town overlooking the water.

Ivy and Shelly brought a few paintings upstairs and placed them around Ivy's room.

A delicate spring landscape of Impressionism here, a colorful rendering of a woman in the Fauvism style with unconstrained brushwork there. Ivy's heart soared as she grouped the paintings.

"Do you want any in your room?" Ivy asked.

"I don't think I could sleep," Shelly said. "What if an earthquake hit and a million dollar painting crashed to the floor?"

"I wish you hadn't put it that way," Ivy said, but she didn't regret her decision. With the paintings she'd brought up, the bedroom glowed with color and life. To her, the paintings fairly vibrated with energy. The vivid blue horses seemed to burst with the desire to be freed from captivity and shared with the world again.

Ivy gazed at each painting in turn. They spoke to her heart and filled her with such joy and inspiration. She would paint again soon, she decided. While she would never be on par with these masters, she could share her artistry, passion, and point of view with others who appreciated the beauty she still saw in the world—the beauty she'd found again at Summer Beach.

"These works have been hidden for decades," Ivy said. "It's almost as if we were guided here to find them, and it's time they were enjoyed again."

"The artists must be smiling down on us."

"What a nice thought," Ivy murmured.

Ivy recalled photographs of this room in the book that Nan had given her. Amelia Erickson also had beautiful art on the walls. Again she wondered how Amelia had come by these, and why she kept them under wraps. Ivy breathed in as she stared at each painting, hardly believing she was in the presence of such greatness.

By tomorrow morning, they would be gone. Seeing the paintings here made Ivy realize how much the room cried out for artwork.

After Ivy and Shelly changed, Shelly insisted on taking photographs of Ivy with the paintings. "When will you ever have this chance again? Remember the *Mona Lisa?*"

Ivy groaned as she recalled trying to view the painting in Paris. "It was worse than a rock concert. I thought we were going to be crushed by the surging crowd. You could've written a book: *Death at the Louvre.*"

Shelly went downstairs to photograph the rest of the paintings. While her sister did that, Ivy went back to her bedroom to change into the sandals her mother had given her. Since her mother would be here soon, she wanted to wear them to show her appreciation.

Ivy slipped behind the antique Chinese screen and into the dressing room. She scooped the jeweled sandals from a shelf and sat on a round, upholstered ottoman to slip them on. As she did, the mirrored closets, shelves, and cubbyholes drew her attention. She rose to explore.

Already she had found two of Amelia's hiding places: the concealed ledge under the library desk and the bricked-up lower level. Amelia was a woman who had harbored secrets. Here, in her most intimate space in the house, would she have had another hiding place?

Ivy tapped on the cedar planks in the closets, hoping to hear a hollow spot. With patience, she combed the closets, tapping the interior walls. In the far corner of the farthest closet, a hollow sound rewarded her.

She ran her fingers along the edge of the tongue-and-groove planks. Smooth notches carved into one piece gave her just enough room to gain leverage with her fingertips. She tugged, but nothing happened.

Stuck.

She got up and retrieved a metal nail file from her cosmetic kit. After positioning it just so, she tapped on the end. The plank popped open, revealing a cubbyhole. In it was another small leather volume with the same feathery writing she'd found earlier. She pulled it out, plucked her glasses from the side table, and sank into a chair to read an undated entry.

My fog lifted some today, and, as I write this, I have the distinct feeling that I have written my thoughts many, many times in a journal such as this, yet I cannot find any such writings in my home. My young maid is of no help, not like Mathilda, who was with me for so many years. Perhaps I hid them or burned them for safety.

Like my mother before me, I have threadbare patches in the fabric of my brain as if the pattern of my memories has been rubbed off. Today my trustee asked me to deposit all my important papers in his care, but I do not know if I have any. He is exasperated with me, but I am more so. For it is I who suffer the daily frustrations. My life is like a novel with missing pages.

Perhaps the trauma of too many wars has taken its toll on me, and my brain erases that which it cannot bear to recall. Yet this is different than before. Although Las Brisas del Mar has been my beloved retreat for many years, I fear I must leave until I am once again well. I only wish that I could recall where the cherished paintings have gone. Did I give them away? Hide them? I am told I do that, but I simply cannot know. Now that the war is over, they must be returned. Someone is waiting for them, but who? I pray I recall soon.

Ivy turned the page, but there were no other entries. She took a photo of the written passage and closed the journal. Perhaps this would help Cecile and Ari untangle the web of mystery.

While Ivy waited for her parents, she hoped to have a few words with the chief and the FBI agents and give them the journal. She opened the door to step outside, but she was immediately inundated with reporters shoving microphones in her face and snapping photos. Ivy flung up her hands.

"Ms. Bay," one reporter called out. "Any comment about the artwork you found?"

"How'd you know those paintings were the real deal?" another asked. "Could they be forgeries?"

"No comment," Ivy muttered, caught off guard. "Please, I can't comment." Horrified that their secret was out, she darted back inside and slammed the door shut.

"Shelly, come quickly!"

Her sister clattered up the staircase from the lower level just as Ivy's phone buzzed. *Bennett Dylan.*

"Bennett, I'm so glad you called. I was just outside…"

"I know. The Chief called me. We've got a media situation on our hands, Ivy. More security is on the way. So am I. Stay put and don't answer the door or your phone for anyone you don't know." He clicked off.

A couple of people peered through a front window and knocked on the pane. Ivy quickly drew the drapery.

"What's going on?" Shelly stared at her wide-eyed.

"When I opened the door, a bunch of reporters and photographers charged me. They're asking about the paintings."

Outside, Ivy could hear the ruckus. Then, "I'm the mayor, let me through," a voice bellowed. "It's me, Bennett," he called to her.

Ivy hurried to open the door.

Before she realized what was happening, Bennett squeezed inside and wrapped his arms around her. "Are you okay?" he asked.

Although Ivy felt safe in his arms, she took a half step back. How easy it would be to fall under his protection. She had to stand on her own feet—now more than ever.

"I was just shocked. How'd they find out?"

"I don't know," Bennett said, shaking his head. "Did either of you say anything?"

"Not a word," Shelly said with vehemence.

"Could anyone have overheard you talking? Maybe at the party last night?"

Ivy shot back, "We didn't even tell our parents, even though we were dying to." She clamped a hand over her mouth. "And they'll be here any minute. I was going to ask

Chief Clarkson like you suggested, but that's when I was ambushed. I asked them to come over for dinner, hoping that they can see the paintings. If not, we can go out for dinner."

"No harm, no foul, right?" Shelly put a hand on her hip. "Now what?"

Before he could answer, another bang on the door erupted. The chief, along with agents Cecile and Ari, spilled inside. Behind them stood Carlotta and Sterling, thoroughly confused at the chaos.

"Do you know these people?" Chief Clarkson demanded.

"Hi, Mom and Dad," Ivy said.

"Come in," Ari said, closing the door after them. "How the hell did this happen? Which one of you called the media?"

"We have no idea," Ivy said, slicing her hands out. "Don't put this on us."

Sterling's deep voice boomed out. "Would someone tell us what's going on? As their father, I'm deeply alarmed."

"Dad, it's okay." Ivy quickly explained. "We found some paintings—stolen masterpieces—on the lower level, which had been bricked up for decades."

"Why didn't you tell us?" Carlotta asked.

"It all happened so quickly this week," Ivy said. "We found it late one night, and the next day I spoke to Bennett and Chief Clarkson. We were sworn to secrecy, and the FBI came right away. But tonight, we wanted you to come and see the artwork before it leaves tomorrow."

Ivy turned to the FBI agents. "I didn't say anything to our parents before, but they're here now. They're in the arts, and it would mean so much to them. And to me."

"I can vouch for them," Bennett said.

"And I found this," Ivy said, stretching out her hand with the palm-sized journal. "I believe this is Amelia's journal, although there is only one entry. It might be helpful."

Cecile took the journal and opened it. A moment later, she looked up. "They can stay," she said, although she and Ari still wore serious expressions.

The entire group trooped downstairs. When Ivy snapped on the lights, her parents gasped.

"Are these real?" Carlotta asked.

"That's what we wondered, too," Ivy said. "In school, I studied the artwork that had been confiscated just before and during the Second World War, so I knew that many pieces had been stolen and were never found." She didn't need to tell them the entire story; they were familiar with it, too.

"How did they end up here?" Sterling asked as he watched Cecile unwrapping a painting for them to see.

"That's what I'd like to find out," Ivy said.

"We must be very gentle with these old works," Cecile said. "But since you are an art lover, I think we can make an exception, no?"

"Your call," Ari said.

Cecile glared at her colleague. "We owe this incredible find to Ivy and Shelly, who came forward with this discovery."

Sterling shook Ari's hand. "We're privileged to view these paintings, thank you. And we're awfully proud of our daughters right now. This will go no further, I assure you."

When Cecile unveiled the first piece, Carlotta and Sterling gasped. "This is almost unfathomable," Carlotta said.

"And these are real?" Sterling asked.

"We're fairly certain," Cecile said. "We'll conduct tests to make sure."

Ivy helped Cecile and Ari, and together they shared each framed print, as well as the canvases in the flat files. Her parents stared, awestruck, at the array before them.

Carlotta placed a hand over her heart. "Never would I have imagined these works here, just a few miles away from us. All these years. What had Mrs. Erickson been thinking to hide all these for so long? She was a well-known collector, a steward of modern art, and a benefactor of artists." She swept her hand around the grouping. "Why would she have concealed these?"

"None of us can say, ma'am," Cecile said. "But we hope to discover her reasons."

"That journal entry indicates that she was holding the artwork for someone," Ivy said. "She meant to return these pieces." Ivy felt a strange kinship to Amelia and wanted her to be absolved of any wrongdoing. But could she? And would Amelia prove innocent or guilty?

Ivy and Shelly watched their parents, who were overcome with emotion, just as they were, at the astonishing discovery.

Suddenly, Cecile spun around with alarm. "Wait, some paintings are missing," she cried. "A Klee, a Kandinsky. A Chagall…"

Acutely embarrassed, Ivy cleared her throat. "They're all still here. I have a few upstairs in my bedroom. I just wanted to enjoy them tonight before they left."

"That's an artist for you," Carlotta said, a smile tugging at her lips.

On Cecile's insistence, they all went upstairs and crowded into Ivy's bedroom. Hastily, Ivy shoved the dirty clothes she'd left on the floor into the linen basket.

"Ivy, you were right. It's much better to view these paintings here," Carlotta said. "In a room, surrounded by the living, as the artists intended."

Cecile nodded. "The work is even more stunning here."

"But it will be even better with proper light and placement," Ivy said, catching the awe in Cecile's voice. Ivy could tell the FBI agent wasn't just a government employee; Cecile was an art lover, too, and devoted to her job. "I hope it won't be long that others can enjoy these, too."

Cecile stopped, speechless before a group of paintings

Ivy had placed in a prime location.

"These are my favorite artists," Ivy said, pressing both hands to her chest. In college, she had conducted research and written papers on these women artists, among others. "They're not as well known, but only because they were women. Just look at the artistry though."

Touching the edges of the canvases and frames, Ivy spoke of each one in turn. The first was a sun-drenched landscape of vivid blues and greens. "Maria Caspar-Filser was a German painter who was inspired by Cézanne, Impressionism, and Expressionism. She infused her work with such wondrous light and color."

Ivy moved beside a sketch and paused in reverence. "Here's a sketch from Emy Roeder, a German sculptor, of a woman emerging from a bath. Much of her work was destroyed, and she suffered greatly for her art."

A dark, unflinching face stared out at them. "This is a captivating portrait from Elfriede Lohse-Wächtler, who struggled with mental health issues. Her work was bold and unflinching. This might be a self-portrait."

Moving on to the last one, a graceful portrait of a woman, Ivy added, "And this is from Russian-born Magda Nachman Acharya, who migrated first to Berlin and then lived out her life in India, where she became a well-respected artist. Her portraits of Indian dancers are exquisite."

Against the incessant roar of the ocean, the small group

gazed at the artworks in quiet admiration.

Shelly said, "Ivy's right. I think these pieces, and the women's stories, are among the most important to share because they've been buried so long. A new generation needs their inspiration."

As Ivy contemplated the artwork, she thought about Amelia and wondered what she would think about this small gathering in her bedroom. She liked to think that Amelia would be relieved and satisfied that these pieces—under her stewardship for so many decades—would now be returned to their owners and shared with the world again. As these thoughts went through her mind, she had an inexplicable feeling that Amelia's spirit was there with them and approving of their actions.

After they had all gazed their fill, Ivy said, "Glass of wine, anyone? I think we should open a bottle."

They gathered in the kitchen, and Ivy opened a cabernet sauvignon from a Sonoma winery for her family. Cecile, Ari, and the chief politely declined.

"Maybe Gert and Gertie can offer us something to go with that," Shelly said as she opened one of the turquoise refrigerators.

Alarm registered on Ari's face. "Who are Gert and Gertie?" he demanded.

If Ari hadn't gone on high alert, Ivy would have laughed. "That's what we call our vintage refrigerators," she said, trying to keep the humor out of her voice. "They're real workhorses. Still running icy cold, too."

"People name cars, so why not appliances?" Shelly brought out an assortment of cheeses and fruit and arranged it on a platter for their guests. She made coffee for those who were still on duty.

"So what do we do with the media camping on our doorstep?" Ivy asked.

"If you would like, I can talk with them—as mayor," Bennett said. "Tell them we will have a press conference in a couple of days."

Cecile nodded. "We'll be finished by then."

Bennett cast a reassuring smile toward Ivy. "That should take some of the heat off, but I can't guarantee that the most tenacious souls won't hang around."

"I'll move them off the property," Chief Clarkson added. "No closer than the curb."

"Thank you all," Ivy said. She was grateful for each person in her kitchen and for the part they had played in assisting her in this unusual saga.

Shelly beamed and gestured. "You know, the media is right outside. If only we could announce the opening of our inn—"

"—iBnB," Ivy and Bennett said, correcting her in unison. Bennett shook his head as though chagrined, though Ivy could tell he didn't really mean it. She understood that he had to follow the city protocol.

Ivy sipped her wine and tried not to think about the

media outside her door. The entire experience of finding the stolen art had been surreal, but then, everything about this house was, too. It was as if Amelia Erickson had been beckoning to her, knowing that her secret would be safe in Ivy's hands. A shiver raced through her. What other secrets did this house contain?

Chapter 26

AS SOON AS Bennett stepped outside on the large front veranda, the media flicked on their lights and cameras. Shielding his eyes against the glare, he readied himself against an onslaught, though he was well accustomed to handling a barrage of questions.

A local writer from the *Summer Beach Breeze* that Bennett knew held out a mini-recorder. "Mayor Dylan, what can you tell us about the stolen art?"

A reporter holding a microphone with Los Angeles station call letters jostled the local reporter aside. Her cameraperson began to film. "Do you know who's responsible for the theft?"

Bennett raised his hand. "Sorry, I have nothing for you tonight, folks. But I promise we'll have a press conference in a couple of days. Let me have your cards, and I'll make sure my office contacts each one of you and gives you an early crack at the story. Best I can do. How's that?"

A few people grumbled, but they quickly produced their cards. He'd keep his word and make sure they all got their stories. Summer Beach was a small town news beat, so he could do that.

Behind him, one of Chief Clarkson's officers was instructing them to move off the property and maintain a proper distance.

Summer Beach residents liked their small town atmosphere. As Bennett watched the media reporters leave, he shoved his hands into his pockets and wondered which one of their circle had divulged information on the paintings.

He didn't like the idea of any one of them having reneged on a promise.

Even though Mitch had served time for burglary, there had been extenuating circumstances. Bennett truly believed that Mitch was dedicated to refraining from any actions that might hinder his freedom.

As for Ivy, she'd come forward with the artwork. If she had wanted to profit from it, she would never have reported the discovery.

That left Shelly. She hadn't accompanied Ivy to report the find. At the party, he'd overheard her talking about her online articles. He could look her up online.

Bennett withdrew the media cards he'd collected. As journalists, none of them would name a source, but maybe one might have bragged about a hot tip.

And Summer Beach was a very small town.

One could overhear a lot at Java Beach.

Chapter 27

EARLY THE NEXT morning, Ivy woke before dawn to watch the sunrise bring life to the brilliant shades of Chagall, the fanciful work of Klee, and the magical artistry of Marc's towering blue horses, among the other paintings she had propped up around her bedroom. Ivy swallowed against a lump in her throat. Knowing the artists' stories brought up a flood of emotion.

But today, time wasn't a commodity to be wasted. She didn't have much more time with these masters.

She kicked off the sheets and padded around the room, viewing the canvases from different angles as the light shifted in the room. To her, painting was more than mere brush strokes on canvas, sketching more than lines on papers. Pausing before each work rejuvenated her creative well-spring.

Creating art fed her soul and brought her joy. To deny this part of her and her unique vision would be to disengage with her human experience.

Gazing at the paintings by the women artists, Ivy decided that at this time in her life—what she hoped was just the midpoint—it was more important than ever to redesign the second half of her life to her taste. The first half of her adult life had been devoted to Jeremy and her daughters, but the rest belonged to her.

Upon reflection, Ivy felt bound to honor the natural talent she'd been given and the time she'd devoted to improving her art. Sharing her journey and instructing others brought her into the world. As she surveyed the works against the rising sun, she felt it imperative to return to teaching and painting again here in Summer Beach. *In the sunroom, facing the ocean.*

Placing her palms together and viewing the artwork lining Amelia Erickson's bedroom, Ivy knew the mysterious collector would be pleased these works had survived and would soon find their way home to their rightful owners. She was relieved that the journal entry revealed Amelia Erickson had been protecting these works of art, rather than coveting them for herself. Ivy knew there was more to the saga, which the heirs to the artwork would want to know.

She did, too.

"I promise I'll share your story when I find it," Ivy whispered into the tendrils of morning light filtering into the bedroom. Downstairs, Ivy could hear her sister in the kitchen. She expelled a deep breath.

The time had come to say good-bye.

A few hours later, Ivy watched as Cecile and Ari oversaw the bittersweet removal of the paintings, including those that had kept her company the night before. Had it only been a few days since they'd discovered these works in the basement?

"That's the end of that," Ivy said, easing into a dusty wingback chair in the drawing room after the FBI agents and police left the house. When she patted the upholstered arm, it released a puff of dust. "Now, we have a lot of work to do here."

She and Shelly had spent the morning arranging groupings of furniture to bring a more personal scale to the grand room—and to keep her mind off the loss of the paintings.

"I think the media attention on the paintings is just the beginning," Shelly said, joining her. "This is a huge discovery. If you thought there was a lot of media here last night, just wait. My email has exploded today."

Ivy was grateful to Bennett for talking to the media last night, but that hadn't stopped her phone from buzzing. "I changed my voice mail recording this morning and turned my phone ringer off, but not before Nan called to say they have a buyer for the chandelier."

"That was fast."

Ivy smiled with relief. "We'll have the money for mattresses, pillows, and other furnishings we need, if we're frugal."

"When have I known you to be any other way?"

Ivy let out a long sigh. "Just once in my lifetime, I'd like to know what it's like not to worry about making ends meet." Although Jeremy had made good money, most of it had been earmarked and spent before it made its way to the shared household account. Bespoke suits, new cars, first-class air tickets—all part of the necessary image for his work he had insisted.

"Living here, we hardly look like we're struggling," Shelly said, waving her hand around the room.

Ivy made a face. "Make no mistake, we're definitely struggling to stay here and keep afloat. Don't go all Jeremy on me."

Shelly nodded soberly. "I really like your furniture placement, by the way."

"Will you help me with the grand ballroom?"

"You bet," Shelly said, stretching.

Staring at another chair, Ivy inclined her head. "Let's try that one near the window instead of the fireplace."

As they were shifting the chair, Poppy arrived.

"Hey aunties, I came as soon as I could," Poppy said. "I know you're anxious to get the guestroom photos posted on the website. Then we can start the media blitz and begin renting these rooms for you."

"Maybe we'll have guests by the time we return from Boston," Shelly said, her eyes widening.

"Are all the guestrooms ready?" Poppy asked.

"Almost," Ivy said. "As I mentioned, we brought up a lot of things from downstairs to fill the rooms. No mattresses yet, but we can stuff pillows under the bedspreads to make it look like there are. Just long enough to take the photos."

"That's a great hack." Poppy nodded enthusiastically. "My brothers and his friends are coming later this afternoon, too. They can help you with the larger pieces downstairs."

Ivy and Shelly spent the rest of the day arranging furniture in each one of the guest bedrooms, as well as the downstairs. One room was furnished with curvy Art Nouveau furnishings, while another one was done in wicker and rattan. In other areas, they mixed up styles for an eclectic look.

Later they would have to give each piece of furniture a good cleaning and send out the fabric covered chairs to be reupholstered.

As they organized and reorganized the rooms, Ivy thought about the paintings she had in storage in Boston that she could use. More than anything, she yearned to work on new pieces inspired by scenes in Summer Beach to add to the mix. Then, once she received the money from the sale of the chandelier from Nan and Arthur, she would order a casual dining room table and consign the ornate dining room table on the lower level to them as well.

In just a few hours, Poppy had photographed every guestroom and uploaded images to the iBnB site. Then she sent photos and details to bloggers she knew in LA and activated the iBnB rental.

"You're live. Now I'll create some keywords for your website," Poppy said, who'd set up at a small table in the library. "And I'll search and see what results appear in top searches for Summer Beach." As Poppy watched her screen, a look of confusion washed over her. "Ivy, there's something you need to see here."

Poppy turned the screen around. "This can't be right. It mentions your name."

The headline read, *Stolen Art Treasures Discovered in Summer Beach Mansion.*

Ivy and Shelly sat next to her. "Actually, it is," said Ivy. They told Poppy the entire story.

"That blows my mind," Poppy said. "I can't believe you kept it a secret these last few days. How exciting is this!"

Ivy glanced at the article again. "This explains why my phone is ringing and my texts are blowing up."

"And my email," Shelly said.

Ivy pressed her lips together with chagrin. "How did they get my number?"

"The internet knows everything," Poppy said. "There

are other apps you can use for family and friends until this dies down."

Ivy handed her phone to her. "Do your magic, please. At least we're getting out of here for a few days." When she'd told Misty that Shelly was coming, too, she'd sounded so happy. When Ivy's daughters were growing up, they had always wanted to emulate their aunt Shelly.

At that, the doorbell chimed, which surprised them all. It seemed to have a *laissez-faire* attitude toward working. Ivy raced to the door.

"Hey," Bennett said, touching her hand. "Can I talk to you?" He peered inside and waved. "Alone."

As soon as she stepped outside, a young man at the curb wielding a camera called out to her. "Are you Ivy Bay Marin?"

She sighed and waved Bennett inside. "In the library." Ivy went inside, and Bennett followed her. "Wonder how long they'll keep that up since the paintings are gone?"

"No idea."

"What's up?" she asked, closing the library door.

"I've come across some disturbing information that I thought you should know about," Bennett said, rocking uncomfortably on his feet. "Looks like Shelly contacted the media about the paintings. That's why they're here."

Ivy's mouth dropped open. *The nerve of him.* "My sister would never do anything like that. Why would you even accuse her? If anyone, I would suspect Mitch. He's the one with a criminal past."

Looking hurt, Bennett put his hands on his hips. "This is exactly what I was afraid of if that got out."

"Well, it's true, isn't it?" she shot back, raising her voice. She turned her back, pacing the length of the library.

"People deserve a second chance, Ivy," he said evenly.

"I'm not saying they don't." She whirled around, fuming. How dare he insinuate her sister? "But why you would suspect Shelly over Mitch?"

"If you don't believe me, look at your sister's blog."

He had to be mistaken. "Why would she post such a story?"

"I don't know. Ask her how much she's been paid from the tabloids that ran with it. The copy is almost verbatim."

"Maybe the site was hacked," Ivy said, raising her voice. "I'm telling you, Shelly wouldn't do that, and I don't appreciate your insinuations."

Just then, Poppy and Shelly opened the library door and came inside. "What's going on in here?" Shelly asked. "I heard my name. Why all the yelling?"

Ivy crossed her arms. "It seems our mayor is poking his nose where it doesn't belong."

Bennett threw up his hands. "I have better places to be." With that, he stalked toward the door. Pausing, he said, "After dealing with your husband, I had hoped you were different. Shame on me."

The door slammed with a finality that shattered Ivy's

hope for even a first date with him.

Incensed, Ivy swung around to her sister. "You won't believe the accusations he just made against you," she sputtered.

"What?" Shelly cried.

Ivy was so angry she could hardly speak. "He says that you alerted the media through a blog post, and accuses you of taking money from tabloids."

"I swear I did nothing of the sort," Shelly said. But as soon as she spoke, her eyes bulged in horror. "Oh no!" she cried, clamping a hand over her mouth. Spinning around, she pounded across the wooden floor to Poppy's laptop.

"What have you done?" Ivy charged after her in disbelief, while Poppy raced to keep up.

Furiously tapping on the keyboard, Shelly pulled up her blog on the screen. "No, no, no! How did this happen?" She sank onto a chair and covered her face. "Oh, Ivy. I'm so sorry, this really is all my fault."

Over Poppy's shoulder, Ivy read the blog post on the screen. *Stolen Masterpieces Uncovered in Summer Beach.* Blood rose in her cheeks, and her chest tightened with the agony of betrayal.

"How *could* you?" Ivy cried out. "We were sworn to secrecy." She thrust her arm out toward the front door. "This is all on you."

Poppy watched the exchange with round eyes.

"This was only a draft." Tears sprang to Shelly's eyes. "I

wasn't going to release it until later." She moaned through her misery. "I-I must have hit the wrong button out of habit. Or maybe it was the wine I had…"

"That's an amateur mistake," Ivy shot back.

"I know, I know," Shelly wailed. "I feel terrible. But I didn't profit off of it."

"Actually, you probably did," Poppy said, leaning toward the screen. "Look how many times it's been shared. Since you have ads on the page, your commission payout will skyrocket."

"I'll donate it to charity," Shelly said, pressing her hands together. "An art school or something. Please, Ivy, believe me. This was a stupid mistake. Look, it's not even finished or edited. Would I publish something like that?"

Ivy paced the length of the room, trying to harness her fury. In her heart, she knew that Shelly spoke the truth. But that didn't ease her anguish over the argument she'd just had with Bennett, nor would it change what he thought of them. She hated that he thought Shelly would deceive her own family, or that she was out to profit however she could. And she wished she could take back what she'd said about Mitch.

"We're in damage control mode," Poppy said, spreading her hands in appeal. "I studied this in my communications class at USC. We have to get ahead of the media and put out a press release."

"I have no idea how to do that," Ivy said through gritted teeth.

"Lucky for you, I do," Poppy said, her fingers flying over the keyboard. "First, Shelly—take down that post and put up a video. I can film you on my phone in two minutes. I'll write a quick script."

"What shall I say?" Shelly said.

"Exactly what you just did. I think I've got most of it. And we'll have a press briefing in the ballroom. We can do it on Skype. All you can speak to is the discovery. The rest of the questions should be directed toward the..."

"FBI's Art Crime Team," Ivy said.

"Good," Poppy said. "Then, you're finished."

Shelly peered at what Poppy was writing. "That's it?"

"For now," Poppy said. "And we'll be sure to put a link to Summer Beach's new Seabreeze Inn. Which will have a link to iBnB, since you're not officially an inn. I got this."

Ivy whirled around. "Poppy! We will not!"

"Relax, Aunt Ivy," Poppy said calmly. "That's standard press release protocol. You'd planned on doing that anyway. Capture the traffic, at least. Build your mailing list. Art lovers are bound to see it."

"But what will Bennett think?"

"After what he accused me of, who cares?" Shelly stubbornly crossed her arms.

But I care, Ivy wanted to shout. Her heart was pounding with anguish.

In a conciliatory tone, Poppy added, "You need to rent

those rooms and generate an income, right? Maybe this isn't how you'd planned to do it, but don't pass up an opportunity. That's what being an entrepreneur is about."

"And that's what we are," Shelly added, hope edging into her voice again. "We have to do that. And Poppy knows how to manage this."

"By the time you two return from Boston, this problem will be under control," Poppy promised, her eyes gleaming at the challenge.

"Do what you have to," Ivy said to Poppy. "But the damage is done," she muttered. Still, they had a point. She wished she could afford to ignore her dwindling bank account, but she couldn't.

And it wouldn't make any difference to Bennett anyway. Not that it mattered anymore, now that he'd shown his true colors again. That relationship would never be.

She turned back to Poppy. "Let's get to work."

Chapter 28

WAITING BY THE baggage carousel at Logan International Airport, Ivy adjusted the scarf and chunky necklace she'd added to her jeans and T-shirt outfit. Shelly had run into a friend and stopped to chat, leaving her alone.

For the past few days, Ivy and Shelly had worked with Poppy to manage the flurry of attention they'd received after Shelly's accidental blog post. Poppy had handled the entire situation like a pro, and Ivy was pleased to have her on their team.

As Ivy watched the carousel for their baggage, she wondered if Misty would meet them here. Ivy had called and left her a message, but she had no idea if Misty had received it. They might be hailing a cab or taking the T—the subway—back to her dark little room at the professor's house, which would seem even smaller now.

That wasn't the worst of it, though. Before they left, Ivy had called Bennett to tell him what had happened, but he'd declined her call and sent her straight to voicemail. *Exactly what Jeremy used to do.* She'd cut off the call without leaving a message. *His loss,* she told herself, but she still ached over it.

Folding her arms, she watched the assortment of bags ride by on the conveyor belt. Her thoughts reeled back to Bennett and that summer of long ago. When she'd finally seen him on the beach again, he'd waved and walked over to her. They talked about college; he was going to the University of San Diego, where she'd also been accepted. Ivy was sure he was going to ask her out, when another girl in a bikini came racing toward him, waving with glee.

"Bennett!"

When he saw the girl, the look on his face was one of unmistakable joy. The girl threw herself into his arms, and he swung her around, laughing. Her blond hair fanned around her bare shoulders, and she began chattering on about a party she was giving and how Bennett had to promise he'd be there with her.

"Of course, I will," he said.

Neither of them looked at Ivy or even thought to invite her.

She was so embarrassed. *He already has a girlfriend.*

Ivy wished she could dissolve into the infinitesimal grains of sand and leave the two of them. With her heart breaking into a thousand pieces, Ivy simply muttered, "See you around." She dashed off before Bennett could make some lame excuse. He wouldn't miss her, and she never wanted to see him again. She felt so stupid for falling in love with a guy without even thinking to ask if he already had a girlfriend.

That was the last time she'd gone to the beach that summer. As for college, she decided to go to school in Boston instead and persuaded her parents to let her go early.

Looking back now, it seemed frivolous to her to have made such a huge decision about her future over a guy, but she had been only seventeen. Her face still burned at the memory. She sighed. She thought about Sunny and the decision she'd made to drop out of school. In retrospect, Ivy understood her daughter's decision more now. Sunny had lost her father; Ivy had only lost a summer crush.

That heartbreak—and Bennett—had changed the course of her Yet, here they were again. How ironic.

Waiting for her luggage to make its appearance on the conveyor belt, Ivy tapped her foot, still thinking about Bennett. This was the first time she'd dared to let herself become interested in a man since Jeremy's death, and it had ended in a disaster even before it began.

Not only that, but Summer Beach was a small town.

And she still had to deal with the zoning change. They could rent rooms on iBnB for a while, but she really wanted to build a business that could increase in value over time. This was her new life, and she was determined to build it on a sturdy foundation. She wondered if Bennett would support her or turn against her.

"Excuse me," said a young, good-looking man standing nearby. He pushed up his glasses on his nose and gave her a timid smile from under a shaggy lock of hair that brushed his forehead. "Is Boston your home?"

"Not anymore."

"Th-that's a shame," he said, stumbling over his words. "I th-thought all the beautiful women lived here."

He's flirting with me. Ivy burst out laughing. "You have to be more original than that."

"I'm kind of rusty," he said sheepishly. "I just got divorced. I haven't dated in twenty years."

"That's okay. I'm kind of rusty, too." They exchanged commiserative grins.

Still, it was nice to be noticed, and the guy wasn't creepy, just awkward. Ivy had to give him credit for courage.

Having Bennett nearby in Summer Beach wasn't ideal, but it was his actions as much as hers that had caused their rift. She straightened her shoulders, determined to make the best of this situation. She had little choice anyway. The damage was done.

She glanced at other men in the baggage terminal. There were plenty of other opportunities, right?

"Mom!"

Ivy turned and waved at her daughter. Misty was dashing through the crowd. Her dark brown hair streamed around her shoulders as she cut through throngs of travelers.

"Misty!" Greeting her eldest daughter with a hug, Ivy wrapped her arms around her and held her as if she'd been away for a year, and not just a couple of weeks.

Ivy kissed her lively girl on the cheek. "I didn't know if you'd be here."

Misty's ambery brown eyes looked perplexed. "Didn't you check your messages?"

"I have an awful lot of messages. I must have missed yours."

"No, Mom. On the *new* app. Poppy texted me about it. Didn't you check it?"

"Guess I forgot." While in disaster mode, she had forgotten to check the app Poppy had downloaded on her phone for her. What kind of early millennial was she? One not as tech-savvy as most. She'd rather have a paintbrush in her hand. Age was no excuse, though. Even as baby boomers, Carlotta and Sterling texted their grandchildren all the time. 'It's the only way we'd ever communicate with them,' her father had said.

"Just happy to see you. Loves you muchly," Ivy said, reverting to their silly talk as she kissed her daughter's other cheek. "What time is your show?"

"Tomorrow at eight in the evening." Misty did a little hop.

Her daughter's excitement was palpable. "Are you nervous?"

"A little. Mostly excited. This could be my big break, Mom. Sometimes talent agents check out these productions, and I really need one."

"I'm so proud of you. I know you'll do well."

The man who'd spoken to Ivy had collected his luggage. Seeing Misty, he paused. "I hope you have a good visit. Is this your friend?"

"My daughter."

"Oh, well then," he said, flustered. "I'll take your advice."

Ivy smiled. "I'm told it gets easier."

As the man grinned and ambled off, Misty's eyes widened. "I don't believe it. I think he was hitting on you."

"How about that?" Ivy tucked a wild strand of hair behind Misty's ear as she had when her daughter was a little girl. "Even at my advanced age."

"I don't mean it that way," Misty said, a corner of her mouth tugging upward. "I've just never thought of you with anyone but Dad."

"Life changes," Ivy said softly. Just how much, she still wondered. "If it didn't, you wouldn't have the chance to step on center stage tomorrow. See how that works?"

"Guess so." Misty glanced around the crowded area. "Where's Aunt Shelly?"

"She saw a friend." Ivy saw her suitcase pop out onto the baggage carousel. She stepped forward.

After they collected the suitcases, Shelly hurried over and greeted Misty. "I hear you're going to be a star tomorrow."

"I'm working on it," Misty said. "And I'm so happy you can see the show. How long will you stay in Boston? Mom's room is super tiny."

"I know, remember?" Shelly said. "But I'm off to New York the morning after your show. Won't take me but a day to pack up my things and ship them back to Summer Beach."

They began walking from the terminal toward Misty's car.

Misty looked surprised. "You're not staying in New York?"

Shelly darted a *mea culpa* glance at Ivy.

There she goes again. Ivy sighed. "Shelly and I will be living in Summer Beach for a while." She'd planned to tell Misty in a different manner, but there it was.

"Wait, I'm confused," Misty said. "Isn't the house up for sale?"

"It hasn't sold, so Shelly and I are fixing it up, and we'll be renting out rooms. Starting when we return."

Misty paused by her car. "Why didn't you tell me any

of this before, Mom?"

"Because I wanted to wait until I saw you."

"Everyone's leaving." Misty's expression drooped. "First Dad, and now you."

"I'd hardly compare the two situations," Ivy said, feeling a surge of guilt. She'd been in such survival mode that she hadn't thought her daughters would miss her much, what with their full lives and goals and penchant for friends and travel.

"But when will I see you again?" Misty asked.

"We hardly saw each other when I was here." After she'd sold the condominium, it was hard to catch up with either of them. Before that, at least they'd come by to do laundry—or drop it off, as Sunny did.

"I came over sometimes," Misty said.

"Now you can come anytime you like for as long as you like," Ivy said, touched that Misty would actually miss her. "We have plenty of rooms. And it's on the beach. It's so beautiful."

"I could understand if Nana and Gramps needed you, but I saw on Facebook that they're sailing around the world," Misty said. "Are you sure they're not too old to do that?"

Misty looked concerned as if the adults in her life had suddenly lost their minds.

"I assure you, they're both in excellent health," Ivy said. "Sixty-eight isn't ancient. And they're experienced sailors.

It's what they love to do. Like your acting and singing."

"I guess so," Misty said, allowing that. "It's just that I was used to things the way they were."

"Change is part of life," Ivy reiterated. "Someday you might be on the stage in New York or London. Think of how your life will change then."

Misty brightened. "Or on a movie set in LA."

"Then she'd be nearby," Shelly said, smiling at Ivy. "Misty, your mom and I really hope you'll come to visit."

"You have a ticket whenever you want," Ivy said. "Plenty of room, too. We still have guest and maid's quarters behind the house that we haven't even started on yet." She hugged her daughter. Even though miles might separate them, her girls were always in her heart. She had confidence that they could stand on their own. Even Sunny, who simply wasn't sure she could yet.

On their way from the airport to Ivy's room, they stopped for lunch at a cafe that had flung its doors open for the late spring sunshine. Sitting outside, they watched the college crew teams practicing on the Charles River.

After they placed their orders—seafood salads all around—Misty said, "Let's call Sunny and give her all the news."

The three women crowded around the screen on Misty's phone.

Moments later, Sunny appeared on the screen. *"Bonjour!"* She was standing in front of an ornately carved stone water fountain with a group of young friends. "Oh, hi Mom. Hi Aunt Shelly. Didn't expect you guys to be on the phone."

"Hi sweetie." Ivy squinted at the scene." It looked like nighttime in Paris. She and Jeremy had visited his relatives there several times. She had to admit, somewhat begrudgingly, that their trips had been magical. "Where are you?"

"In the Marais having dinner. Can I call you guys tomorrow?"

Misty cut in. "Sunny, wait. I called to tell you that Mom and Aunt Shelly are moving to Summer Beach."

Sunny looked crestfallen. "Why? I'm coming back soon."

"You can crash on our couch," Misty said. She had an apartment that she shared with a friend from college.

Ivy wished she could hug her younger daughter. Sunny's expression tore at her heart, but Ivy had made the decision she knew she must. "I thought you were planning to leave Boston anyway."

"Yeah, probably..." Sunny's voice trailed off. "I just didn't think you were going to run away from home after Dad died. Do you think that's what Dad would have wanted?"

Shelly shot Ivy a sympathetic look.

Trembling with anger at her husband, Ivy started to say that Jeremy wouldn't have cared where she lived. Someday she might share the truth with her daughters but now was not the time. They still thought the Summer Beach house was just an investment he'd made. Technically, that was true. Besides, her girls had a different relationship with their father than she had. Would they ever understand?

Instead of answering Sunny's question, Ivy simply said, "I'm doing what's best for me right now. By renting out rooms, I can pay the taxes and save the house from a forced tax sale. Once I manage that, then I'll see." One step at a time, she decided, though it would be challenging to deal with Sunny, who was the more sensitive and volatile of her two daughters.

"But what about all my stuff?" Sunny wailed.

"It's in storage, and I'll leave the key with Misty." Ivy paused. "You can visit Summer Beach anytime, or stay if you want. We can always use an extra hand to help with guests."

Sunny gave a dramatic sigh. "Whatever, Mom. I just don't think you belong there, or should be washing other people's dirty towels and sheets. What would Dad think?"

Misty shot her mother a look of apology for Sunny, then leaned toward the screen. "He'd be proud that Mom is doing so well without him. We should be, too."

Ivy mouthed *thank you* to Misty.

Sunny was quiet for a moment, then she said, "Hey, I've got to go. We're going out to a club. Aunt Shelly, Misty, I'll see you soon," she called out, blowing them a kiss as she hung up.

Shelly touched her hand. "She's only thinking of herself right now, but she'll be okay."

Misty watched their exchange. "I'm sorry, Mom. I know this is tough on you."

"The worst of it is over," Ivy said, smoothing her hand over her daughter's. "Onward and upward."

After lunch, Misty dropped them off at the professor's home. With her car idling at the curb, she said, "I've got great seats for you. Check in with the box office when you arrive."

"Will do. Thanks, my darling," Ivy said. "Awfully proud of you."

Waving, Misty rushed off to the theatre to get into makeup and costume for the dress rehearsal.

Ivy walked around the back of the professor's house. Shelly trailed her in silence.

"Won't take long to pack what I have," Ivy said, slipping her key into the side entry door. Two or three hours— at the most—to pack what she had here in boxes to ship, and tomorrow afternoon at her storage facility to ship her art, along with photographs that she'd saved.

"Do you still have much in storage?" Shelly asked.

"I sold most of the furniture from the flat. Storage in Boston is expensive, and my furniture was too large to fit into a small condo anyway." She would leave Sunny's belongings in a smaller unit as she'd promised.

Shelly twisted her hair into a messy bun and sat on the

bed. "What am I going to do with all my winter clothing?"

"I plan to keep a few pieces, but also to donate a lot to the homeless shelter." Ivy had little need for a full wardrobe of sweaters, snow boots, and coats at Summer Beach. "Making a clean break."

"Since I've never had much, I don't have much to go through," Shelly said. "I'll give away some of my books, send a few boxes by UPS, and be on my way. It still feels weird to be leaving New York for good. I have to see a couple of friends, too."

Ivy sat next to her. "Does that include Ezzra?" She knew how persuasive he could be, and Shelly seemed fragile right now.

Shelly hesitated. "Just to say good-bye."

"Do you think that's wise?" Ivy asked as gently as she could.

"I have to." Shelly gave her a lopsided grin. "I need closure, but I promise I'll resist. When your flight stops in New York, I'll be there."

Bumping her shoulder, Ivy said, "You'd better be. I need my partner at the Seabreeze Inn."

The next evening, after Ivy and Shelly had spent the day sorting through the last boxes of Ivy's life with Jeremy and dropped off bundles of winter clothing at the shelter, they changed and took a taxi to the theater for Misty's big debut performance.

When the curtain parted and the stage lights went up, Ivy clutched Shelly's hand. "I know Misty is talented, but I'm so scared for my baby."

Shelly squeezed her hand and whispered, "This is what she loves to do. She'll be great."

And Misty was. By the time the production was over, and the cast took their bows, Ivy was beaming with pride. When Misty skipped out to take her bow, the applause intensified, and the audience rose to their feet. A few fans tossed flowers onto the stage, and she picked them up and waved.

"Bravo!" Ivy and Shelly called out. They blew kisses to Misty and snapped photos.

Ivy was so proud of her daughter. She had always encouraged her daughters to follow their dreams. Now Misty was on her way.

"Bravo!" Ivy raised her hands toward the stage, clapping for Misty. It was time for Ivy to follow her dreams, too. And Sunny just needed to find hers.

Just then, her phone flashed a message from iBnB across the screen. Ivy turned to Shelly and let out a scream. "We just rented a room!"

"When?" Shelly asked.

"The day after we return!"

"Woo-hoo!"

Waving at Misty, Ivy and Shelly jumped up and down. The next chapter of their lives was just beginning. Maybe they didn't have the partners in life they'd thought they would, but even so, Ivy couldn't be more excited.

As Ivy and Shelly waited in the theater lobby with a bouquet of red roses for Misty, Ivy glanced at the booking request on her phone. With a satisfied smile, she tapped an acceptance.

"It's official," Ivy said. "The Seabreeze Inn will be open for business when we return."

"We shouldn't call it that just yet." Shelly frowned. "Remember what Bennett said?"

"Who?"

"I'm serious."

"So am I." Ivy brushed her hair over her shoulder. "I'm filing the papers at the zoning office when we return. We'll have an open house and invite all the neighbors and the reporter for the *Summer Beach Breeze*. When they hear our plan for the community, they'll support us."

Ivy had read that some cities were banning iBnB rentals within city limits to maintain exclusivity, so it was essential to have the proper zoning to operate as an inn, even though they would be subject to more regulations. Her heart quickened as she thought of the lengthy process.

After the charges Bennett had made against Shelly, Ivy wondered if he would try to block their request for a zoning change. Darla, their neighbor, was another challenge to convince. Were there others who would feel the same?

Chapter 29

IN THE SIDE garden that Shelly had brought back from the wild, Ivy snipped stalks of Hawaiian red ginger, orange birds of paradise, and lacy green ferns in anticipation of their first guests. She admired the colors against the yellow linen sundress she wore and thought what a vivid still life the armload she carried would make, especially framed by the brilliant blue sky above. It seemed unseasonably warm today as if summer couldn't wait to arrive. Turning her face toward the sun, she thought it was a perfect day for new beginnings.

Ivy glanced toward the ocean, where a few solitary souls strolled the water's edge. Some people had leashed dogs nipping at the waves, while others stopped to contemplate the swell of the sea. If the heat kept up, the summer crowds would come early.

She paused, fixing the image of a young couple with a yellow Labrador trotting beside them in her mind. He carried a little girl on his shoulders.

She would sketch that later today, she decided.

Carrying her bundle of flowers, Ivy hurried to the front of the house where Shelly was watering a riotous mix of flowers she had just planted on the slope leading to the front steps. Purple and pink petunias were nestled within a border of white alyssum, along with pink hibiscus and lavender buddleia bushes to attract butterflies.

On their flight back from Boston, Shelly had been uncharacteristically quiet. Ivy didn't know if she was upset over Ezzra or Mitch—or both. Each time she tried to coax conversation out of her, Shelly shut down. But now, out here, surrounded by the nature she loved, Shelly seemed better. For the time being, at least.

Shelly looked up as Ivy approached. "Are you sure the room is ready for the guests?"

"I've triple checked." Ivy pressed a hand to her warm forehead. "I also opened the windows to let the sea breezes in." She paused. "This is really happening, isn't it? Our first rental, our first day in business."

"My insides are leaping like crazed grasshoppers." Shelly redirected the water nozzle toward another group of new plantings. "I'm giving these plants an extra drink before I leave them. It's awfully dry for this time of year. We haven't even gotten to the June gloom yet, and it's already feeling like summer."

"Feels like hot Santa Ana winds." Ivy met Shelly's eyes. "I hate to say this, but Mom always said unseasonal heat feels like earthquake weather."

"Don't even say that," Shelly said. "Besides, we're not directly on a fault line here. But we should stock up on bottled water and supplies, just in case."

"And sunscreen." Ivy looked at Shelly's handiwork, which enlivened the entrance and appealed to her artistic sense. "You're doing wonders with the yard. And these plantings are gorgeous." Ivy really meant it, and she could see that Shelly appreciated her taking notice of her efforts.

"You should paint these flowers. Those bare walls inside are screaming for artwork."

"I set up my easel and paint in the atrium sunroom," Ivy said. She'd even dabbled a bit the day before, and it had felt good.

"Our shipments should arrive soon," Ivy added. "I'll hang those first." Fortunately, most of her paintings of the New England coastline had already been packed from her first move. It was easy to ship them. She'd also brought a couple of small paintings back on the plane.

Shelly sprayed a light veil of water over the freshly planted flowers. "I have a more elaborate plan in mind for a tropical seaside garden to chronical and video, but this was quick."

Shelly's mood seemed to have improved, but Ivy still detected a trace of melancholy.

Just then, a car arrived at the curb, and Ivy motioned the guests into the long, curved drive. "Here they are."

"No more late night dance parties in the kitchen, I guess," Shelly said. "Or we could invite guests to join us."

"Darla would love that." Ivy thought of how Bennett and Mitch had walked in on them that crazy night when they were blasting music, dancing, and attacking the brick wall. The past couple of weeks had been a stress-filled blur, but she'd also had more fun than she'd had in a long time, despite her problems with Bennett.

"Dang, we'll have to invite Darla to the open house, won't we?" Shelly flicked the water nozzle off and bent down to pat dirt around the base of a petunia.

"We should." Ivy glanced next door. "But I don't know whether to spike her Sea Breeze juice cocktail and risk a vitriolic rage, or serve her a virgin cocktail…and still risk a vitriolic rage."

"I see your point." Shelly brushed dirt from her hands. "While you see the guests in, I'll pour the juice." She hurried around the back toward the kitchen.

Ivy watched Shelly go and wondered what she could do to help her. She turned to welcome the new guests.

"Welcome to the Seabreeze Inn," Ivy said to the young

couple that got out of the car. They wore beach attire, and the easy way they slung their arms around each other as they walked toward her reminded her of herself and Jeremy when they were their age.

The fond, unbidden memory surprised her. Humans were neither all good nor all bad—they were just human and fallible, herself included. With a full life to look forward to now, her anger at him was lessening.

And after Bennett, she needed to face the fact that she might never find another person to spend her life with.

With gravel crunching under her sandals, she took a step toward the couple. "You must be the Calloways. Please come in."

"Megan and Josh," the young woman said. They greeted her and followed her inside.

While Ivy quickly stuffed her bundle of flowers into the cut-crystal vase in the foyer, Megan slowly turned around, her eyes sparkling as she took in the soaring ceiling and honeyed parquet floors.

Ivy and Shelly had redesigned the ballroom into a reception room, and they'd opened the bank of French doors on the long veranda to catch the ocean breeze. Chairs facing the sea would be a nice addition, Ivy thought, making a mental note.

Ivy and Shelly had grouped the furnishings they'd found on the lower level into small conversation areas to bring the scale of the room down to a more personal level.

Shelly added an array of interior plants, including orchids, potted palms, fiddle-leaf fig trees, and other tropical plants. With large windows and sunlight streaming inside, the room took on an airy greenhouse feeling.

"Wow, your home is amazing," Megan said.

Ivy was thrilled. As soon as she had stepped off the plane from back east, she had purchased mattresses and bedding for each guest room. This had cost a small fortune, but Nan had wired the money from the sale of the chandelier to Ivy's bank account. She expected the expense would pay for itself many times over. Per Poppy, a fire pit was also on its way. Next week, the pool would be inspected and filled, and the piano tuned.

"We weren't too sure about this place," Josh said. "In the photos, it looked huge, but you don't have any reviews yet. And right on the beach? Wow. Thought it might be a scam, but then we saw Shelly Bay's video and thought, why not? My wife follows her gardening channel online. She feels like she knows her."

Thinking of Poppy's online videos, Ivy grinned.

Shelly bustled in holding a bamboo tray with two rose-colored drinks in blue-rimmed, hand-blown Mexican bubble glasses topped with lime wedges. "Specialty of the house—virgin Sea Breeze cocktails."

"It's *you*," Megan said, delighted to see Shelly. "I love your videos. You make everything seem so easy and fun. And your arrangements are so different."

Shelly thanked her, and they chatted while Megan and Josh accepted the icy drinks.

"Delicious," Josh announced.

Ivy led them upstairs to their room. Against antique wicker chairs, she'd placed marine blue-and-white cushions with a pop of pink pillows. A white duvet covered the bed, and with the shutters and windows open, sheer white curtains fluttered in the breeze. In the background, the low roar of the ocean was naturally mesmerizing.

In her storage facility, Ivy had found two small canvases she'd painted years ago of Massachusetts beaches, not long after she'd arrived in Boston. Though the shorelines were rocky, in each one the sea was a majestic, curling marine blue kissed with windblown whitecaps. The artwork seemed at home in this room, and Ivy imagined that Amelia would have approved.

"This is beautiful," Megan said, easing onto the edge of the fluffy, summer-weight down comforter. "We might never leave."

Ivy smiled, remembering a time when she was first married and was exploring the east coast with Jeremy. From Maine, Rhode Island, Nantucket, and Martha's Vineyard to South Carolina, Georgia, and Florida. Lobster rolls, Maryland crab cakes, clam chowder. Another unbidden memory, she realized. She shook herself out of it by plumping a pillow on the love seat.

"Where's a good place for breakfast?" Josh asked.

"All the locals go to Java Beach," Ivy said. She hadn't seen Mitch since they'd returned, and Ivy wondered if Shelly was still keeping her distance from him. "Be sure to sit outside on the beach. You'll have a great view." She was already speaking like a local.

"We came to get away from the rain in Seattle," Megan said. "What's fun to do around here?"

"Besides the beach, you can wander through Antique Times or stroll through the marina. For quick meals, Rosa's has good fish tacos. And while you're at Java Beach, ask Mitch about his whale watching trips."

Megan and Josh were staring at Ivy's paintings. "We saw the news about the stolen paintings," Megan said. "Is this one...?"

"Not at all," Ivy said, laughing. "Those are with the FBI's Art Crime Team, and they'll be returned to their rightful owners or their heirs." Ivy nodded at the seascape. "That's one of my paintings."

Megan perked up. "I love to paint, too."

"I'll be giving classes here soon." The prospect of a future here filled Ivy with such joy, but they had to fill the rest of the rooms first. And fast.

After making sure the couple was comfortable, Ivy left them and joined Shelly downstairs on the veranda, where Shelly was sitting on the steps, digging her toes into the silky sand and sipping a Sea Breeze. Ivy sat beside her.

"We've done it," Ivy said. "Our first guests. And the

Sea Breezes were a nice touch."

Shelly offered her a rosy-orange colored juice cocktail. "Brought you one."

"Virgin or fully loaded?"

"It's not cocktail hour yet," Shelly said, staring at the ocean. "I thought we could serve these at the open house."

"Buttering up the neighbors?"

"Absolutely."

Ivy lifted her face to the light ocean breeze, letting it cool her skin, while the sun hovered in the midday sky, bathing her in golden sunshine. As she enjoyed the warmth of the spring sun, she remarked, "So this is our life now."

Shelly nudged her. "Way to land on your feet, sis. You were always the smart one."

"So are you."

"Sometimes I wonder," Shelly said, scrunching her eyes against the sun.

"I have no doubt. When I left Boston on the connecting flight to New York, I was so worried that you wouldn't get on the flight." Ivy stretched out her legs. "That you would have stayed with Ezzra. You didn't tell me what happened when you saw him."

Shelly turned up a corner of her mouth. "Oh, he tried, but I'd heard all those lines before. I told him he needed a new audience."

"See?" Ivy smirked. "Smart." Shelly only shrugged, and Ivy could tell she was still upset. "Do you miss him?"

Shelly clasped her knees and stared ahead at the swelling waves. "It's funny. He's not the one I really miss."

Mitch. Ivy caught her meaning, but what could she say?

Lifting her chin, Shelly slid a gaze toward her sister. She held out her fist. "Rock, paper, scissors to see which of us goes to invite Darla."

"You're on," Ivy said.

Ivy crossed the lawn to Darla's house. She'd lost the rock, paper, scissors game, so here she was, calling on the local dragon lady. Ivy forced a pleasant look on her face and knocked.

Darla answered. The older woman had yet another rhinestone visor clamped around her dark blue hair. Ivy wondered just how many of those she had.

"Now what is it?" Darla asked with a sneer.

Ivy handed her an invitation flyer that Poppy had composed and printed. "We're having an open house, and we'd like you to come and join us."

Darla narrowed her eyes. "You're not going to have that loud music, are you?"

Ivy suppressed a laugh. "We plan to show everyone the work we've done on the property and talk about the future of the Seabreeze house." Recalling Shelly's warning, she made a point not to call it an inn just yet. That would only antagonize Darla, and Ivy wanted her—and all the other residents—to hear their entire plan first. And they needed Darla's approval, even though they ran the risk that she would complain the loudest.

"I saw some people get out of a car earlier. I hope they're quiet," Darla said.

"They're our iBnB guests. Very nice young couple. And quiet."

"Humph." Darla crossed her arms.

"Lots of people here rent rooms to guests," Ivy said. "If we can't, we'll have to sell the house or lose it in a tax sale to a deep-pocketed developer. You know better than I what that means."

"I fought your husband, and I can do it again."

"But is that what you want? Wouldn't you rather see people enjoying the home? I plan to teach art classes, Shelly is going to lead garden tours, and we'll invite authors in to speak. We want to be part of the community and share this magnificent old home for years to come."

Darla looked like she was considering her message, so Ivy pressed on, hoping she was making progress against a potential seismic upheaval at the open house.

"A lot of your friends will be there. Nan and Arthur from the antique shop, and Mitch from Java Beach." Ivy remembered that he had spoken in her defense the first day they'd arrived.

"Maybe I'll stop by." Darla snatched the invitation from her hand.

"We'd sure like that. Since we're neighbors—"

Darla slammed the door.

A dire warning stirred inside of her. Did that woman ever have a good day? If so, Ivy thought, please let it be the day of the open house.

Ivy continued knocking on neighbors' doors. Shelly had selected another street. Finally, Ivy decided to visit Mitch at Java Beach. Although she still had some reservations, she wanted to make an effort. According to Bennett, Mitch had reformed, but then, Ivy had no idea about the details as to why he had served time in prison, aside from burglary. She hadn't asked.

The coffee shop was busy, and Ivy waited in line. When Ivy stepped up to the counter, Mitch simply said, "What'll it be?"

"Hey, Mitch. Coffee of the day, please. She took an invitation from her purse. "We'd like for you to come to our open house, see what we've done to it, and hear about plans for the future."

"I'm pretty swamped."

"And we were hoping you could provide coffee and pastries," she quickly added. "For about 50 to 100." Would Shelly be angry about this? She'd sure seemed happier around Mitch. That would be worth the cost.

"Well—"

"Good, it's settled then." Ivy beamed and opened her purse.

Mitch held up his hands. "I didn't say I'd do it."

Her eyes flicked across his pastry case. "Your cream cheese pastries are the best, everyone says so. I can't believe you make them here." She raised her eyes to his. She wasn't above begging on behalf of her sister. "Please?"

He heaved a great sigh. "All right. But only if you're sure Shelly is okay with this."

"Of course. It was her suggestion."

Mitch raised his brow.

"Well, I could tell that was what she was thinking, even if she wouldn't say it."

"I shouldn't be doing this, but—"

"Thank you, Mitch." Shelly would be livid when she found out, but Ivy hoped she'd eventually come around. What would her sister do—storm out in the middle of the open house? Ivy blew out a breath. *Yes, she might.*

Chapter 30

ADMIRING THE FRESH flowers that lined the walkway, Bennett climbed the steps to Las Brisas del Mar. Or, as the invitation Darla had given him referred to it, the Seabreeze house. Same meaning, fresh look, he supposed. His only interest was how their scheme would affect the community. He wouldn't have even attended had it not been for Darla. Neither Ivy nor Shelly had actually invited him.

Which didn't bother him in the least.

Not much, anyway.

At the top of the steps, Ivy stood greeting guests. She wore a soft pink sundress that fluttered around her legs. Her hair was lighter, probably lightened in the sun. This past week, he'd seen her walking on the beach in the morning, and he'd done his best to avoid her.

His gut tightened. Okay, maybe the lack of invitation bothered him more than a little. But he was the mayor, and he was bound to learn about this open house from his constituents. He figured he should hear about it firsthand.

When she saw him, she caught her breath. "Oh, you're here."

"Darla invited me."

Ivy blinked. The light streaks in her hair framed her deep green eyes. "Darla's inside."

"Thanks," he said, as anxious to tear his gaze from her face as she was to be rid of him. Yet everything about her drew him back. Her perfume was fresh and delicate, and her shoulders glowed with the sun's kiss. For a split second, he imagined lifting a pink strap and kissing that shoulder. He opened his mouth to say something.

"Yes?" Ivy stared at him.

"I…" It was as if his brain had disconnected from his mouth. "I think you've done a good job on the flowers."

"That was Shelly, but thanks."

"Yeah. Well, you can tell her for me." He winced at his ineptness. *Good job.* That's what his sister used to say to Logan when he was a toddler. What was it about Ivy Bay that left him so tongue-tied?

"Tell her yourself," Ivy said. "She's right over there." Swiftly, she turned away from him to greet another guest.

Bennett made his way through the sizeable crowd that had already gathered in the ballroom, which had been redesigned with smaller groups of antique chairs anchored with rugs and a bevy of plants. The sisters had talent. He had to give credit where it was due.

Catching snippets of conversation around him, it was clear that guests were curious about the plans for the estate, while others were eager to learn more about the stolen art saga. Others, like Darla, were concerned about the traffic and noise an inn would bring to Summer Beach. As usual, everyone had an opinion.

Scanning the crowd, Bennett saw Nan and Arthur, who were admiring the antiques. The owner of Blossoms, Imani, was laughing with Shelly. Jen and George, the couple who owned Nailed It, were talking to Flint Bay. Beside him, Bennett noticed other Bay family members, including Ivy's parents, Carlotta and Sterling. He nodded cordially toward them.

Jim Boz, head of the planning and zoning department, approached him. "Hey, boss. Darla invite you, too?"

"The invitation said all were welcome. Looks like Darla rallied the town."

Boz chuckled. "Give her an inch…"

Shelly sailed toward them, a tray in her hand. "Care for a virgin Sea Breeze? Specialty of the house. Cranberry and grapefruit juice with lime. Very refreshing." She plucked one and handed it to Bennett.

He gripped the glass, grateful for something to do with his hands. "I heard you got your first guests."

Shelly grinned. "Bet you've been talking to Darla. I think she's been tracking our guests' every move."

"Word travels fast in this town." Bennett sipped the juice concoction and nodded approvingly.

"That's why we're having an open house," Shelly said. "So the word will spread like wildfire." She handed him a printed Sea Breeze recipe card from a stack. "Take one of these, too."

Chief Clarkson joined their group. "Someone say wildfire?" he asked, frowning.

"Just as it relates to the Summer Beach gossip line," Shelly said, handing the chief a juice cocktail.

"We take fires seriously in California," the chief said. "Had a brush fire on the ridge this morning, but it's under control. Not too far from your place, Bennett."

"Hot weather, low humidity, and stiff winds are a bad recipe for dangerous fire conditions," Bennett said.

Shelly shuddered. "Fires, earthquakes. Might as well throw in a tsunami, too."

"Had a water spout off the coast last year," Boz offered. "Didn't you know those are the seasons of the California coast?" He chuckled. "But the mayor here runs a disaster preparedness class every year."

"Even in paradise, you have to be ready for a potential disaster." Through an open butler's pantry door, Bennett saw Mitch unpacking coffee and pastries. "Excuse me, I need to speak to Mitch."

At the mention of his name, Shelly's face paled, and she hurried off. Bennett wondered what had transpired between them.

"Hey, didn't expect to see you here," Bennett said, tapping the card Shelly had given him.

Mitch shook his head. "Ivy wouldn't take no for an answer. Figured I might as well join the club. Looks like a big crowd."

"Everyone is curious." Bennett eyed his friend. "Looks like you are, too."

Mitch shrugged off his comment. "Hey, I'm here to do business and keep my head down. Shelly stopped returning my calls, but business is business. Complicated women are just that. Complicated."

"Couldn't agree more." As Bennett watched Ivy greet other guests, glowing rays from the setting sun streamed through the windows, bathing her in burnished golden light.

When she turned toward him, he suddenly realized why she seemed so familiar to him. In that particular light and in that diaphanous pink dress, she looked as she had years ago on the beach, bathed in moonlight and dancing around the summer bonfire in a pink sundress. There was no doubt in his mind now. Ivy had been his first crush.

Although they'd hardly spoken, he'd lost his heart to

her. All summer he had lived yearning to catch a glimpse of her, hoping every day that she would be at the beach with her friends. Yet when he'd finally found the courage to ask her out, she'd disappeared. He'd searched for her, but her friends said she was on her way back east.

A lot had changed in his life since then, but he'd never forgotten her, or how heartbroken he'd been when she'd left. She had been his impossible dream.

No wonder she had his emotions tied up in knots.

Chapter 31

"THANK YOU ALL for coming," Ivy said as she gazed across the converted ballroom, which comfortably held the crowd that had gathered. Feeling confident, she raised her glass, taking care not to catch Bennett's strangely intense gaze.

Instead, Ivy looked at her mother, who had a proud smile on her face. "Here's to a new chapter of Amelia Erickson's Las Brisas del Mar, which we now call the Seabreeze house. A place for gathering and relaxing on the shores of Summer Beach."

"Here, here," Nan said as she began clapping. Arthur joined in, as did many other people.

When the applause subsided, Ivy went on. "Speaking of Seabreeze, we're hoping for a cool breeze right now, in fact."

A chuckle rippled across the crowd. "An early summer," someone called out.

Ivy fanned herself. "And please welcome our first iBnB guests, Megan and Josh from Seattle, who have joined us, too." She fluttered her fingers in a little wave to the young couple, who were seated nearby.

As it turned out, Megan was a documentary filmmaker, and an idea was quickly forming in Ivy's mind. Amelia Erickson was a fascinating character shrouded in mystery. Maybe there was a story there for Megan.

Ivy refocused her attention and carried on. "Our ultimate goal is to turn this house into a gathering place for the community," she said. "This summer, I'll host painting classes, and Shelly will give gardening instruction and tours. But we want to do even more for the community."

Shelly put her tray down and joined her. "Amelia Erickson was a patron of the arts," Shelly said. "We want to continue her legacy by welcoming artists of all kinds. We'd like to host book clubs and authors in the library and musicians in the music room. We can host dinner parties and small events, and also provide lodging for your friends and family members. But to do all that, we need to be more than an iBnB host."

"We need your support to transform our vision into the new Seabreeze Inn," Ivy added, letting her passion imbue her delivery. "I've already filed the paperwork for rezoning, and I hope we can count on your support to realize our vision, which will be such an asset to the community."

A murmur rose across the crowd, and Ivy cast a glance at Darla. Her arm shot up, nearly dislodging her sparkly visor.

Here we go, Ivy thought. "Yes, Darla?"

"What about the noise and parking? This is a residential neighborhood." Darla's tone was already confrontational.

"Just across the street is the beginning of the town's seaside village," Ivy said, summoning every bit of patience she could. "And if we're given permission, we can enlarge our parking court on the side of the property, safely out of view of your home, Darla. And we'll be sure to adhere to noise curfews."

"More than anything, we want to be good neighbors," Shelly said. "This is also our home."

Without meaning to, Ivy caught Bennett's gaze. Feeling heat rise in her cheeks, she averted her eyes and took another question.

"What we really want to know about is all that artwork you found," Jen said. Her husband elbowed her good-naturedly in the ribs as she spoke. "Did you get to keep any of it?"

Ivy laughed. "We wish, but no, we turned over everything we found to the FBI, who will be tracking down the rightful owners and heirs."

Behind her, a sudden hot breeze lifted the sheer curtains at a tall window, sending yards of fabric billowing out in a cloud of white. A stack of paper napkins ruffled in the gust like a deck of cards and took flight. Poppy dashed to catch them. Ivy brushed her windblown hair back in place. "Wow, what a gust. Must be the Santa Ana winds. Any other questions?"

"May we tour the house?" Jen asked.

"This floor is open, and we left guestrooms upstairs open for you to look at, too." Ivy grinned at her new friends and neighbors. "Except for Josh and Megan's room."

Shelly added, "And be sure to say hello to Gert and Gertie in the kitchen, our twin turquoise refrigerators. They're old, but they're as chill as ever."

"If you want to talk to Shelly or me, we're around the house a lot, so come and visit." Ivy stepped into the crowd, which was already flowing throughout the downstairs rooms.

She was proud of how Shelly was handling herself. Her sister was talking to neighbors, though Ivy noticed that she had been avoiding Mitch. She wondered how she could get them together.

Outside, the wind was picking up, and Ivy saw a chair blow over. Motioning to Poppy, she asked her to secure the chair and close a couple of windows.

After talking with a few guests, Ivy sought out her parents. "Mom, Dad, what did you think?"

"We thought you presented your side very well," Carlotta said. "You have your detractors, but you'll just have to win them over." She nodded toward Darla and lowered her voice. "She's not a fan of yours."

"How well we know. Darla doesn't like many people in town. Except Mitch, for some reason." Ivy sighed. "Think we have a chance?"

"There's always a chance," Sterling replied. "Start documenting and collecting data on your community service and guest reviews. Be ready to defend your vision."

Suddenly, an even stronger gust blew over a potted palm tree. Poppy raced to the windows to close them.

"It's the devil winds," Sterling called out. "Santa Ana winds are blowing hot inland air through the canyons. We'd better secure the windows on that side of the house, or you'll have half of Summer Beach's sand on your floors to clean up." Her father took Flint's sons with him to make sure the windblown side of the house was tightly closed.

Ivy cast a worried look outside, where palm trees were bending against the heated onslaught. *Santa Ana winds.* They were right to be worried. SoCal writer Joan Didion once wrote that these hellish blows delivered "incendiary dryness." It had been a long time since Ivy had felt the wrath of these winds, but she hadn't forgotten.

Overhead, the chandeliers began to flicker. Ivy gazed up just as the lights snapped off. Though it was barely dusk and not too dim inside yet, they'd soon have a problem. She saw Bennett head outside and remembered that he kept lanterns in an emergency kit in his truck.

"Everybody stay calm. We'll check the power," Ivy called out. A circuit breaker had probably been tripped. She'd seen a breaker box in the kitchen.

"I'll get the flashlights we bought ready," Shelly said.

Ivy started after Bennett, who was striding toward the kitchen. Since he'd cleaned the house before they moved in, he knew where the breaker box was.

When she reached Bennett, he was already inspecting the breakers, which were in a metal box inside the kitchen and behind a door. He hardly gave her a glance. "Everything's fine here. There's another one outside."

"I appreciate this—" She stopped. Bennett was already out the door.

Ivy hurried after him outside, where the wind whipped her hair around her face.

Bennett looked around. "I don't see any lights on at your neighbors. I'll bet the problem is farther up channel. We may have a general power outage in the neighborhood." Bennett pulled his phone from his pocket and made a call.

Crossing her arms, Ivy waited for him, drumming her fingers on her arm and growing perturbed. He didn't seem to care whether she waited for him or not. But this was her house, her lights, and her party. She needed to know what was going on and what to tell people.

When he hung up, she asked, "So?"

"Citywide outage."

"How long will the power be off?"

"I'm no expert, but once the fellows find the problem and take care of it, I imagine you won't be put out for too much longer." He turned to go back inside.

"You were right, but Shelly made a mistake," Ivy blurted out. "It was a draft blog post she was working on that wasn't supposed to go out. And I'm sorry I accused Mitch."

Bennett paused at the door. "Well, okay then."

"Is that really all you have to say to me?"

He stopped and turned back to her. He remained quiet for a long moment as if contemplating a momentous statement. Instead, he said, "This was a nice gesture—opening the house and inviting your neighbors and the community in like this."

Ivy continued tapping her fingers. "What about us? Can I count on your support to operate as an inn in the future?"

"Ivy, you have to understand the process for zoning changes. I'm not the sole decision-maker."

She stepped squarely in front of him and put her hands on her hips. Though she tried to remain calm, her heart was hammering. "But you do have a voice in the matter. And an opinion."

Finally, Bennett looked her in the eye. "I think you've made a compelling argument, and your intentions toward the community seem honorable."

He had on his mayor's mask, and that disturbed her. "I sense there's something more that you're not saying."

"I'll be straight with you," he said, his voice dropping a notch. "Your husband stirred up the residents and cost this community a lot of money. You can hardly blame them if they don't fall into your arms the first time you ask them for a favor. You and your sister have to prove yourselves. You're the newcomers."

Ivy nodded. What he said made a lot of sense, even though it wasn't what she wanted to hear. "And we will. Thanks for the advice."

Figuring there was nothing more she could say, Ivy twisted her windblown hair from her face and turned to go back inside.

Suddenly, an enormous, sun-dried palm frond with sharp, spiky edges hurled toward her. Bennett pulled her aside, though an edge of the frond scraped her bare shoulder.

"Watch out," Bennett cried as another one blew toward them. Grabbing her arm, he spun her into the safety of his arms and pressed his back against the house for shelter.

"Ouch," she cried, pressing into him. Above her, palm trees were arched in the wind, their large, dried fronds peeling off and taking flight in the gusts. "Those fronds are dangerous."

Holding her in his arms, he looked at her shoulder.

"Not too bad, but you need a bandage on that. Do you have a first-aid kit?" He pulled a white cotton handkerchief from his sports coat.

Ivy winced as he pressed the cloth against her skin to stem the trickles of blood oozing from the scrape. "Not yet. It's on the list."

"What am I going to do with you?" he murmured.

He was so close she could feel his breath on her cheek. "What do you mean by that?" Ivy stared into his hazel eyes. Her heart was beating so hard she was sure he could hear it.

Bennett applied the slightest pressure to the small of her back and lowered his eyes.

For a split second, Ivy lost her focus, and lifted her face to his, imagining the feel of his lips on hers.

Only a breath of space separated them.

"You need to see to your guests," he said brusquely and pulled away. "But first, I'll put a bandage on your shoulder. Come with me to the truck."

Taking her hand, Bennett led her into the wind. "Watch the fronds," he called out, though the winds whipped his voice into the air. He kept his head down and pulled her close to him.

As the stiff wind tangled her skirt around her legs, Ivy clung to him. Whitecaps formed on the ocean, and late afternoon beachgoers raced after hats and umbrellas skipping across the sand like tumbleweeds. The wind held fine particles of sand…and a whiff of smoke.

Bennett unlocked the cab of the pickup and helped her up. She waited, untangling her hair from her earrings and eyelashes while he opened a first aid kit.

"I can do that," she said.

"You have another scratch on your back that you won't be able to reach." Working deftly, he cleaned her wound and applied ointment.

Grateful for his gentle touch, Ivy watched him work. "You enjoy being of service to others, don't you?"

He paused, his gaze encompassing her face before finally settling on her lips. "At the end of the day, what else is there? The journey is awfully lonely if you have to go it alone."

"Which you've been doing for a while." For all their differences, the loss of their spouses was what they had in common. She touched his forearm. "I need to know. Does it get any easier?"

"The pain mellows, but the person who is gone remains forever rooted in your life." He peeled off a bandage. "Hold still." With a swift motion, he applied the bandage.

Ivy drew a breath, summoning her courage. "Do you think there will ever be room for another relationship to take root?"

While she waited for Bennett to answer the wind whistled through the cab, its force rocking the SUV.

After smoothing the edges of the bandage, Bennett let his hand linger on her shoulder. "I'd grown to think not.

But lately I've seen widowed friends remarry and find happiness again. I think what they've found is good—even better—in many ways."

They sat shoulder to shoulder while the wind pummeled the vehicle. "Why is that, do you think?"

"More experience, more maturity. Realizing that their one true love was human, too." He chuckled. "As much as I loved Jackie, she drove me crazy at times with her incessant talking. But then, I also loved that about her, too. She had a lot of friends and was so informed on so many subjects." He paused, searching her eyes. "Do you know what I mean?"

"I do. Jeremy had his faults, too. Only I didn't realize the most egregious of them until after he'd died." She quirked her lips to the side. "He stole the pleasure of screaming at him from me. Not that we had that sort of relationship. Not at all, actually, which makes it so surreal to think about what I know now."

Bennett shook his head. "I can only imagine." Glancing out the window, he said, "We should get back inside."

Ivy twisted her hair to one side to secure it against the wind. "Ready."

Bennett took her hand, and they raced head-down through a fine spray of sand and leaves blasting them like confetti. The smell of smoke was stronger now, and dark plumes rose from the high ridge that separated Summer Beach from the rest of the county. Bennett glanced up. "Oh, crap."

Behind them, waves roared against the wind and droplets took flight, pelting them until they reached the house. They burst through the door, panting and flinging bits of debris from their hair and clothing.

Chief Clarkson strode towards them, his face a grim mask. "Mayor, we've had a report of fire up on the ridge."

Bennett's lips parted. "How bad is it?"

"We're evacuating the area," the chief said. "Your house, too."

Chapter 32

TURNING TO IVY, Bennett gripped her hands with a ferocity that surprised her. "I've got to go. I'm a volunteer firefighter, and those are my neighbors."

As she realized the magnitude of his words, her heartbeat quickened. "Be safe," she pleaded. She couldn't lose him now.

With a last, searching look at her face, Bennett raced from the house.

A moment later, Mitch rushed past. "Right behind you, Bennett," he called out.

The chief looked outside, where an errant shower of embers twinkled like fireflies but could spark a destructive fire. "With these high winds, cinders can sail through the air and skip blocks. You're close to the sea, but don't be fooled. Keep watch, and make sure your guests get to safety."

Ivy rushed into the reception room to check on everyone. Jen and George from the hardware shop were handing out flashlights and lanterns to the remaining people, and Sterling was making sure people knew how to use them.

Shelly fell in step beside her. "Last week I cleared a lot of brush around the house, but we need to be preemptive with these swirling embers. We need a team outside to douse the trees and roof."

Ivy recalled the actions their father once took when a fire threatened their neighborhood years ago. "Dad, Flint," she called out. "Going to need your help outside." She and Shelly quickly explained.

"Sure thing," Flint said. "Got a hose?"

"We have several in the shed behind the house," Shelly said.

Ivy knew the strong wind could haphazardly whip burning embers into the rafters, sending flames through an attic and engulfing a house in minutes. "Shelly and I can start hosing down the roof and rafters of the main house."

Sterling turned to his son. "Flint, you and I need to find the exterior spigots and get the hoses distributed."

As Ivy and Shelly spoke with their family, their iBnB guests, Megan and Josh, appeared beside them.

"What can we do to help?" Josh asked.

"Help me with the trees," Shelly said, taking charge of them. "Wet down their leaves and branches." She glanced through a window and frowned. "Our neighbor Darla has huge eucalyptus trees in her yard. With their natural oil, those trees flare like roman candles when embers touch their branches. Please go help her first."

Boz rushed to them. "Many folks here can't leave. Their homes are up on the ridge. Can you put them up? Doubt if they'll be going anywhere tonight."

"Absolutely," Ivy said. She clapped her hands over the din of worried conversation. "Excuse me, neighbors. If you've been evacuated, or can't get to your house, we have plenty of room here. Might be a little dusty, still, but you can spend the night and stay as long as you need to." She spied Poppy near the entrance. "Poppy can show you where to go and make you comfortable."

Poppy waved her hand, and a few people made their way to her.

"And if you're hungry," Carlotta said, "don't forget we have plenty of coffee and pastries, compliments of Mitch."

Ivy knew she could count on her mother and Poppy to take care of their guests. She paused, eyeing the tall windows. "And could everyone help close the shutters and drapes to guard against broken windows?"

Shelly tugged her sleeve. "They'll be okay. Let's go."

Ivy kicked off her heels and shoved her feet into a pair of gardening boots she'd left by the back door, and Shelly did the same. Ivy secured her hair with a rubber band and shrugged into a windbreaker. They pushed outside behind their father and brother and nephews, their heads down against the hot, relentless wind.

Flint looked back at them. "We've had a long drought. Fires have been bad in California for a while." Motioning to his son and nephews, he called out, "This way, guys."

Shelly quickly directed them to the water spigots around the property and the hoses inside the shed. Ivy grabbed a hose that was already connected and turned on the nozzle. The wind wasn't making their job any easier, and within minutes, Ivy was nearly as wet as the roof and rafters from the back spray.

"Over here," Shelly yelled above the wind. From the ridgeline above them that crashed into the sea, embers were raining down around the pool and onto the atrium sunroom off the veranda. Ivy whirled around and blasted the sizzling embers with a strong jet of water.

Next door, she could see Josh and Megan helping Darla, and she turned her spray onto the eucalyptus tree branches that hung onto their side of the property line.

"Beautiful tree, but that needs to come down," Shelly called out. "Too close to the house, too much of a hazard."

As dusk encroached, Ivy watched for bright specks in the gloomy sky. Though the fire on the ridge above them raged, the winds died down. Ashes fluttered down like snowflakes, coating the yard and their hair and clothing.

Seeing how her family had quickly come together to help touched Ivy's heart. She was so grateful for their help, and she realized how much she had missed having her family nearby. Even if she couldn't save the beach house from the ravages of fire or a tax sale, she knew this is where she belonged. From restoring the paintings to families to offering shelter to those who needed it, this is where she could make a difference in people's lives.

Overhead, an engine droned, and everyone tilted their heads back. Ivy let out a whoop. An aircraft was flying into the billowing charcoal clouds above the ridge. Opening its lower hull, the plane dropped sheets of water onto the blaze. Ivy whooped with joy. She had heard that the larger city of San Diego had invested in airplanes and helicopters capable of night flights to defend against fire.

"Hallelujah!" Sterling bellowed, thrusting his fist into the air while the family cheered.

This was only the first drop. Ivy watched as the plane circled around to reload. A long night stretched ahead of them all.

As the moon rose in the sky, the Bay family continued to keep watch on the property and on all those within the walls of the Seabreeze Inn.

Though she was relieved, Ivy wondered about how Bennett and Mitch were faring. She was concerned that they were so close to the fire. The danger of a wind-whipped tornado of fire worried her; too many firefighters had perished in such circumstances.

Still, she and her family were facing down dangers here, too. She couldn't let her mind drift; she could only pray that Bennett and Mitch were safe.

Chapter 33

A FEW HOURS later, tired and bedraggled, the family tromped into the house. They'd heard from a neighbor that the fire was contained, though it would still burn throughout the night. Since the wind had decreased, the most pressing danger that would cause the fire to spread had subsided.

Ivy slumped onto a stool in the kitchen. It was almost midnight now, and looking at her clothing, she began to laugh. The sundress she'd taken such pains to iron was a soggy, ash-streaked mess that reeked of smoke. "What a grand opening party this turned out to be."

"But we're still standing," Shelly said, giving her a high five.

Her father and brothers and the nephews were stepping out of soggy shoes that had once been nice, too. Sterling chuckled at the sight. "Ivy and Shelly always did know how to throw memorable parties."

"I think we're out of the crushed ice we bought for the party," Ivy said. She was exhausted, and her shoulder throbbed with pain. The rigid end of the palm frond had slammed onto her harder than she'd realized. "My shoulder is a wreck. Any ice cubes left in Gert or Gertie?"

"I don't know, but I sure could use a stiff Sea Breeze now." Shelly rubbed soot from her eyes. Ash streaks crisscrossed her face like hash marks.

"I'm on it," Poppy said. She opened the freezer and pulled out a couple of antique, silver-toned ice trays. Staring at them for a moment, she said, "I have no idea how to work these contraptions, but there's ice in there if we can knock it out."

"You kids are so techy you forget how to work things," Carlotta said. With a swift jerk on the handle, the ice jolted from the tray. "See?"

"Impressive," Poppy said. "And after seeing you and Gramps in action tonight against the fire, I guess we shouldn't be worried about you two sailing around the world."

"Tell that to my daughters," Ivy said, accepting a bundle of ice wrapped in a dishtowel from her mother. She eased it onto her shoulder, shivering from the intense cold.

"Will they visit soon?" Carlotta asked.

"Not likely," Ivy replied.

Poppy brightened. "I saw Misty's opening night photos on social media. And Sunny's still globetrotting."

Ivy looked around at her disheveled family. "Take a photo. We need to show them how much fun we're having out here." Around her, the weary family burst out laughing, partly in relief from the stress of the day. They flung their arms around each other while Poppy snapped a few photos.

Shelly made a face. "Since we put our first guests to work saving Darla's house, I guess we shouldn't charge them."

Ivy wiped tears of laughter from her streaked face. "What a great investment this place is turning out to be."

"Hey, we're just getting started," Shelly shot back. "And already we have a full house. Think of the reviews we could get."

They were still laughing from sheer stress and exhaustion when Bennett and Mitch walked in. Both men were covered in soot and grime. Bennett made his way toward Ivy.

"Hey," Mitch said, his voice somber. "Did as much as we could up there on the ridge. On the way back, I realized I left my phone here. Anyone see an extra one?"

"Here it is. I was wondering who this belonged to," Poppy said, scooping up his phone and handing it back to him.

"Thanks," he said, trying to catch Shelly's eye.

"You look like you could use something cold to drink," Shelly said. She spun off the stool and hurried toward the fridge.

Ivy couldn't help but wonder where that relationship might go. She turned her attention to Bennett, who also looked exhausted. His shoulders were slumped, and his eyes were bloodshot.

Ivy put down the ice pack on the counter. "How's your home?" she asked Bennett, touching his hand.

He ran an ash-streaked hand through his sooty hair and exhaled. "Going to need a lot of repair." His voice sounded even deeper and more gravelly. "Smoke damage is pretty bad, but the house is still standing. Can't say as much for my garage. The palm trees went up in flames, and the fire jumped to the garage."

"I'm so sorry to hear that," Ivy said. "Do you think you've lost much?"

"I'm insured. Photos are digital. I needed new clothes anyway." He shrugged. "Life is so much more important than things."

That was something they both understood.

Her father interjected, "Any homes lost?"

"Three," Bennett said. "Everyone made it out, thank goodness. We even got the pets to safety."

"Got a place to stay tonight?" Flint asked.

Looking lost, Bennett shrugged. "I'll find a motel or

something—"

"Absolutely not," Shelly cut in. "You'll stay here with us."

Poppy piped up. "We've got a full house, but I saved a room for you. Thought you might need it, though I'm sorry that you do." To Ivy, she added, "It's a room near yours, Ivy. His name is on the door."

A spark of gratitude lit Bennett's dull eyes. "Really appreciate it. I'm in desperate need of a shower."

"Ditto," Ivy said, twisting up a corner of her mouth. They were both weary, and their clothes and hair were filthy after having fought to protect their home and others' against the ravages of wind-whipped flames.

"I'll show you to your room." Ivy dragged herself off the stool.

Bennett touched her arm as she stood. "How's your shoulder?"

"Didn't notice it until I stopped, and now it's aching like mad." She answered the question in his eyes. "We turned on the hoses, spraying down the exterior and trees, including Darla's, to keep flying embers from causing trouble."

"Smart." A smile curved his lips. "I'll bet she appreciated that."

"How can you ever tell?" Ivy replied. Even though Darla was difficult at best, it was the right thing to do for the woman. Neighbors looked out for each other—even the grumpy ones.

Ivy led Bennett toward the rear staircase that had been intended for staff use. The thought of having him so close under her roof sent a torrent of conflicting emotions tumbling through her. Yesterday she would have wanted to strangle Shelly for extending the invitation, but now her limbs were tingling with a strange type of energy she hadn't felt in a long time

"Can't tell you how much I appreciate this," Bennett said when they reached the door to the guest room. "I won't be here long. I'll find a place to stay tomorrow."

Ivy opened the door and led him into the blue-and-white nautical-themed room. No matter how she'd felt about him before, she was struck by the man who stood before her now. His raw emotions were etched on his face. Filled with compassion for what he'd been through tonight—and in the past—she ran her hand along his shoulder. "Please don't go. You're welcome here for as long as you like."

"I really couldn't…"

She widened her eyes in protest. "Why not? Do you think I'm trying to bribe a public official?" When he didn't answer, she added, "I'm really not. You need a place to stay, and we have more than enough room. Besides, I need someone to help me hang paintings."

"Well…as long as they're not stolen."

"They're all mine. You're looking at the artist." As she

gazed into his eyes, a flush gathered in her chest.

"And she's never looked better." Bennett lifted an ashy strand of hair from her face and trailed his fingers along her smudged cheek in a gentle stroke.

Turning into the palm of his hand, Ivy let out a sigh. A feeling that this was *so right* washed over her. She'd truly come home to Summer Beach. With a slight movement that felt entirely natural, she lifted her face to his.

Before she could even process what was happening, their lips met with warmth and softness, and in the next moment, they were in each other's arms, each filling a need in the other as they deepened their kiss. Their bodies melded together, and in their close embrace, time ceased to be.

When they finally eased back from each other to catch their breath, Ivy caught a glimpse of them in the old-fashioned mirrored vanity. "Oh, look at us." She shook her head. "We're a filthy mess."

"Don't look." Bennett brought her face back to his. "Right here is the perfect view."

And so it was. When she looked into his eyes, she saw a possible future for them, though she had no idea how they would work out their lives. While the renovation of her house might be well underway, the restoration of her life was just beginning.

"I'm glad you're here," she said.

"So am I." A look of wonder crossed his face. "When I woke up this morning, I never could have imagined that I would end the day like this, here with you." He teased her lips with his tongue. "My first summer love from all those years ago."

"You remembered," she said with awe.

"Not until tonight. I wanted to ask you out back then, but when I finally got my courage up, you disappeared."

"Here we are again." Amazed that he recalled that last day on the beach, she laughed softly. "You were my summer crush, too. I remember that day. But there was another girl there, too."

"My cousin from Texas," he said, nodding. "She'd just arrived with my uncle and his wife."

"Wait a minute," Ivy said. "*Not* your girlfriend?"

Bennett shook his head. "Only my exuberant cousin. I searched all over for you. Your friends told me you'd moved away to college." He tucked a strand of hair behind her ear. "I'd hoped to see you at the university here. I looked for you."

"How I wish I'd known." Ivy stroked his face. How different their lives might have been if she hadn't acted so impetuously. Although she was still far from perfect now, she had changed; they both had. And now, life was serving them another chance. Maybe someday she'd tell Bennett how heartbroken she had been.

"And do you still play your guitar on the beach?" she asked.

A smile curved his lips. "I'll play it for you."

Ivy kissed him again softly. Though challenges still loomed ahead, she couldn't wait to see how their summer would unfold.

She had a feeling the saga of her new life at the Seabreeze Inn was only just beginning.

Thank You!

THANK YOU FOR reading *Seabreeze Inn*, and I hope you enjoyed it. Continue the *Seabreeze Inn* saga with Ivy and Shelly in the next book, *Seabreeze Summer*. As the first guests of summer descend on *Summer Beach*, Ivy and Shelly continue to find that the life of an innkeeper is fraught with surprises.

To learn when *Seabreeze Summer* is available, please join my VIP Readers Club at JanMoran.com. You might also enjoy reading my *Love California* series, beginning with *Flawless*.

Seabreeze Inn Recipes

Compliments of Ivy and Shelly Bay

Sea Breeze and Bay Breeze Coolers are refreshing tonics that conjure beachside sunsets. These fruit juice blends are just as yummy without alcohol, too. Adjust the ratios of juices for taste as desired.

Note: The original Sea Breeze recipe is thought to have originated in the 1920s, possibly at The Savoy hotel in London. Made with gin, apricot brandy, grenadine, and lemon juice, it was quite different.

Seabreeze Inn

Sea Breeze Cooler

4 oz. cranberry juice drink
1 oz. Ruby red grapefruit juice drink
1 oz. vodka (optional)
Lime wedges

Mix together juices and add vodka if desired. Serve in a chilled glass with a wedge of lime over ice. Squeeze the lime into the juice for extra tartness.

Serving suggestions: This juice cocktail is a refreshing pop of color at summer parties. Serve in mason jars, highball glasses, or any unusual glassware.

Bay Breeze Cooler (or Hawaiian Sea Breeze)

3 oz. cranberry juice drink
3 oz. pineapple juice
1 oz. vodka (optional)
Lime wedges

Similar to the Sea Breeze, the Bay Breeze packs a cool tropical punch. Mint makes a refreshing garnish.

Of course, always drink responsibly and don't drive and drink.

Jan's Books

Contemporary
The Summer Beach Series:
Seabreeze Inn
Seabreeze Summer
And more to come...

The Love, California Series:
Flawless
Beauty Mark
Runway
Essence
Style
Sparkle

20th Century Historical
The Winemakers: A Novel of Wine and Secrets
Scent of Triumph: A Novel of Perfume and Passion
Life is a Cabernet: A Wine Novella for The Winemakers

Nonfiction
Vintage Perfumes

To learn of Jan's new books first and get special offers, join Jan's
VIP Readers Club at www.JanMoran.com and get a free read.

About the Author

JAN MORAN IS a writer living in generally sunny southern California. A few of her favorite things include a fine cup of coffee, dark chocolate, fresh flowers, laughter, and music that touches her soul. She loves to travel just about anywhere, though her favorite places for inspiration are those rich with history and mystery and set against snowy mountains, palm-treed beaches, or sparkly city lights. Jan is originally from Austin, Texas, and a trace of a drawl still survives to this day, although she has lived in California for years.

Many of her books are available as audiobooks, and her historical fiction has been widely translated into German,

Italian, Polish, Dutch, Turkish, Russian, Bulgarian, Portuguese, and Lithuanian, among other languages.

Visit Jan at JanMoran.com. If you enjoyed this book, please consider leaving a brief review online for your fellow readers where you purchased this book, or on Goodreads. Thank you!